TWILIGHT OF A GODDESS

TWILIGHT OF A GODDESS

Christopher Nicole

This first world edition published 2010
in Great Britain and in the USA by
SEVERN HOUSE PUBLISHERS LTD of
9–15 High Street, Sutton, Surrey, England, SM1 1DF.
Trade paperback edition first published
in Great Britain and the USA 2011 by
SEVERN HOUSE PUBLISHERS LTD.

British Library Cataloguing in Publication Data

Nicole, Christopher.
  Twilight of a goddess.
  1. Digby, Jane Elizabeth, 1807–1881 – Marriage – Fiction.
  2. Digby, Jane Elizabeth, 1807–1881 – Sexual behaviour –
  Fiction. 3. Digby, Jane Elizabeth, 1807–1881 – Travel –
  Arabian Peninsula – Fiction. 4. Ellenborough, Edward Law,
  Earl of, 1790–1871 – Fiction. 5. Biographical fiction.
  I. Title
  823.9'14–dc22

ISBN-13: 978-0-7278-6956-2   (cased)
ISBN-13: 978-1-84751-286-4   (trade paper)

Except where actual historical events and characters are being
described for the storyline of this novel, all situations in this
publication are fictitious and any resemblance to living persons
is purely coincidental.

All Severn House titles are printed on acid-free paper.

Severn House Publishers support The Forest Stewardship Council [FSC],
the leading international forest certification organisation. All our titles that
are printed on Greenpeace-approved FSC-certified paper carry the FSC logo.

Mixed Sources
Product group from well-managed
forests and other controlled sources
www.fsc.org Cert no. SA-COC-1565
© 1996 Forest Stewardship Council
FSC

Typeset by Palimpsest Book Produ
Falkirk, Stirlingshire, Scotland.
Printed and bound in Great Britai
MPG Books Group, Bodmin, Cor

'She's beautiful, and therefore to be wooed,
She is a woman, and therefore to be won.'
William Shakespeare

JANE DIGBY was the most beautiful woman of the nineteenth century. She was also the most notorious, as she became the centre of an enormous scandal when her husband divorced her for adultery. But her remarkable life was only beginning.

Contents

The Crisis

This is not an apology. It is a statement. My critics, and they are legion, have described my life as a series of mistakes, inspired by lust and compounded by a perpetual immaturity. I feel only pity for such people, so embedded in the hypocritical conventions of their limited society, they have always been afraid of attempting to *live*, and seek and, if they are fortunate, even find, the ultimate love. That has been my quest, from my earliest memory, and whatever the disasters that have from time to time overtaken me, having at last achieved my goal, I regret not a moment of it.

But the vicissitudes had first to be survived.

'Oooh, la la!' Emma exclaimed. Emma was French, and inclined to overreact to a crisis, although there are few ladies' maids who will not overreact to the door of their mistresses' bathing chamber being thrown open to admit a man. But then she realized that the man was my husband, and her agitation subsided into a simper as she abandoned her position beside the tub to retreat across the room.

Karl replaced her. He was a splendid figure of a man, in his mid-thirties, tall and well built, with strong features and glowing red hair and moustache. As Baron von Venningen he was also one of the wealthiest men in Germany, his estates stretching far beyond the confines of Bavaria into Baden and Hesse-Darmstadt. Had our circumstances been different, I could have loved him – he certainly loved me – and I did respect him and enjoyed his company.

But at this moment he was not his usual ebullient, good-humoured self, despite the fact that he was gazing at a sight just about every man in Europe would have given a year of his life to witness: the Baroness von Venningen sitting naked in her tub.

I write this in no spirit of hubris. When, at the age of seventeen,

I had 'come out' and been presented at court, the King, George IV – better and infamously remembered as the Prince Regent – had acclaimed me as the most beautiful woman he had ever seen – and he was a connoisseur – words that had overnight made me the darling of London society. Now, ten years on, I was approaching my apogee, the possessor of a tall, slender, and yet strong body, suitably adorned with those attributes so dear to the male sex – but then, I was four times a mother, even if I had nothing to show for it. My face, it has been said, could have been carved by a Greek god. My complexion has been described as pure milk with just a trace of strawberries. My hair, a lustrous Titian, was, even when secured on the top of my head, compelling in its colour and wavy sheen. And I have been told that my eyes, wide set, large and a deep blue – some call it violet – could bewitch Satan himself. As to the truth of this, I cannot say, but I did know that I could use them to attract or reject as I chose.

All of these attributes I could see every time I looked in the mirror, and as I regard hypocrisy as the lowest form of human behaviour, I will admit that this constantly available image certainly affected my view of life. But at that moment, I was interested rather than concerned at Karl's obvious agitation. What can a man, one of the wealthiest in the land, and possessed of such a wife – well, partly – have to be agitated about? So I enquired, 'Charles?' – I preferred to use the English form of his name – 'Whatever can the matter be?'

'Jane!' he declared. 'You are impossible! Sitting in your bath, when we leave Munich in an hour.'

This was news to me, and unwelcome news, as well. 'Leave Munich? To go where?'

'Mannheim. We are going to stay with Mama for a while.'

I was appalled. The Dowager Baroness von Venningen had never troubled to conceal her dislike for me; she regarded me as a loose woman. Well, she had a point, in the context of her family background and upbringing. But now that I was married to her son I was disinclined to put up with her monumental sniffs and snide remarks. As Karl well knew.

'She will be delighted with your news,' he said, placatingly.

I glared at him, and then looked at Emma, who was petrified.

'I met Dr Bruening, yesterday,' Karl explained.

At least my maid had not let me down. But my physician . . .

'I assume that you were going to inform me, at some stage,' he continued.

I was on the defensive, at least temporarily: he was my husband. 'I wished to be sure.'

'Well, he is sure. And I congratulate you. Now please make haste.'

I sought refuge in unassailable facts. 'I cannot leave Munich without the King's permission.'

'The King is not here. And will not be returning for another month. And by then you will be in no proper condition to grace his bed. Nor will you be for the next year. Mannheim will be the perfect place for your confinement. It is quiet there.'

You mean it is like a grave, I thought angrily. I was strongly tempted simply to refuse to go, even if I recognized the truth of what he had been saying. But I was in an invidious position. It was the popular concept that as the King's *maîtresse en titre* I was the most powerful woman in the kingdom, far more so than the now redundant Queen Theresa, and this was largely true: because of his adoration, Ludwig could refuse me nothing.

But there was a caveat. Convention demanded that I should have a husband. I had never been sure how much influence Ludwig had used to bring this about. Karl swore that he had fallen in love with me at first sight, and the evidence of his devotion was so strong that I believed him; he had followed me around Europe for two years, begging me to marry him. And I had never attempted to deceive him. He knew of the scandal that haunted my past, and he knew that I was the King's mistress, and he knew that, charming and virile as he was, I did not love him, certainly by my, perhaps extreme, standards.

Yet the fact remained that he was now my husband, and in Germany, far more than in England, husbands exercised total power over their wives. This had not seemed important as long as the King had been available to override his decisions. But as he had reminded me, the King was not here. Nor could I be certain that Ludwig *would* support me in what could develop into another scandal, certainly when he no longer had the use of my body. So I accepted defeat for the moment. 'Very well,' I said, and stood up. 'My towel, Emma.'

*   *   *

Yet the seeds of rebellion had been planted by this cavalier treatment. Actually, they had always been there. How could they not be? I am the granddaughter of Thomas Coke of Holkham in Norfolk, the richest man in England, and one of the most powerful; even if he never aspired to political office, he was variously known as the King of East Anglia, or the Vice-King of England.

Grandpa had maintained a lifelong and often violently verbal opposition to the House of Hanover, which he despised, and the Tory administration it supported. He also lived his life as he chose, without regard for convention or social niceties, or criticism, reaching an outrageous crescendo when, at the age of sixty-eight and a widower for some thirty years, he married his god-daughter, Anne Keppel, who was eighteen, and at the time my best friend – and immediately became a father all over again. Although we were to become estranged, as a girl I worshipped him, and while I do not think I consciously set out to emulate him, he certainly influenced my character.

But in my case, my rebellious nature was alleviated – there are those who have said aggravated – by my equally romantic streak. As a girl I devoured the books in Holkham's vast library. These even included works by the promising young female novelist Jane Austen – I am not sure that Grandpa approves of women writing books – but they certainly encouraged my ambitions. I wanted only to love, but the man had to love me in similar fashion, throwing all aside to share my life. Thus, I fell in love with the poet Byron, or at least, his portrait; I never saw him in the flesh. But I adored his poetry. In this regard I was entirely following fashion. Best of all, however, I feasted on history, and the great women who had adorned it. My absolute favourite was Zenobia, who, following the death of her husband, had in the third century ruled the desert kingdom of Palmyra in the name of her son, and had defied even the might of Rome for some years.

I dreamed, but given my ebullience and overconfidence, I soon sought to translate dreams into deeds. In my early teens, I indulged in more than one adventure, which even included an attempted elopement with one of Grandpa's grooms, from which I now know I was fortunate to escape unscathed. This was very upsetting for my long-suffering mother, who was Grandpa's eldest daughter; my father being a captain in the Navy, I did not see

as much of him as I would have liked. Thus, immediately following
my sensational presentation – someone gave me the title of Aurora,
the Queen of the Dawn – she started looking for a husband
for me.

I was delighted; a husband was all I wanted from life, at that
time. And I was even more delighted with her choice. Edward
Law, Lord Ellenborough, was tall, handsome, independently
wealthy, and a rising politician. Sadly, this was of the Tory persua-
sion rather than the Whig – which did not please Grandpa – but
his dislike was overshadowed, in my eyes, by the fact that Edward
appeared to fall in love with me at first sight. As I was certainly
prepared to love him.

I looked forward to a long life of domestic bliss, enjoying his
embrace and thus bearing his children. I wanted nothing more. The
shock was therefore the greater when, on our honeymoon, I discovered that I was to be an appendage of his political ambitions,
nothing more; a hostess for his dinner parties, but otherwise not
allowed to interfere with or encumber in any way the tenor of his
life. I was not even required to manage his household; he had a
long-standing and efficient housekeeper. As for amatory discourse,
he regarded that as a frivolous and somewhat vulgar waste of time,
only to be undertaken for the necessary business of supplying an
heir for his title and fortune. In fact, when I finally did fulfil his
requirements and produced a son, he informed me that he would
no longer require the use of my body, for any purpose whatsoever, and moved out of the bedchamber we had hitherto shared.
And out of my life, so far as I was concerned.

I have been told that my fate was no different to that of most
married women, certainly of my class. But other married women,
even those who are also aristocrats by birth and upbringing, are
not the granddaughters of Tom Coke of Holkham. Disappointment soon turned to anger, and anger to rebellion. As Edward
showed no interest in what I did with my time, I struck out on
my own, and joined the Almack's set, frequenting the famous
rooms where London society regularly gathered to talk, and drink,
and dance . . . and discover the joys of illicit love.

Immediately I regained my position as toast of the town, and
one thing, in my angry and frustrated state, soon led to another.

These early affairs were of course well known to my friends; every lady in Society was required to have a lover, just as every gentleman had to have a mistress. But the social rule was discretion. One did not flaunt one's beau, but rather met secretly, and if the word soon got around it never produced more than a quiet smile – even if eyebrows were raised when it was whispered that my first lover was my first cousin, George Anson, great-grandson of the famous admiral, and son of Mama's younger sister.

However, the excesses of the Regency being behind us, *the* golden rule was that one never allowed oneself to become pregnant. Thus, one's husband, even if he might learn of your liaisons, lacking concrete proof, was seldom willing to undertake the scandal, and the expense, of a divorce.

But clandestine affairs seemed to me the height of hypocrisy. I so desperately wanted to love, and even more, to *be* loved, without reservation or secrecy. And so eventually I met, at Almack's, the man of whom I had always dreamed.

His name was Prince Felix von Schwarzenberg. He was a scion of one of Austria's oldest aristocratic families, and the handsomest man I had ever met – or ever would. As he felt the same way about me, within a fortnight we were lovers. I was so enchanted that I threw caution to the wind. If I endeavoured to keep my regular visits to his apartments secret, we went everywhere together, and our mutual adoration was obvious to all. Felix, if entirely orthodox in his approach, was yet the most consummate lover I had known . . . or at that time could imagine: I was only just twenty-one when our liaison commenced.

The gossip certainly reached Edward's ears, but he continued to appear to ignore it, until, lost in passion, I one night omitted to take my usual precautions. Even Edward could not ignore my pregnancy, and he, more than anyone else, knew the babe could not be his: he had not visited my bed in over a year. The ensuing divorce was the scandal of the 1820s. I was vilified as a harlot throughout the land. My friends abandoned me; I had broken their code. Even my family, with the exception of dearest Mama, did not wish to know me. I shrugged all of this off. I was about to join Felix in Paris, and begin a new life, as his wife and the mother of his child. Or so I supposed.

However, to my great good fortune, the immediate business had a surprising and profitable ending. The case had to be heard before Parliament, as the only court in the land authorized to terminate a marriage – which of course meant that such a proceeding was only available to the very wealthy – and while I continued to be condemned on all sides, Edward also came in for a good deal of criticism, it being felt that he had contributed to my delinquency by his neglect of me. Thus, still anxious to make his way to high office, he could not let his wife live on the charity of her family, and so made me a remarkable offer; he would settle on me an income of eight hundred pounds a year for the rest of my life, if I swore to leave England forever, and never attempt to see or contact my son.

The first of these conditions I was planning to do anyway. The second brought me close to heartbreak, until I realized that whether I accepted his terms or not, I would not be allowed to see my son. So I took the money and ran. Eight hundred a year did not make me an heiress, but I was a reasonably wealthy woman, and for the first time in my life I was absolutely my own mistress. The episode ended tragically in any event, as within a year little Arthur was dead, of some sudden, and as far as I was informed, totally obscure ailment.

I wept, but I had in front of me Paris, my daughter, and Felix.

I soon discovered that I was no more welcome in Parisian society than I had been in London; my reputation had spread across the Channel. But I remained confident that this would change, the moment I became the Princess von Schwarzenberg, as Felix had promised would happen as soon as my divorce was final. But this event came and went. Felix explained the difficulties he was encountering in wishing to marry a divorcee who was also a Protestant. Matters like this can usually be overcome by greasing a few well-placed ecclesiastical palms; what apparently could not be overcome was his family's opposition to his wishing to marry a fallen woman. The family now enlisted the help of the Austrian chancellor, Metternich, who ordered Felix back to Vienna. Faced with the same choice that had confronted me, he chose the prudent, if dishonourable course, and abandoned me. He had of course had the use of my body for more than two years, which is a long time for most men to remain interested.

I was absolutely shattered. I had given up everything for this man, and was now left lonely and unwanted. Mama determined to assist me by suggesting I leave Paris for Munich; the British ambassador to the Bavarian court was an old family friend who she knew was sympathetic to my situation. So to Munich I went, to discover that I was no more acceptable to Bavarian society than I had been to Paris or London.

Once again despair, my only joy being my daughter Mathilde. And then a most remarkable thing happened. I was seated in a restaurant one afternoon when King Ludwig passed by; he was fond of strolling amongst his people. He was well known as a connoisseur of beautiful women, but as he later confessed, he had never seen anyone to equal me. Thus, to my consternation, he left his entourage in order to speak with me.

Initially I resisted his advances; incredibly, I was still in love with Felix, and I had no desire to engage in another surreptitious liaison, even with a king. But he persevered, and he possessed, unwittingly, a powerful ally. When in Paris I had once visited a fortune-teller, a famous lady named Madame Normande, who after examining my hand, proclaimed that I would have love affairs with *three* kings. I naturally treated this as arrant claptrap . . . but here was a king knocking on my door!

On the other hand, in his letters Felix gave every evidence of still being in love with me. In my innocence I did not understand that all *he* wanted was to have his daughter. And at last, still hoping for a miracle, I allowed Mathilde to visit Vienna, to see her father, only to discover that she would not be coming back. And there was nothing I could do about it; she was his daughter, and I had no rights in Austria, certainly when opposed to a family like the Schwarzenbergs.

Once again, despair, this time utter. But Ludwig had slowly been realizing that *he* wanted me more than anything else, and so he invited me to become his official mistress, raising me in one movement from the social gutter to being the most powerful woman in the country; I was called the Bavarian Madame de Pompadour! This change of fortune I could not resist, and the husband he found for me was very acceptable. Or had been until this sudden realization that I was still someone else's property. And I did not actually love either of them.

★   ★   ★

The main reason I had not immediately confided my situation to Karl was that it posed quite a question, if only in *my* mind. Naturally I had ceased to take any precautions once I was a married woman, and I had not even done so after visiting Ludwig – I was required to do so for 'private conversation', several times a week. The same went for Karl, of course. I was a busy girl that winter. So . . .?

Karl naturally had no doubt that the babe was his, and so off we went to Mannheim in hope that my condition would lead to a reconciliation with his mother. This did not happen. Both the old lady and her eldest daughter, Mimi, were as disagreeable as ever, openly trying to make trouble between my husband and me, and while this failed, Karl could see that I was acutely unhappy, and we soon left . . . but not to return to Munich. Instead we went to another of his properties, the castle at Grombach, where I spent the summer awaiting my confinement. This did not disturb me, as I would have been unable to take my place in society in any event, and neither would I have been able to visit Ludwig. But I was somewhat put out, when I wrote the King to inform him of my condition, and asked if I might name the babe after him, he requested me not to do so. I therefore dropped the idea, and as it was a girl the matter did not arise again. But I was decidedly disturbed when he also declined to act as godfather. Perhaps I was unwise to suggest it, but we had been so intimate over the previous two years it did not occur to me that protocol still had any part to play in our relationship.

I could not of course take offence, but entirely accepted his decision, and we arranged for Count Alfred Obendorf, a chamberlain, to act instead. We spent a pleasant summer, and a most maternal winter and spring. I wrote Ludwig regularly, and he responded as lovingly as ever, and by the autumn I was looking forward to a return to Munich and a resumption of my old position. To my dismay, Karl refused to do this, and instead determined to spend some time at another of his castles, this being Weinheim, a watering place some twelve miles north of Heidelberg, for my health, he claimed. I could not doubt that he was deliberately keeping me away from the capital . . . and Ludwig.

I was very unhappy about this. I could not do anything about it at that time, but I grew increasingly bored and thus irritable . . . and rebellious. In the spring of 1835 I was beginning to come within sight of the dreaded landmark of thirty, with all the suggestions of looming diminution in my beauty and energy and, most importantly, my passion. Many people supposed that I had filled much of my twenty-eight years with high adventure, but from my point of view they had been entirely wasted. My feelings were aggravated by the fear that in my absence, for all his continued protestations of love, Ludwig would discover some new lady love and my position would be usurped. No doubt fortunately, in most cases, the future is hidden from us. I could not possibly suspect, much less expect, that I still had more than forty years of health and beauty and energy and passion before me, or that I would soon embark upon adventures granted to few people and even fewer women.

However, at the time I was only aware of the tedium of Weinheim, which was now beginning to resemble a prison. This led to quarrels with Karl, who became quite aggressive whenever I suggested that we should return to Munich, and accused me of having the mind of a frivolous young girl. Shades of Edward! I do not really know what would have happened had our return not been forced by the news that Phillip von Venningen, Karl's younger brother, was seriously ill and not thought likely to survive. Karl felt obliged to hurry to his brother's bedside, which happened to be in Munich, and I was happy to accompany him. Unfortunately, things did not turn out as I had hoped. I had never actually spent a summer in Munich, and thus it had not really registered with me that, unlike London, the Bavarian capital shuts up shop for the summer. All the notables leave for their country estates, and the King and his Court troop up into the Alps. Thus, I was bereft of any congenial company, and instead found myself surrounded by Venningens, hurrying to be at the last days of their brother and son. Things improved when Ludwig and his entourage returned in September, and I was able to resume my visits to the Nymphenburg with no evidence of any rival. In addition, there was a continuous round of festivals and celebrations, and naturally the Baron and Baroness von Venningen were invited to attend all of the important functions. It was at the first of these that I met Spiro!

His full name was Count Spiridion Theotoky, from which it will be gathered that he was Greek. Munich at this time was full of Greeks; since the elevation of Ludwig's younger son, Prince Otto, to the throne in Athens – it had been felt by the great powers that a country, which had so recently achieved its freedom after four centuries of Turkish rule, should be a monarchy, and have as its king a member of a royal house *not* one of the Powers – it had become de rigueur for any aspiring Greek nobleman both to speak German and become intimately acquainted with German culture. Owing to my prolonged absence from the capital I had been unaware of this. Equally, our Greek guests had been unaware of me, except by reputation. Now I beheld quite the most handsome man I had seen, since Felix, his black hair, strong features and splendid moustache topping a tall and powerful body, fascinatingly displayed by his frilled white fustanella – which necessarily meant that his splendid legs were revealed in white stockings – and his crimson tunic, heavily laced with gold thread. And what did he see? I may claim that at twenty-eight I was on the threshold of my greatest beauty. There can be no doubt that he liked what he was looking at as much as I did. The only jarring note was that I recognized immediately that he was younger than I, but as it turned out, this was only a matter of four years.

He danced with a gusto to match his looks, while peering at me with burning eyes. Again, shades of Felix! 'Baroness,' he said. 'I have dreamed of this from the moment I first heard your name.'

'Dreamed of what?' I asked.

'Of holding you in my arms.'

'I am flattered.'

At that moment the music stopped. 'I must see you again,' he said.

'I doubt my husband would approve.'

'It is your approval I seek.'

It was too long since anyone had addressed me with such fervour. 'I ride in the park every morning at ten,' I told him.

★   ★   ★

Spiro was most attractive, and his compliments most welcome, even if I found his tendency to smoke in public, and without permission, a trifle off-putting, but I did not at that moment seek more than a flirtation. As I tried to explain to Ludwig. The King was not at the ball, but he had his agents everywhere, and he soon learned not only of my dancing with the young Greek Count, but also of us riding together in the park.

'You should be more discreet,' he grumbled.

'Is the young man dangerous?'

'Any young man is dangerous, around you.'

'It is sweet of you to say that,' I remarked, truthfully. 'Tell me about him. Has he a good background?'

'In Greek circles, the very best. His family have been prominent in Corfu for centuries. His father fought in the War of Independence, and is a wealthy and powerful man. I believe at the moment he is a provincial governor. But this boy has the reputation of being irresponsibly romantic. You would do well to keep him at arm's length.'

Even after our long affair he could not appreciate that he might just as well have dropped a lighted match into a basket of waste paper, on two counts, one by his description of Spiro, and the other by attempting to forbid me to see him. While shrouding everything in glory was the fact that he was Greek, and his family, if not himself, had fought for the freedom of that enchanted land. Perhaps alongside Byron! In addition, I felt I owed myself an adventure for the long months of boredom I had recently endured. Thus, Spiro and I continued to ride together, and we continued to meet at balls and soirées. With every meeting Spiro's language became more inflammatory. 'A kiss,' he said one night as we waltzed. 'A kiss from you, my dearest Baroness, and I would die a happy man.'

'And if you do not get it?'

'I shall die in misery.'

'That would be most unfortunate,' I agreed, and, the music at that moment stopping, with us adjacent to one of the doors on to the terrace, I stepped through this into the gloom.

It was early October, but there was a chill. This did not matter, as a moment later I was in his arms. It was the most delicious feeling I had known since the first time I had shared a bed with

Felix. Of course there is no feeling superior to that of being naked in the arms of a naked man, provided one is in love with the man. But being held tight and kissed when wearing a ball gown must be a close second. While his hands set to roaming, I did not demur, and reciprocated in kind, which seemed to delight him. 'Oh, Ianthe' – this being my name in Greek – 'Ianthe,' he muttered in my ear. 'I must have you.'

His hands were now lifting my skirts, and I suspect that within a few seconds we would have achieved our joint goal, but at that moment the doors opened again, and another couple emerged from the heat of the ballroom. This pair, with whom I had a nodding acquaintance, did not appear to have carnal matters in mind, but advanced to the balustrade to look out at the night. In doing this, they failed to notice us, tucked in as we were against a buttress. This gave us a few precious seconds to restore ourselves to some order, and step apart, for when they turned, they did see us. 'Why, Baroness von Venningen,' the woman said. 'Are you not cold?'

'I am now,' I agreed.

She was peering into the gloom. 'And Count Theotoky, is it not?'

'Your servant, madam,' Spiro said, with considerable aplomb. She simpered, her companion cleared his throat, and they returned inside. 'Will they gossip?' Spiro asked.

'I am sure of it. We should return as well, so that it will remain gossip.'

He held my hands. 'But Ianthe . . . just now . . . I am on fire.' Well, so was I. 'I must see you again. I must . . .'

I kissed him. 'Send me a note, giving your address, and when you will be at home. Alone.'

He gasped. 'You will come to me?'

'If I can.'

I was reaching back to the madness of my youth. But then, I had no desire to grow old, in either mind or body. As for the risk . . . what was life without danger? Without experience? Without romance? Perhaps I told myself, that I would have one last fling before settling down to that life of humdrum domesticity which was all Karl was offering. The note arrived the next day, and aroused no comment, as Karl assumed it was from the King. It contained, as I had requested, Spiro's address, which, rather inconveniently, was at a hotel, and a time, three o'clock, which was even more inconvenient, for Ludwig was in the habit of sending for me in the afternoons, which Karl spent mostly with his brother. But I had created this situation, and I was not in the mood to pass it up. Besides, Ludwig's summons had become very irregular, and hardly more than once a week. It was certainly worth taking the chance. I told Emma that should His Majesty send for me, she was to tell the messenger that I was not feeling very well, and had taken myself for a walk. She seemed a little upset by this, but only because she could not imagine anyone not being eager to attend a king.

I left her to it and visited the hotel. No one questioned my purpose, and Spiro was waiting in the lobby. We talked for a few minutes as if we had met by chance, then went up the stairs together. Again, no one appeared very interested – the hotel was quite busy – but that we were overlooked cannot be doubted. Again I knew I was taking the most outrageous risk, but this was my mood. At that moment my only concern was that the deed itself would be worth it.

I need not have worried. We entered the suite, I bracing myself for an encounter with Spiro's valet, but he had sent the fellow off. He closed the door while I took off my hat, and I was in his arms, and then lying on the bed while he undressed me. When I moved to reciprocate, he shook his head. 'Just lie there,' he commanded, 'I wish to look at you.' Which he did, as he stripped, while I also enjoyed what I was looking at. Then he lay on his back on the bed beside me. As he had not yet touched me, apart from our kiss, I was uncertain what might be going to happen next. Then he stroked my arm. 'Will you not come to me?' he asked.

I was momentarily nonplussed. Then I realized that he wanted me to straddle him. Would you believe that I had never done this before? For all their fervour, Felix, Karl and the King had been the most orthodox of men, while Edward had sought only to complete the event, to his own satisfaction, as rapidly as possible. I thus approached what might be termed my new situation with some caution.

'Do not fear,' he said. 'Whenever you are ready.'

He was certainly ready. Aided by my weight he seemed to go in forever, and to embrace every one of my sexual organs while doing so. 'Don't move,' he said

That was next to impossible, but I did my best, while he took over the operation. I do believe I climaxed before him, but he certainly climaxed as well and we enjoyed quite an explosion. Then at last I was allowed to dismount and lie beside him. 'I love you,' he said. 'I adore you. I want you, always.' Well, I certainly wanted to renew my experience, as often as possible. 'When will you come again?' he asked.

'I do not think I can do that.'

'But . . .' he rose on his elbow in dismay.

'We will meet again,' I assured him. 'Soon. I will work it out and let you know.'

'Soon,' he reminded me.

I returned home in a whirl of exultation, to find a very despondent Emma. 'The King sent for you, milady. And as you instructed, I told the equerry you had gone for a walk. He did not seem to be very pleased.'

Oh, dear, I thought, and hastily wrote Ludwig a note. I do not know if he replied, because suddenly things were off at a gallop once more, but I suspect he did not. As he undoubtedly soon discovered where I had been that afternoon, he could consider me not only as having taken a new love when I was supposed to be his mistress, but also that I had lied to him.

It had never occurred to me that Karl might also be having me watched – I would have been furious had I known – but he did not come home until after I was in bed that night, for which I was grateful as I was pondering ways and means of having another meeting with Spiro. I pretended to be asleep when he came in, thus we did not speak until breakfast the following morning, when he said, without preamble, 'I would like you packed by lunchtime. We are returning to Weinheim this afternoon.'

I spilt my tea. 'Weinheim? We cannot leave Munich. What about Phillip?'

'I have done all I can for Phillip. Now I must start considering my own family. Bertha is not looking well. The city air obviously does not agree with her.' As we had named our daughter.

'Bertha is perfectly well,' I snapped.

We gazed at each other. 'I have said she isn't.' Karl spoke quietly enough. 'I have decided that we shall return to Weinheim this afternoon.'

'*You* have decided?' I cried. 'Well, I have no desire to leave Munich. And I hate Weinheim. It is the most boring place on earth. I am staying here.'

'You are coming to Weinheim. You are my wife. You will do as I say.'

Was this the man who had followed me around Europe for two years like a faithful dog? 'I shall have to consult the King.'

'The King, any king, has no power or right to come between a man and his wife. Even Ludwig understands that.'

I knew that at this moment he was probably right, if not for the reason of protocol he supposed. But I tried to keep calm. 'You are reneging on our agreement.'

'What agreement? I asked you to marry me. I offered you my name, my rank, my wealth, and my love, accepting that I must share you with the King. And now you have all of those things. Kindly act as if you appreciate them.'

I was speechless. But as with two years previously, there was nothing I could do. Karl was entirely within his legal rights to take me wherever he wanted, even to lock me up, if he chose. My mistake had been to suppose that a man who had always seemed to me to be the epitome of a gentleman could never behave like this. But if I had lost a battle, the war was still there to be won. I did not at that moment actually contemplate leaving him, and my home and my child, for a second time. I knew that such a repeat performance would not only end my position with the King, but there could be no return to social acceptance. But I would see Spiro again, I was determined, let Karl do what he might.

I went upstairs and told Emma to pack, then I sat at my desk and wrote Spiro a note, explaining the situation and telling him that if he could find himself in Heidelberg I would come to him, no matter what. This I had Emma deliver to his hotel before she hurried back to be in time for our departure.

What did I hope for? It is difficult to be sure of my emotions. In sending him that note there was undoubtedly a half-wish that he would not follow it up, would say to himself it is too dangerous to become further involved, and thus was not worthy of any further thoughts on my part. If he *did* follow it up, then he sought more than my body.

It will be seen, therefore, that if I could not resist the challenge of discovering how deeply he felt for me, I was throwing the whole affair into the lap of the gods, and would abide by their decision. Not that I intended to forgive Karl for his high-handed behaviour. Because there was a most important factor he had overlooked. He might be able physically to command me, as long as I was in his clutches, but if I ever escaped those clutches, he had no hold on me, as would have been the case in most marriages. He had never inquired into my finances, and I had never confided them to him, nor had he objected when I had broken with convention and had a clause inserted into our marriage contract to the effect that, contrary to accepted custom, my money remained out of his control. In addition, I had received, entirely without requesting them, several large financial gifts from Ludwig, I was still in receipt of my eight hundred pounds a year, and as I had had no reason to spend any of my own money throughout the two years of our marriage, and had indeed never, since arriving in Munich, and despite my tendency to extravagance, found it necessary to spend all my income, I had a tidy sum awaiting me in my bank in Zurich, whenever I had the urge, or the need, to claim it.

And the gods were on my side, or perhaps, they were still intent on luring me to destruction, as they saw it. A week after our arrival at Weinheim, I received a note.

It contained but an address, in Heidelberg itself. My heart swelled to bursting. But immediately my brain was assessing the possibilities and the problems of my next step. Obviously I could not allow Spiro to approach me too closely: on the continent cuckolded husbands are more inclined, and are encouraged, to deal with such matters at the point of a pistol rather than a divorce court, and I knew Karl to be a very good shot. Indeed, during our first summer at Weinheim we had often practised together, and I could estimate that he was very nearly as good as I. In any event, I had no more desire to have him killed, or even wounded, than I wished to have him wound or kill Spiro. But my fertile mind quickly found an answer. Since our return to Weinheim, Karl and I had maintained what might be described as an armed truce. He had asserted his prerogatives as my husband on the night of our arrival, but I had been so obviously disinterested that he had not touched me again. While, as I had been some-what agitated while waiting to see whether, or not, Spiro was going to respond, I was very obviously not at my best. Now, I knew that only a few miles away there was the spa of Schwetzingen, where an old palace which had once belonged to the Electors Palatine had been converted into a luxurious hotel for the use of those wishing, and were able to pay, to take the waters. This was my objective.

So the day after receiving Spiro's letter. I took a purgative. Needless to say, being me, I overdid it, and as a result was very ill; indeed the doctor Karl called in began to mutter about cholera! However, the next day I began to recover, but he willingly agreed that what I needed was a course of the waters. Karl who, bless his heart, had been thoroughly alarmed by my symptoms, also agreed – he naturally had no idea that Spiro was in the vicinity – and in addition he was reassured by my decision to leave Bonzo behind, as he knew I never went anywhere for any length of time without my dog, a Dachshund which had been a present from Ludwig. So off I went to Schwetzingen to regain my health. Nor did he raise any objections when I took with me my favourite gelding, which I had named Indefatigable, in view of his re-markable staying power; he knew how much store I set by my morning ride.

I needed to act a role, and this I did to perfection. From dawn till supper I was the most decorous of ladies. I slept late, took Indefatigable for a brief ride when I arose, enjoyed the waters in the afternoon, spent the early evening with the other ladies, all eager to be seen speaking with the famous Baroness von Venningen, and retired early. Then I dressed in my habit, left Emma to hold the fort – in her usual highly nervous state – and stole down the back staircases to the stables. On my first day I discovered a willing groom, prepared to assist me both because of my beauty and the liberal donation I offered him. He had Indefatigable waiting, and I was away into the night, down the five-odd miles to the city. I was invariably at the rooms Spiro had taken by midnight, stayed in his arms until the first cock-crow, and then remounted and was back at Schwetzingen before the hotel had begun to stir.

This was quite the most glorious week of my life to that point, and certainly mentally prepared me for the even more glorious days that lay ahead. While our love-making was divine. But, inevitably, it came to a dramatic, and some would say, calamitous end, as equally inevitably the night arrived when we had a more than usually exhausting session, with the result that we fell asleep in each other's arms, and when we awoke the cock had been crowing for some time. I leapt out of bed, dragged on my clothes, kissed Spiro, and dashed out into the dawn. It yet wanted half an hour to daybreak, but the sky was definitely lightening as I approached Schwetzingen, at the gallop, and rounding a bend, I beheld before me a large open wagon filled with fruit for the market, and parked right across the road, with its driver fast asleep on the ground beside it. To my right was a water-filled ditch, to my left a thick hedge. Neither would do either me or my mount any good, nor would attempting to stop him at this juncture. I have never been afraid of the highest fence, nor was I now. 'Away, away!' I shouted at Indefatigable, at the same time using my whip, a very unusual recourse for me.

He responded magnificently, rising like a bird, and we soared over the startled driver, who, unfortunately, had been awakened by the galloping hooves. Although I wore my habit, I rode astride for these midnight trysts, and therefore what he saw, rising above him, was a panting horse's belly, booted legs, flying skirts, and tumbling red-gold hair. I don't think he saw my face or identi-fied me but what he did see was sufficient for him to dine out on for the rest of the week, and perhaps for the rest of his life. Meanwhile, Indefatigable and I had landed safely on the far side of the wagon, although my hat had come off – I did not waste the time going back for it although it was a new silk – and we were in Schwetzingen fifteen minutes later. But by now it was broad daylight, and before I could hand Indefatigable to his groom and regain my suite I was accosted by the manager. 'My dear Baroness,' he asked. 'Whatever is the matter?'

'Why should anything be the matter?'

'Well . . .' he looked at my somewhat disordered habit, and my exposed hair.

'I went for an early morning ride,' I told him. 'I often do this. If it is any business of yours.'

'Well, of course it is not, milady. Shall I send someone to look for your hat?'

'I have other hats,' I told him, coldly. He bowed, and withdrew, abashed. I have no doubt that I could have survived his curiosity, but by that evening the wagon driver was at the inn and relating his strange adventure. Some of the hotel servants were in the hostelry to listen to him, and they brought the tale back home, as it were, whence it reached the ears of the manager. I have no idea what he really made of it, but he found himself in possession of certain facts that seemed to require explanation. That I should take a pre-dawn ride was unusual. That I – because he easily identified me from the mention of my hair – should do so at such a mad gallop that involved the risk of jumping a large wagon could be called a dangerous eccentricity.

Unaware of all of this, I retired to bed, exhausted but happy, awoke and dressed, went downstairs to see that Indefatigable was all right – in the circumstances I had decided not to exercise him, or me, that morning – and encountered Karl, just arriving, and intending to stay, for he was accompanied by his valet and several boxes. 'Why, Charles!' I cried. 'What a pleasant surprise! What brings you to Schwetzingen?'

'Why, the ball,' he said.

'The ball?' I asked, stupidly.

'Did you not know there is to be a ball here, tomorrow night?'

'Ah . . .' now I recalled it being mentioned. But it had not interested me.

'And as you are looking so well,' he went on, 'so totally re-covered from your illness, after the ball we shall go back to Weinheim, together.'

I was totally confounded, but not at that moment alarmed. I still had no idea that he had virtually been summoned by the manager. He made no mention of my pre-dawn ride, and I was still certain he did not know of Spiro's proximity. It seemed to me that this was the merest mischance, and would have to be ridden through, as it were. But for the moment I was hamstrung until I could work out a new arrangement. I scribbled a note telling Spiro that I would not be coming tonight, and that he should await a longer letter from me in a day or two, but it was well into the afternoon before I was able to get down to the stables and hand it to my faithful groom. Wilhelm promised to deliver it as soon as he got off duty, but I now know that he did not reach Heidelberg until the following morning, by which time Spiro was in a frenzy of anxiety.

Meanwhile, I attended my husband all that day, and that night, being as loving a wife as I could, submitting to him while I dreamed that he was Spiro. We went for a ride together the next day, and then took the waters together until it was time to dress for the ball. That done we descended the stairs arm in arm, and were, as always, the centre of attraction. We waltzed together. Then Karl graciously allowed me to partner other men, until we got together again for a dance just before midnight. But this had scarcely commenced when I heard Karl mutter an exclamation, and turning in his arms to see what had disturbed him, I found myself staring at Spiro.

The Flight

I released Karl, my mind spinning. Spiro looked at me then turned and left the room. His expression was a mixture of anger and despair. I could only think that he assumed my behaviour meant that I was in the act of ending our relationship, and without consideration I ran behind him. People stared at me as I burst past them, holding my skirts in both hands, and hurried down the stairs, all but tripping in my haste. On the drive, Spiro was just getting into his carriage, on which there were two grooms. 'Wait!' I shouted. Already on the step, he turned to look back. 'I will come with you,' I panted, reaching him. He gave me his hand and plucked me inside beside him. 'Where can we go?' I asked.

He tapped on the hatch. 'Frankfurt! Haste. I have friends there. But . . . you are running away with me!'

'I could not let you go. I will not.'

He kissed me. 'You will never cease to amaze me. What about your things?'

'We can send for them later. Or I can buy new things.'

'But what about your child? Your dog?' He knew how fond I was of Bonzo.

'Them too. Later.' We snuggled against each other. The future was too uncertain. Not that I was afraid of again becoming an outcast, providing only I could be sure of this man's love. But the future had still to be reached. We had not been on the road an hour, and were indeed in the vicinity of Weinheim, when one of the coachmen opened the hatch. 'We are being followed, milord.'

Spiro released me to sit up. 'How many?'

'There is one man, milord.'

We looked at each other, the same thought passing through each of our minds. 'Can you not go faster?' Spiro asked.

'We cannot outrun him, milord. This is a heavy vehicle, and the horses are tired.'

'Well, then . . .' He pulled out a pistol case from under his cloak, which lay on the seat opposite.

'No!' I said. 'You cannot shoot my husband.'

'What would you have me do? It is very likely that he intends to shoot *me*.'

I chewed my lip for a moment. 'Let me talk with him.'

'Do you not suppose he might attack you?'

'He will not do that.' I tapped on the hatch. 'Stop.'

'Milord?' asked the coachman.

'Yes,' Spiro said. 'Stop the coach.' To my alarm, he finished loading the pistol. The reins were pulled, the brake was applied, and we came to a halt. Spiro opened the door and stepped down, and I followed. Now the hoof beats were quite loud, and a few moments later Karl came in sight, urging his panting horse right up to us before drawing rein.

He dismounted. 'You, sir, are guilty of abduction.'

I stepped forward. 'Please, Charles, can we not discuss this?'

He ignored me, as he had now seen the pistol Spiro held. 'To which you intend to add murder.'

'I have two pistols,' Spiro said.

'Then give me one and let us settle this business now.'

I was aghast. While I knew Karl to be a good shot, I had no idea of Spiro's capabilities in that direction. 'You cannot,' I declared.

'It is out of your hands,' Karl told me. 'Unless you abandon this fellow and come with me now.'

'You will find that difficult with but one horse,' Spiro pointed out.

I tried to interject a note of sanity into the proceedings. 'You cannot fight a duel. There are no witnesses and no doctor. If one of you is hit, the other may well be charged with murder.'

'We have witnesses,' Karl insisted. 'Yourself and these fellows.'

Both the grooms had climbed down to see what was going on. 'You expect me to stand by and watch you shoot each other?' I inquired.

'The situation is of your creation, madam.'

Spiro had finished loading the second pistol. I was very tempted to snatch one of them and take control; I had no doubt that I could. But before I could act he had handed the second weapon to Karl. 'Who will count?'

'You may,' Karl said.

'Very well. At the count of ten.' He turned away, and Karl did also, standing with his back almost against Spiro's; both men held their pistols upright against their shoulders. I had no idea what to do. For all the darkness, which should make accurate shooting difficult, I had a strong feeling that someone was going to get hurt. Perhaps seriously. I had to reflect that men were the most absurd creatures.

'Commence,' Karl invited.

'One.' Spiro said. Both men began walking. 'Two – three – four – five – six – seven – eight – nine – ten!'

They turned together, levelled their pistols, and fired. Karl never moved. Spiro gave a startled exclamation, and fell. I imagine I gave a startled exclamation as well, or possibly a shriek, and ran forward to kneel beside him; his white shirt front was covered in blood. 'Oh, my God!' I said. 'Spiro!'

'I am dead,' he declared.

'I do not think so,' I said. I did not know a great deal about wounds at that time, but I could see there was no pulse in the blood which suggested that the bullet had not hit anything vital, and his voice was strong.

Karl had come forward to stand above him. 'Is he bad?'

'We must get him to a doctor. Oh, Spiro!'

'I am dying,' Spiro said again. 'Is that you, Venningen?'

'I am here. I did not mean to kill you.'

'I wish you to know that I never dishonoured your wife.'

I had to suppose that the Greeks had different ideas on honour to us. But Karl took him seriously, and dropped to his knees. 'What?' he demanded. 'What?' Spiro gave a great sigh, and his head sagged. 'My God, I have killed an innocent man.'

'He is not dead,' I said, as Spiro was still breathing, heavily. 'But you will have killed him if we do not get him to a doctor. He is losing blood.'

'We will take him to Weinheim,' Karl decided. 'It is only a mile from here.'

★   ★   ★

Spiro made the journey in the back of his coach with his head on my breast and my arms tight round his body, with the result that although I had torn strips from my gown to bandage him, I was as bloody as he by the time we arrived. We put him to bed while a messenger was sent into the town to fetch the doctor. That worthy arrived and after removing the bandages and examining the wound – Spiro had recovered consciousness but did not seem to know what was going on – informed us that while the bullet had exited, the count had two broken ribs, had lost a great deal of blood, and would have to remain in bed for at least a fortnight. 'But his life?' Karl asked, anxiously.

'He appears to have a strong constitution, so I do not feel he is at risk unless infection sets in. That is always a danger. However . . .' He looked from Karl to me; he did not know the reason for Spiro's wound or which of us, if either, was prepared to take responsibility for his recovery.

'I will nurse him,' I said. 'He is an old friend.'

'Very good. However . . .' Another anxious glance. 'I must report this incident.'

'I will report the incident,' Karl said.

'As you wish, milord.' Now he looked at my dress. 'Is the Baroness also hurt?'

I was tempted to say, not yet. But I actually said, 'It is Count Theotoky's blood, not mine.'

'Very good. I will call again tomorrow.'

I found those very reassuring words. The servants had naturally been awakened by the hullabaloo, and Bonzo was barking excitedly, but with the departure of the doctor they settled down again, and it was obvious that there was going to have to be a confrontation with my husband.

I retired to my bedchamber to change my clothes – poor Emma was still stranded at Schwetzingen – and was in déshabillé when the door opened. 'I thought I had killed him,' Karl said. 'Should I have killed him?'

'I think that would have been most unfortunate,' I replied, choosing my words with care.

'Was he telling the truth?'

'He thought he was dying, and sought to protect my honour.'

Karl came towards me. I was standing by the bed. I braced

myself, unsure how I should react to what was coming, principally because I did not know what was coming. If I felt that Karl had reneged on at least our prenuptial understanding there could be no doubt that in the eyes of either the law or society he was entitled to punish me, perhaps severely, for my behaviour, some of which had taken place in the most public of places. But I was not in the mood to receive a whipping.

My fears were groundless. Karl was simply not that kind of man. 'Would you have run away with him?' he asked, standing immediately before me.

'I *was* running away with him,' I pointed out, still braced for action.

He sighed, and sat on the bed. 'Why? Tell me why, Jane?'

I sat beside him. 'It is not something that can be explained.'

He held my hands. 'I have given you all that I have to give.'

'I appreciate everything that you have given me, Charles. And I most solemnly regret that I have not been able to respond in kind. But . . . I have never attempted to conceal my nature from you.'

'I accepted that you could never love me as you loved Schwarzenberg. But I cannot believe that you still love him, after the way he treated you.'

'I do not. But you mistook the situation. It is freedom I am in love with, freedom to go as I please, dress as I please, act as I please . . .'

'And love as it takes your fancy?'

I would not lower my eyes. 'Yes.'

We gazed at each other for several seconds, and again I braced myself. But he said, 'If I give you that freedom, will you stay with me and be my wife? Be the mother of my, our children? I will this day write my agent in Palermo and arrange for Heribert to be returned to us. Will you not like to see your son again?'

Heribert was the son I had borne for Karl three years before. On discovering my pregnancy I had fled Munich for Sicily, both to conceal my condition from Ludwig and from Felix, with whom I was still hoping for a reconciliation. Karl had followed me, and we had jointly determined to have the babe fostered until our situation became clear; at that time I had had neither the intention nor the desire to marry him. Now . . . I needed time. 'Will your mother not object to receiving a bastard grandson? She did so once.'

'Heribert is no longer a bastard. He is my son and heir.'

'And Spiro?'

'That is up to you.'

Was I being offered everything I had always wanted? Could it be true? I knew that Karl was the most honest of men, and that he honestly believed he had honoured our prenuptial agreement. If I still hesitated it was because of the doubts within myself. But it was not an offer that could be rejected, without at least being sampled. I took Karl in my arms.

However we might have arranged things, if not to our mutual satisfaction, at least to our mutual acceptance, there remained the world, and above all, the King. Before we had even got Spiro home the rumours had started flying; my tumultuous departure from Schwetzingen and Karl's pursuit had been seen by too many people, while the fact of the duel became widely known the moment Karl made his report, and was circulated, in a garbled fashion, which grew more garbled with the telling. I was concerned more about what might get back to England, and wrote Mama an explanation. But I was even more concerned about Ludwig's reaction, and wrote him as well, asking him if he would like to hear my version, which would necessarily be the true one. I had not received a reply by the time we left Weinheim for Paris just after Christmas, where Heribert was to be delivered. Yet I could not believe that his undoubted anger at the misbehaviour of the woman known to be his mistress, and therefore a blow to his pride, would last very long.

In fact, as I later learned, while he was offended by my running off with a Greek, which had involved, as he saw it, a betrayal of his love and position, the reason he did not reply to me during 1836 was that he had other, possibly more important, things on his mind. For young Otto had quickly proved himself quite unfit to be a king, and certainly to rule over such a turbulent society as that of Greece. The country was apparently on the verge of revolt, and Ludwig had to hurry off in an attempt to set things right and to instil some common sense into his son's brain and behaviour. One of the solutions to the problem he chose was to find Otto a wife. The idea might have been sound enough, but his choice of a bride was to prove catastrophic, as I was to discover.

And what of the principal actors in what, looking back, one has to consider as an *opéra bouffe*? I did not believe our arrangement would work, but I was prepared to give it a try, my resolve strengthened by a reply from Mama, begging me, for all our sakes, to settle down as a good wife and mother. I had not, of course, told her of the arrangement between Karl and myself. I knew she would never be able to understand such a situation involving her own daughter. At home, however, things did not go as smoothly. Karl was apparently content to settle for half a loaf, as he had done vis-à-vis the King. Spiro, on the other hand, found it difficult to understand what was going on, this situation being entirely out of his experience.

In the first instance, this was not a problem, because his wound took longer to heal than we had hoped. I was concerned because he would not give up smoking, nor would he give us an address for his father, and in fact made it clear that he did not wish his family informed of his mishap. I could not be sure whether he did not wish them to know of his involvement with a married woman or whether he did not want them to learn that he had been bested in a duel. But as he grew stronger he became increasingly uneasy about his position. He gave every indication of being as much in love with me as ever, and I certainly still found him as compellingly attractive as ever, even if it was some time before we could have sex together. But having to share the house with Karl disturbed him. I had never told him of my relations with Ludwig, and therefore he was unaware that Karl had in effect been sharing me with another man throughout our married life and even before. Thus, Spiro found Karl's somewhat pointed daily absences from the castle disconcerting.

My own position, looked at superficially, was perfection. In reality it was far from satisfactory. I had agreed to remain at Karl's side, and he, true as always to his word, and convinced that Spiro was but a passing fancy, made no attempt to interfere in our relationship, although perhaps he called upon me to fulfil my conjugal duties more often than had been usual in recent months. But I have never been happy living a lie. However, we maintained a facade of civilized, if irregular, living, and Spiro, now recovered, accompanied us to Paris in the new year to collect Heribert. We intended to keep a very low profile, and Paris is a very large city, but as luck would have it, on almost our very first day there, when Spiro and I went for a walk, we bumped into the Austrian diplomat Aponyi, who I had met in London years before, an inveterate gossip who knew all about my liaison with Felix. There were few people I disliked more. But the damage was done. Within twenty-four hours the entire capital was ringing with the news that the notorious Baroness von Venningen, well remembered as the even more notorious Lady Ellenborough, was flaunting her new lover, *with her husband in tow.*

This embarrassed Spiro, still concerned that the news of his ambiguous situation might reach Greece. In addition, with the arrival of Heribert he became the fourth side of a square rather than the third of a triangle. I had to be overjoyed again to hold in my arms the son I thought I had lost forever, and wished to spend as much time as possible with him. I had no intention of excluding Spiro from my company in any way, but he could not help but be aware that he was not the boy's father, and, perhaps more importantly, that Heribert's very presence indicated a strong link binding me to Karl. The result was that when we left Paris in the spring, he elected to remain.

I did my best to change his mind, and even shed a few tears, but he was adamant. And I was caught in my own snare. As Karl gently reminded me, while he had agreed to allow me to have a lover, my part of the bargain was to be his wife and the mother of his children. It was not his fault if my chosen lover wished to follow his own path. He also understood that I was not a promiscuous woman, only from time to time subject to violent and irresistible passions for any man who presented an aura of romantic adventure and who would sweep me off my feet; he knew nothing of the new and immensely stimulating sexual mores to which Spiro had introduced me. It followed, therefore, that all he had to do, he supposed, was separate me entirely from temptation. We thus returned to Weinheim, where I had previously lived for eighteen months without straying, however frustrated I might have become.

I did not object at the time. I actually felt like a little domesticity, and Heribert required a lot of attention; his foster parents had been, shall I say, several classes below that of the future Baron von Venningen, possessor of enormous wealth. But as usual I was sure that I could never love another man as I loved Spiro. I was heartbroken to have lost him, but I was certain this was temporary, convinced that he loved me as much as I loved him.

But for the moment I spent a very quiet and indeed pleasant summer. To my great pleasure, Mama and Papa came to visit, undoubtedly encouraged by Karl to set the seal on my rehabilitation, but also to satisfy themselves that their wayward offspring had at last settled down. Spiro's name was never mentioned. They seemed delighted with both Heribert and Bertha, and invited us to visit them the next year. Mama was certain that Edward could not object, and in any event, she held that now I was securely married to a wealthy man, it would not matter if he did. As in other directions, she could not appreciate that having my own money was a vital part of that desire for freedom that was so important to me.

In the event no objections were raised; Edward was in the early stages of being appointed Governor-General of India. More important to me was the failure of Ludwig to answer any of my letters. Unaware of his preoccupation with affairs of state, I began to realize that our long liaison was over. I could not in all honesty regret this. I was immensely grateful to him for raising me, however selfishly, from the mental gutter into which I had sunk following my betrayal by Felix, to a position of wealth and prestige, but I had never loved him with the passion that was so important to me. Thus, at the end of the year I wrote him formally, dropping my usual address of Lewis in favour of Your Majesty, and begging his forgiveness for any embarrassment I might have caused him. This, at last, after several months, elicited a reply – he was now back in Munich – but it was the last time I ever heard from him. Ours had been a strange romance, but, as I have related earlier, I am proud that I never sought anything from him other than his affection and support. I suppose he was justified in feeling aggrieved that I had gone off with Spiro, but he could not live without a beautiful woman at his call, and in his efforts to replace me he embarked upon a road which led to his destruction.

I am of course referring to the woman Eliza Gilbert, who called herself Lola Montez, an exhibitionist who had sensationalized herself across Europe by performing a dance in which she pretended to be searching for a spider beneath her clothing, before arriving in Munich in 1846. She was already embarked on this career when Ludwig and I parted company, although they had not yet met. But when they did, he went overboard for her as he had for me. Even when he discovered her to be the most grasping and avaricious of women he seemed unable to break her hold on him. Unlike me, she devoted herself entirely to him, not from love, but because he was the quickest route to power and prosperity – she was wont to illustrate the power by laying into anyone who displeased her with a horsewhip. The upshot was that she became the most hated woman in the country, where I had been the best loved, and it has been estimated by many historians that it was her constant presence at the King's side when, in 1848, the tide of revolution swept across Europe, that was more responsible than anything else for Ludwig's forced abdication and his eventual descent into an unhappy grave. But by then I was far away. And it had been his decision to end our relationship.

Our visit to England was not a great success. Perhaps fortunately, its gossip value was overshadowed by the death of Sailor Bill and the succession of the seventeen-year-old Victoria. At this early stage of her life the Queen was both attractive and eager to please, or so I understand; however, it was not considered proper that the notorious Lady Ellenborough, even if I was now the only slightly risqué Baroness von Venningen, and accompanied by my husband, should be presented to Her Majesty. This decision was made by Willy Lamb, husband of the unhappy Caro – now dead – who was the current Prime Minister. But the whole attitude of the country, or at least Society had changed when the Parliamentary reformers took power, admitting to the Commons the middle classes who were both prurient and inhibited. Almack's was no more. The great ladies who had ruled it with their iron laws were either dead or in their dotage. Morality was the keyword.

My immediate family welcomed me and made me feel at home, even Kenelm, my younger brother, who was now a minister of the Church, and was married to a young woman named Caroline Sheppard, and already a father. My elder brother, Edward, still awaiting his uncle's estate – the old fellow refused to die – had just married John Fox-Strangeway's sister Theresa Anna . . . we arrived just after the wedding, which was perhaps fortunate. I felt that he was a bit stiff, but he and his wife did their best to be kind.

However, my old nurse, Margaret Steel, who I had always called Steely, was still about – Mama seemed to have taken her on permanently – and she was perhaps the woman I most detested in all the world. While to the rest of the family I remained anathema. The Ansons did not wish to know, and when I expressed a desire to revisit dear Holkham I was advised that this was not possible, as Grandpa, who had just been ennobled as the Earl of Leicester – I assume this long-delayed acceptance of a peerage had been at the urging of my step-grandma Anne who was thus now a countess – had forbidden my name to be mentioned. I was happy to get back to Bavaria.

But I was not in a happy frame of mind. This was partly because I was realizing that I could never again make England my home. But where was my home? Bavaria to me was Munich. In fact, all Germany, perhaps all Europe, as I knew it at that time, was centred in Munich – and I was not allowed to live there. In vain did I explain to Karl that my romance with the King was over, although having obtained that one reply I continued to write him from time to time. But Karl regarded Munich as containing too many temptations for me. He did do something which he hoped would please me: he sold Weinheim. He knew I had never been happy there and I was glad to see it go. But from Weinheim we moved to Mannheim! Not only did this put us in far too close contact with his family, but the city itself entirely lacked either entertainment or conversation. We did visit Munich briefly, in the spring of 1838, as Karl had business there. I wrote Ludwig to inform him and expressed a hope that we might meet, but he never deigned to answer.

The conclusion of my liaison with the King marked another end – or was it a beginning? – of an aspect of my life. As I have indicated, I was not unhappy, in a physical or mental sense; I merely felt a great emptiness. My days were composed of doing the same things over and over again. Even my sexual encounters with Karl, handsome and vigorous as he was, left me feeling utterly uninvolved. I did my best to fulfil my part of our bargain, but of course Karl could not fulfil his, simply because there was no one of our acquaintance, as he took care to ensure, with whom I had the slightest desire to fall in love. But he overlooked the possibility that I might still *be* in love. Spiro kept in touch, very brief notes, but containing heartfelt expressions of adoration, and more to the point, his current address: he continued to live in Paris. Every time I received one of his letters and recalled the fervour of his love-making, I went into a frenzy of frustrated desire. Until the day came that I could stand it no longer.

It was the spring of 1839. Karl happened to be away for a few days. I told Emma to pack our bags – I could only take a few of my things – kissed the two children farewell, tucked Bonzo under my arm, and took the coach for Paris.

I knew that I was surrendering to an irresistible impulse, as I had done so often before in my life. I knew that nearly every woman in my circumstances would have accepted her situation and attempted to make the best of it. I knew that I was once again breaking every rule of morality and society, and I could be fairly certain that in doing so I was putting myself beyond the pale of acceptance, certainly in Western Europe. I knew that all the old accusations that I was a wanton and an unnatural mother would reappear; what could be described as giddiness in a twenty-year-old could not be accepted in a mature woman of thirty-two. I did not even know what I was going to, what I was actually sacrificing home and children and respectability for. Yet I was certain that Spiro could make me happy, and I felt more sure of his love than of anyone before him – except for poor Karl, and he, alas, could *not* make me happy.

I did not inform Emma of where we were going – I wished it kept a secret until we got there – and she was in a state of some agitation by the time, after a week on the road in a hired coach, overnighting at unfashionable inns, we clattered over the cobbles and arrived at the last address I had been given. But I was in some agitation myself. I had not informed Spiro of my decision to join him, and now I suddenly wondered if he would

be happy to see me, in view of the inevitable scandal that was
going to ensue, or indeed even if he was still at this address.
However, I kept my nerves under control, stepped down, and
rang the bell. It was late afternoon, and the streets were busy, my
appearance, as always, attracting a great deal of attention. Emma
joined me at the door, carrying Bonzo and, looking more
concerned than ever; Bonzo in fact was the calmest of the three
of us. 'Is this a hotel, milady?' she inquired.

'No,' I replied. 'Be patient.' A moment later the bolts were
drawn, and we were confronted by a flunkey, not very well dressed,
and looking bewildered at the sight of me. 'Is Count Theotoky
at home?' I asked.

I spoke French, as I was in France, but he did not appear to
understand me. So I tried English and then German and then
Italian, with no success. This somewhat elongated and quite un-
successful conversation attracted even more attention, and in turn
agitated my coachman, who began to show a strong tendency to
be off, if I would pay him the agreed fee. I could not permit
that until I had ascertained that we were not going to have to
continue our journey, but fortunately at this juncture one of the
onlookers thought fit to intervene. 'He is Greek,' this worthy
explained. 'He speaks only Greek.'

'Ah,' I said. But that was the information I sought. A non-
French speaking Greek servant in the centre of Paris had to have
a Greek master. I therefore stepped past the bewildered man
before he could stop me. 'Halloo!' I called up the stairs. 'Is anyone
home?'

A door opened above me, and Spiro came down the stairs,
wearing a smoking jacket and slippers and looking as bewildered
as his servant. 'Ianthe?' he asked. 'Oh, Ianthe!'

'Aren't you pleased to see me?'

'Ianthe.' He folded me in his arms. The crowd, pressing ever
closer, applauded as only the French can do in the presence of
l'amour, the coachman smiled and brought down my box, Bonzo
barked happily . . . only Emma looked scandalized.

'Oh, Ianthe, Ianthe,' Spiro said, when we had managed to disperse
the crowd and get upstairs to the privacy of his rooms. 'If only
you had let me know you were coming.'

'It was a spur of the moment decision. Are you saying that there is another woman on the premises?' I felt it important to know exactly where I stood.

'I cannot afford another woman,' he said dolefully. 'In fact, I cannot afford a woman at all. I thought you were one of my creditors.'

'Do you have many creditors?'

'They are innumerable.'

I could tell from looking about me that the apartment was neither very well furnished nor very clean. But a situation which was at once a challenge and also one I could control was just what I wanted at that moment. 'Well,' I said. 'If you will let me stay, I will deal with both your creditors and any other problems you may have.'

'Let you stay? Oh, Ianthe . . .' Another hug. 'This is bliss. But . . . stay? For how long?'

'Shall we say . . . the rest of our lives?'

'Ianthe! But . . . Venningen!'

'I have left Charles.'

'Will he not follow you?'

'He must first of all discover where I have gone.'

'He will do this.'

'Do not worry. I will not let him take me back.'

He held my hands. 'There will be a great scandal.'

'I have survived great scandals before. But you . . .'

'I will be damned.' I held my breath; could he possibly be another Felix Schwarzenberg? In which case I was the one damned. 'But it will be worth it, to hold you in my arms. Did you say, forever?'

'Forever,' I told him, 'starts now.'

Half an hour later I was in paradise. But Spiro, being a man, was still consumed with anxiety. 'My landlady . . .'

'I hope she is not also your mistress.'

'That crone? But she is very religious, very strait-laced. She will not approve. And she hates dogs.'

'Does it matter? I think we should seek other accommodation in any event.'

'I owe her six months' rent. I am only allowed to stay because

I keep telling her I am expecting money from Greece. If she throws us out she will keep all of my things.'

'Well, then, we must not let her throw us out until you can settle your debts.'

He sighed. 'I do not know when that will be. My allowance takes a long time to reach here, when it comes at all. And when she discovers I am keeping a woman up here . . . and a dog . . .'

'I have told you, I will take care of it. You will go downstairs and speak with your landlady, and tell her that your niece has come to visit Paris, and will have to stay with you until she can find a place of her own. With her dog.'

'My niece?'

'Do I not look young enough to be your niece? Next you will tell her that your allowance will definitely be here in a fortnight, at which time you will liquidate all your debts.'

'But when the money does not come . . .'

'The money will be here in a fortnight. I will write my bank tomorrow morning.'

'Your bank? Venningen would never permit that.'

'Charles has nothing to do with it. This is *my* bank. My money.'

'I cannot possibly allow you to pay my debts.'

'Are we not going to get married?'

'Oh, you darling. But you are already married.'

'I will get a divorce.'

'Is that possible?'

'Everything is possible. In any event, it is the intention that matters. So, as of this moment, your problems are my problems, which I will be happy to solve.'

'But my debts . . . they are enormous. I have written my father asking for help. But . . . we are not a wealthy family, in terms of money. We have much land, but in Greece there is little income.'

'So how much is involved? Can you give me a figure, preferably in English pounds?'

He gave one of his sighs. 'In English pounds? It will not be less than four hundred.'

And after five years of marriage and of being a king's mistress I had a great deal more than four *thousand* pounds on deposit in Zurich. I kissed him. 'Your debts will be paid.'

*   *   *

I was happy. When I had left Edward, and he had settled my income on me, I had, for the first time in my life, felt utterly free, in a physical and financial sense. But I had still been emotionally tied to a love that had evaded me every time I had sought to grasp it. Now I was truly free. It was not that I did not love Spiro. I think I loved him even more than I had loved Felix. At that time I could not imagine us ever parting. But I was in total control, emotionally, mentally, and above all, financially, almost as if I were the husband. It was a position I had always wished to be in, and now I had achieved my goal. Which is not to say that there were not difficulties ahead. The first occurred the very next morning, when I was confronted by Emma. 'I must leave your service, milady,' she said.

I'm afraid I goggled at her. What she was saying made no sense. 'Is your family in trouble?'

'No, milady. But I cannot remain here.'

'I agree with you. But we intend to find better accommodation as soon as possible.'

'Count Theotoky will continue to live with you?'

'That is why I came here, Emma. To live with the Count.'

'But, milady, you are the Baroness von Venningen.'

'And you think that to change my name to the Countess Theotoky would be a retrograde step? Actually, in terms of titles, I think I could be moving up. But my dear girl, a title is only as good as the man, or woman who possesses it. I have been betrayed by a prince, abandoned by a king. I like my count better.'

'But you are still married to the Baron, milady.'

'I have just indicated that I intend to change that, as soon as possible.'

'But until it becomes possible, milady, you will be living in sin.'

'Oh, for Heaven's sake, Emma, I have spent half my life living in sin, as you call it. I was living in sin when you came into my employ.'

'Not so, milady. You were having an amour. You were not sharing a house, on a permanent basis, with a man who was not your husband.'

I was speechless, partly with outrage and partly with amazement that a woman of her class should be so prepared to separate hairs as it were. But, being in a triumphalist mood, I was not prepared to discuss my situation. 'Then you had better leave,' I told her. She was clearly taken aback by such a peremptory dismissal, but she was too stubborn to ask for reinstatement, and so we parted company, after ten years. I was sorry to see her go, because, willy-nilly, one shares a great deal with one's maid, and they had been a tumultuous ten years, but I realized that as I was about to begin a new life, which I anticipated, correctly as it turned out, would be entirely different to the old, it was probably best to make a fresh start in every direction.

I did not immediately replace her, for all the inconvenience of lacking a maid and having to cope with my clothes and my toilette, not to mention Bonzo's nocturnal habits, on my own. Instead, as soon as my money arrived and Spiro's debts were settled, we left Paris for an extended holiday at Honfleur, on the Channel coast. It was well into spring, the weather was warm and our situation was delightful. Not surprisingly, by the time we returned to Paris in the summer, I was pregnant, although I did not yet know it.

Paris this summer was entirely distracted by the news that Bonaparte, or at least his body, was to be returned from St Helena for a state funeral in Les Invalides. The return did not take place until the following year, but everyone was in a state of patriotic excitement.

Spiro and I had hitherto enjoyed a relieving anonymity, which lasted until we started to house-hunt, which we did as the Count and Countess Theotoky. For all the time he had lived in the capital, Spiro had necessarily kept a low profile, as he had lacked the funds to indulge in high society, and as he was neither a poet, a journalist, a sculptor nor an actor, he had made no impact on the Left Bank cafes either. But when we had found a house, No. 83, Place Bourbon, and I started to accompany him to the theatre and the opera, tongues began to wag.

People wondered where we had come from and why our coming had not been announced. But soon enough we encoun-tered those who remembered Lady Ellenborough. Then others remembered that Lady Ellenborough had married Baron von Venningen, and they began to wonder where and how a Greek count fitted into the picture, and rapidly arrived at the right conclusion. The scandal naturally spread across the Channel, and once again I was damned. Sadly, this time the damnation spread to my immediate family. I only learned this later, but although Mama did her best to defend me, Papa joined Grandpa in forbidding my name to be mentioned in his presence, and had all my portraits, even a couple of miniatures, removed from the house.

But despite this sad news, I was happy. My pregnancy could be shared and enjoyed with my lover, in such contrast to the secrecy that had necessarily shrouded so many of my previous confinements, but more than this I was delightedly learning more and more about Spiro, and most of it I liked. I discovered that his family, if lacking the wealth normally associated with position, was every bit as prominent in Greek politics and society as were the Cokes in England, and that he would, in the course of time, be required to take on high office. With me at his side? I found the idea most attractive, if only because it would be a slap in the face for my many detractors. But the man himself had hidden depths, and for all his public persona of gay irresponsibility was deeply interested in literature, in every form – his hobby was bookbinding – and he also aspired to write poetry of his own. If only he did not smoke incessantly, but as I was to discover, this was a national pastime. He also, at my request, taught me to speak, read, and write Greek, a difficult subject, mainly because of its alphabet. But with my gift for languages I rapidly mastered it, enjoying every moment of my lessons.

By Christmas, I had dropped out of circulation as I was then six months pregnant. The moment I became aware of my condition I wrote Karl and formally asked for a divorce. But he did not reply, and on 21 March 1840 I gave birth to a son. He was baptized John Henry, Count Theotoky, but in my desire to become more Greek than the Greeks themselves I always called him Leonidas, that immortal name which is the foundation stone of Grecian romantic history. Spiro was delighted, and now began to make serious plans for our future.

Somewhat to my concern, these required strict adherence to Greek protocol. Thus, in the first instance, although I was a twice married woman, and in fact still *was* a married woman, he did not feel he could officially set our relationship in motion, as it were, until he had informed my parents of his intentions and obtained their consent. I could see no prospect of this happening and had to warn him that he was setting himself up for a considerable snub. But he was adamant, and off he went. I could not accompany him as Leonidas was still at my breast, so I had to wait patiently for his return, being looked after by Giorgio, his man, who was delighted when I bought him a proper livery.

To complete my household, I now found myself a new maid, named Eugenie. She was a statuesque young woman in her middle twenties, with dark hair and handsome features, and an effervescent personality. More importantly, she did not demur when I informed her that we would soon be leaving France for Greece. Indeed, she seemed quite excited at the prospect. Poor girl, she had no idea what she was letting herself in for. But then, neither did I. And she became my most faithful companion, remaining at my side through thick and thin.

I therefore felt I had completed as many arrangements as I could pending some sort of reply from Karl and Spiro's return from England, when one morning Giorgio came into my sitting room to announce, 'There is a gentleman to see you, milady.'

He could never get accustomed to using a tray, and merely held out the card, which I took without great interest, and then rose in temporary alarm: the name on the card was Karl, Baron von Venningen.

I quickly got my nerves under control. 'Is he alone?'

'Yes, milady.'

Which did not mean there was not going to be a scene. But at least Leonidas was safely in his cot upstairs. I did not wish Karl to see the boy, or even to know of his existence, as I was very aware that so long as I was legally his wife, any child I might produce was also legally his, if he chose to recognize it. Having had such a chequered maternal career, I was absolutely determined to keep Leonidas at my side until he was grown to manhood. 'You may show the Baron in, Giorgio,' I said. 'But stay close.'

I faced the door, and a moment later, Karl. 'You're looking well,' he remarked.

'As are you.'

He came closer. 'Are you alone?'

'Apart from Giorgio. My servant,' I replied meaningfully. 'And my maid.'

'Theotoky is not here?'

'At the moment, no. He is away, briefly, on business. Would you like a glass of wine? I'm afraid it's only sherry.'

'Of course. It is all you drink during the day, is it not?' I poured, and he raised his glass. 'What memories this brings back.'

'Please sit down,' I suggested, and did so myself, in a some-what isolated straight chair, so that he could not get too close to me. 'You must excuse my appearance.' My hair was loose, and I wore a house gown. 'What brings you to Paris?'

He sat opposite me. 'You.'

'You did not reply to my letter.'

'I thought it best not to. I understood that you needed to flap your wings. Now that you have done so, I would like you to come back with me.'

'I am not going to do that, Charles. I asked you for a divorce. I am doing so again, now.'

'You realize that you are universally condemned?'

'I have been condemned before. For responding to my feel-ings rather than behaving like a stuffed dummy.'

'It has become a serious business. An order has been issued, declaring that should you cease to be the Baroness von Venningen, you are forbidden to set foot in Bavaria, or indeed in any German state, again, on pain of immediate imprisonment.'

'You had that order issued?'

'No, I did not. But I have an idea who did.'

'Ludwig? I cannot believe it.'

'I would say it was almost certainly him. He regards you as having betrayed him. So, will you come back with me?'

Not for the first time in my life, I had a strong sense of déjà vu. Karl could have been Mama, pleading with me to abandon Felix, unaware that I could not do so because I was bearing, or in this case had already borne, his child. But as with Mama, I was not going to give in. 'No,' I said.

'You may see him as often as you like. Just be my wife.'

'Spiro cannot accept that arrangement. He wishes me to be *his* wife.'

'And his wishes are more important than mine?'

'To me, at this moment, yes. Will you divorce me?'

'I have explained that if I do that, you will be damned from one end of Germany to the other.'

'If it is my fate to be damned, then so be it. I intend to enjoy my journey to Hell.'

For several moments he stared at me so intently I anticipated an attempt to take me by force. But I knew that Giorgio was close by. And after those moments Karl said, quietly, 'I will send you your belongings.' Then he bowed and left the room without another word. After I had heard the door bang, I wept.

Spiro was back a few days later, to my great relief. But his visit had been no easier. 'Your mother was very charming, and even appeared to be sympathetic,' he told me. 'But it was all she could do to prevent your father ordering me from the house.'

'But you did obtain the permission you sought, to marry me whenever possible?'

'I was given to understand that as you had left his control he was no longer interested in what you did. That is outrageous behaviour from a father.'

'Well, I suppose one could say that I have been guilty of outrageous behaviour as a daughter. Now let me tell you my news.'

I brought him up to date. 'The devil,' he commented. 'Will he make trouble?'

'I do not think so. He appears to have accepted that I will not return to him. But he still will not divorce me.'

'You must be my wife before we return to Greece. My family is very strict.' Another case of déjà vu, and this *was* profoundly depressing. 'However,' Spiro went on, hesitantly, 'there might be a way.' He paused, gazing at me.

'Tell me what it is, and I shall do it.'

'It would mean renouncing your religion. Joining the Orthodox Church.'

I considered, but only for a few seconds. I believe in God but I have never blindly accepted the various tenets proclaimed by mortal men in His name. And as I had already been accused of breaking every moral and ethical tenet known to man – and was to break a few more in the coming years – I cannot claim to be a religious person. If I had a motto it would be Apollo's 'Know

Thyself' and to this I have faithfully kept. But I knew that I would not be welcomed in any Anglican communion, and while I had been prepared to accept Roman Catholicism if it would have enabled me to marry Felix, I had entirely gone off that idea. Thus, taking another step away from what might be called my religious roots did not seem a terrible crime. If . . . 'Will that help us?' I asked.

'Certainly. The Greek Orthodox Church does not recognize any act of the Roman Catholic Church as valid. And this attitude includes the Anglican Communion. If you were to join our communion, your previous marriages would not be recognized as having ever existed, and therefore there would no longer be any necessity for you to seek a divorce.'

'What a splendid idea,' I said.

Besides, it was a new adventure, of the spirit rather than the body, and even more besides, I had already determined to adopt Greece and its people and customs entirely as my own.

Joining the Greek communion took some time, and involved a great deal of study as well as long hours spent closeted with various black-robed priests, some of whom were quite young, and several of whom seemed to be more interested in my physical rather than my spiritual salvation. I merely smiled and fluttered my eyelashes at them, which seemed to drive them even more into a tizzy. Of course I cannot pretend to have understood all the nuances of this, to me, new faith, and I found their belief in iconography off-putting, but by the time I was accepted into the Orthodox communion I was as fluent in Greek as in English.

I also spent my spare time well, and my money, buying various items I felt I might have difficulty in obtaining in Greece, such as some splendid saddles – I had abandoned all my horse furniture in Mannheim – as well as a grand piano. I also commissioned a full dinner service for a hundred people, each piece bearing the Theotoky crest. Spiro regarded all of these items with some unease, not because of the expense – he had come to regard my pocket as bottomless – but because he felt they indicated that I was not truly aware of what I was going to. 'Tinos,' he attempted to explain, 'which is where my father is governor, is a very small and primitive island.

There is nothing there like Paris, or Munich, or London. Or the English countryside.'

'I shall adore it,' I promised him. 'It is Greek.'

He was more enthusiastic, even if more taken aback, when I discovered in a gunsmith's shop, some pistols unlike anything I had ever seen before. 'They come from America,' the proprietor told me. 'They are made by a man named Samuel Colt.'

'Why do they have such a bulge in the middle?'

'That is the chamber. It holds six bullets. You cock it just like an ordinary pistol, you see, but as you squeeze the trigger, when the hammer falls and discharges the shot, the chamber automatically revolves to present the next bullet. The pistol is called a "revolver".'

'You mean it will fire six times without being reloaded?'

'That is exactly it, Madame.'

'I must have one. No, two.'

He rubbed his hands. 'I have a matching pair. The handles are pearl.'

'That sounds perfect.'

'And cartridges? They do not fire ball, you see, but rifled bullets. This gives them several times the range, and the accuracy, of an ordinary pistol.'

'Six boxes.'

'I did not know you knew anything about firearms,' Spiro remarked.

'I adore firearms. When I was a girl I was regarded as the best shot in Norfolk. That is a county in England. Let us find somewhere appropriate, and I will show you.'

We were now ready to be married, but there remained one potential obstacle to be overcome, about which I will admit that I was apprehensive. I have been accused of living my entire life as a giddy adolescent, and I will admit that there have been several occasions when I have considered that the action of the moment far outweighed *any* possible repercussions. But in one direction I have never wavered an inch. As I have mentioned, since leaving Edward I have been the sole mistress of my financial affairs. I had no intention of relinquishing control of this situation, whatever rights of husbands established by Greek law. Now I was going to a profoundly poor country, where, my bankers informed me, the cost of living was about one tenth of that in Paris. In other words, if my eight hundred a year was comfortable in Paris, it would become the equivalent of a staggering eight *thousand* a year in Greece, which, they also informed me, would make me just about the wealthiest person, male or female, in the country – not excluding the King! I therefore put this to Spiro, with, as I have said, some apprehension as to his response. I made it clear that while I would willingly devote my income to the well-being of him, and his family, if need be, its disposition must remain always in my hands, although I did offer to make him a personal allowance of a hundred pounds a year – again a fortune in Greece – to be spent as he chose. In the event I was entirely relieved. Like Karl, Spiro agreed that a legal document should be drawn up establishing our arrangement beyond risk of contradiction. And so, all the bookwork having been brought to a satisfactory conclusion, Spiro and I were married in Marseilles, in March 1841, and a few days later, accompanied by Leonidas, Eugenie, Giorgio, and Bonzo, we sailed for Greece.

The Land of Dreams

As I was now turning my back on Western Europe forever, except for one or two fleeting visits, it may be as well to conclude the fates of the various men who had up till now filled my life.

Edward did not prove a success as Governor-General of India; there are, indeed, those who lay the outbreak of the Indian Mutiny, some years later, at the door of his high-handed actions.

Due to the British habit of never admitting they have made a mistake, he was allowed a triumphant return to England, and was even, at the end of his political career, created Viscount Seaham. Think of it, I could have equalled step-grandma Anne, and been a countess in England rather than Greece. But only if I had remained married to Edward, and that is not a fate I could wish upon any woman. He never did marry again, although he has only recently died.

Felix had an altogether different career. He did eventually marry, the Princess Windisgratz, and remained prominent in Austrian politics with the result that when Metternich was forced to flee Vienna following the revolution of 1848, he found himself Chancellor, charged with ending the revolt. This he did in a most typical fashion, surrounding the city, which was in the hands of the insurgents, with the army and bombarding it into submission, this although his pregnant wife was within the walls! He died only a couple of years later.

And Karl, dear Karl, remained true to his love. When he discovered that I had exited by the back door, as it were, and that I had borne Spiro a son, he did institute divorce proceedings, which included an affidavit that Leonidas was not and could not be his son, as I had left his bed several months before the child could have been conceived. These steps were no doubt necessary to negate any risk of Leonidas ever claiming part of the Venningen inheritance, but they did not affect his love for me. Indeed, he

wrote me a most charming letter in which he stated, unequivo-
cally that he would always welcome me back if I chose to return.
He never married again, and to my great pleasure Heribert has
inherited.

But at the time I was only concerned that I was again sailing on
the Mediterranean; the previous occasion had been my visit to Sicily
in 1831. And this time I was neither pregnant nor apprehensive of
the future. I had my husband and lover always at my side, my son
always within touching distance, my faithful dog at my feet, and only
the present mattered. Even when the weather proved entirely different
to my previous experience of it and we were overtaken by strong
winds, I delighted in being on deck, watching the great tumbling
waves and feeling the spray dashing against my cheeks. However, for
all my utter happiness, I was concerned at Spiro's uneasiness as we
approached his ancestral home. There were apparently two reasons
for this. 'You understand,' he said, when the storm had blown itself
out, as we sat on the afterdeck while the ship ghosted along before
light airs and over calm seas, 'that Tinos, where my father is presently
governor, is a very small island.'

He had raised this matter before, and my answer was the same.
'I can hardly wait to see it. How long will we stay there?'

'I have told my father six months.'

'Oh, splendid. Why cannot we make our home there?'

'Because our family home is in Corfu. That is where we shall
live after our visit to Tinos. Corfu is a splendid place, very English.
You will love it.'

That wasn't exactly what I wanted to hear. My ambition was
to turn my back on all things English. 'And Tinos is not splendid?'

'Well, it is. But it is, well . . . it is not good horse country. All
up and down. And there is not much company.'

'It sounds exciting. As for company, why, I will have you, and
Leonidas, and your father.' He had informed me that his mother
was dead.

Which brought us to his second problem. 'We need to talk
about my father. My whole family.'

Oh, no, I thought. 'You told me they would approve of me,
once I joined your religion.'

'Oh, they will. They do.'

'They haven't met me.'

'I have told them all about you.' I turned my head. 'Well, not everything.'

'I think you should tell me exactly what you have told your family.'

'Well, they know you are the Lady Ellenborough, who was forced to flee from her cruel and licentious husband, and who I met living in Paris.'

I realized that he must have got together with Aponyi during his sojourn in the French capital, and not for the first time reflected that: *had* Edward been cruel and licentious, or at least licentious, I might well have still been his wife. 'Go on.' I could hardly wait to hear what else he had told them.

'That is it.'

I considered. 'I left Edward twelve years ago. What am I supposed to have done during those years?'

'I did not think it appropriate to go into dates.'

'You mean they know nothing of Prince Schwarzenberg?'

'No, no, they would not approve of that.'

'Or of Charles? I was his wife. In his eyes I am still his wife.'

'They would not be able to understand that.'

'And King Ludwig?'

'Good heavens, no. Nothing must ever be said of that. His son is King of Greece. Did you not know that?'

'I did know it. But surely there is not the slightest chance of us living in Greece and *him* not knowing it.'

'News travels slowly in Greece. What we need to do is keep a low profile. And in time, who knows.' He tapped his nose.

Had I been concentrating on any matters other than myself, I might have found this a trifle sinister. But I was still trying to find out exactly where I stood in Theotoky eyes. 'And my children? I have had six.'

'*Six?* And you are still the most beautiful woman in Europe? In the world?'

I kissed him. 'I seem to have a natural facility for it.'

'Does that figure include Leonidas?'

'Yes.'

'But the others . . . they are not likely to come seeking you?'

'I'm afraid not. Two are dead, and the others . . .' I sighed. 'I doubt they even know who their mother is.'

'That is a relief. As far as my family know, Leonidas is your first and only, so far. It would be best if they were to continue to think that.' He held my hands. 'You are not angry? I did as I thought best. I would hate anything to come between us, and I am so anxious to have my family welcome you.'

How could I be angry after such an appeal? In any event, at that time I loved him too dearly ever to be angry with him. Besides, I was being offered a gift available to very few people, the opportunity to begin my life all over again, with an absolutely clean slate. This was a most attractive prospect. Perhaps in my heart I knew that one can never truly banish the past, but being the optimist that I am I felt sure that if it *were* possible, I was the woman to manage it. 'I will make them love me,' I promised him.

This was actually very easy to do, certainly as regards his father: Johanne Theotoky took one look at his daughter-in-law and fell, head over heels. He was old enough to be my father, but it was very simple to discern where Spiro got his looks and his personality, and I cannot imagine what might have happened had I visited Tinos as a tourist instead of as Spiro's wife! As it was, Johanne welcomed me into the intimacy of his home with, quite literally, open arms. I am not often flustered by masculine attention, but his greeting quite took my breath away.

I use the word intimate advisedly, because I found myself plunged into a world I had not previously experienced. The island, and everything in it, was, as Spiro had warned, very small. This went for the governor's residence as well, although it was by far the largest and grandest on the island. It was situated in the very centre of the town, wall by wall with all the other houses, and was gained by trudging up a very narrow, steep and slippery cobbled street. The houses themselves made a delightful picture, in their pastel shades and traces of Byzantine architecture, but it was impossible to sneeze without the entire island being aware of it. Equally was it impossible to get the smell of tobacco out of one's nostrils, for where in England no gentleman would smoke in the presence of a lady without being granted permission, in Greece no gentleman would consider himself a gentleman, or, apparently, be so considered by his womenfolk, without a strong-smelling cigar clenched between his teeth, the stronger smelling the better. Actually, having lived with Spiro for a year and suffered his habit for that time, I was prepared for this, and I even gave some thought to joining in what appeared to be the national pastime, if only in self-protection, but decided against it, principally because I rapidly observed that the teeth so employed were stained an ugly brown, and I have always been proud of the whiteness of my teeth.

But the intimacy without was nothing compared with the intimacy within. Spiro and I at least had a bedroom to ourselves, but we were required to share it with Leonidas, not to mention Bonzo. Johanne also had a room to himself, but the servants, in whose midst Eugenie found herself, slept as and where they might, all over the remainder of the house. As there was no such thing as a water closet on the island, the privy being an evil-smelling hut at the end of the garden, had I not brought with me a china chamber pot I would often have found myself *in extremis*. Equally I quickly realized that my expensive Paris purchases would be quite out of place in these surroundings, and left them packed up for the time being. This especially applied to my new saddles, for there was not a horse on the island, nor anywhere to ride one if there had been; it all went either straight up or straight down, and even mules had a difficult time.

All in all, I had not been on Tinos twenty-four hours before I understood Spiro's apprehension. But in fact I loved it. Everything about it appealed to that longing for primitiveness I had always possessed but never yet had the opportunity to indulge. My only disappointment was that there was no view of the sea from the governor's residence, but that was scarcely important when the coast could be reached by a five minute walk. And on these walks one became aware of the delicious smell of the island for the slopes were covered in wild herbs of every description, rosemary, thyme, oregano, and above all, basil. Basil, indeed, could be described as Tinos's national flower, and when I landed I was presented with a bouquet of it. But the island itself was a never-ceasing source of interest. Like all Greece it was a treasure house of antiquities, from ancient ruins to still discoverable artefacts which might date back to Homeric times.

But my principal joy, apart from Spiro, who continued to be everything I had ever wanted in a man, was my son. On Tinos, far removed from social distractions, I for the first time discovered the true joy of motherhood. I had loved all of my other children, but in the English upper-class society into which I had been born and grew up, maternal love was always once removed from its object, separated as it was by an army of nannies. Obviously this was very convenient for the mother, and I must be honest here and confess that it was probably more convenient for me than anyone else. But even before we had sailed from Marseilles I had resolved, after so many mishaps, to take every possible care, and lavish every possible affection on my son, and this resolution was enhanced when we reached Tinos, where I found I had the time to indulge it. Spiro would have employed local women, but I declined and cared for Leonidas myself, changed his nappies, bathed him, fed him and cuddled him, assisted only by Eugenie, who, like me, seemed to take to her new life with enthusiasm, aided, I have no doubt by the even more enthusiastic attention of the Tinos males, who found the very well-endowed young Frenchwoman a considerable change from their more usual bedmates. To a man they also cast passionate glances at me whenever I left the house, but I was clearly not interested in them, and there was no one bold enough to risk the anger of the Governor's son by approaching me uninvited.

When not caring for Leonidas, and on occasion even while doing so, I also discovered the pleasures of Greek cuisine, so unlike anything I had ever known before, with every menu containing items such as pigeon or octopus, all enhanced by the variety of herbs I have mentioned. The wine was equally strange to me, and while I must confess that I never did acquire a taste for retsina, I found the more normal wine very palatable. Most of our supply we obtained from the neighbouring island of Santorini, which was of peculiar interest to me, as some historians have identified Santorini with Plato's Atlantis, destroyed by an earthquake several thousand years before the birth of Christ. The facts of the earthquake are self-evident, and there are also historians who claim that the blast was so vast it was also responsible for the collapse of the Cretan Empire, once the dominant factor in Aegean civilization.

We were not entirely lacking in society. The doctor, an Italian named Zallony, was good company, and there was a little foreign colony on the neighbouring island of Siros, which we visited from time to time. The British consul, a Mr Wilkinson, was most pleasant to me, but I never felt fully at ease in his company, as I did not know how much he knew of my background, and thus what he might be saying behind my back. However, I regard my sojourn on Tinos as one of the happiest periods of my life. But an even happier period was now upon me. Having prolonged our stay with Spiro's father for very nearly a year, in the spring of 1842 we moved on to Corfu.

I was agog to see my new home, in which, as usual, I expected to spend the rest of my life. My only regret was that we made the journey by sea; travelling from Tinos in the Aegean Sea to Corfu in the Ionian meant that we were skirting the country rather than plunging into its heart, as I would have preferred. Apparently the interior was so primitive, lacking roads and filled with bandits, that it was quicker and safer to go by sea, even if this meant retracing our route round the Peloponnese before turning up into the Ionian Sea.

But to my delight, Corfu was a paradise, certainly if one's name was Theotoky. No stronger contrast to Tinos could be imagined, and while I had thoroughly enjoyed my long, primitive honeymoon, this was actually the life to which I had been born and intended to enjoy. The island was far larger than Tinos, and instead of being composed of slippery rocks, however fragrantly interspersed with sweet-smelling brush, was a vista of rolling green hills and neat little copses. It could almost have been an English county. Then there was its situation. The Ionian Sea might not possess the 'wine-dark' quality of the Aegean, but it was more lively, and even more steeped in history. From the shore of Corfu one could almost make out the naval battlegrounds of Actium and Lepanto, the one where the romantic dream of Antony and Cleopatra had been shattered, the other where the might of the Ottoman Empire had suffered its first defeat by the combined navies of Christendom. While only a few miles across the water there rose the mountains of Albania, perhaps the most remote and therefore fascinating part of Europe, into which fastnesses Byron had once ventured.

The history of Corfu as a Venetian colony had been tumultuous;

since the destruction of Venice itself as a power by Bonaparte in 1797 the island had fallen into foreign hands: Russian, French and now British. This last, from my point of view, was Corfu's only drawback, but far from being ostracized the beautiful Countess Theotoky was welcomed by the ex-patriot colony, and the High Commissioner himself, Lord Nugent, came to call. Sadly, the one obvious contribution of the British to Corcyrean scenery was the enormous High Commissioner's palace, which I assume was intended to overawe the populace with a constant reminder of Britain's wealth and power, and which was certainly grand but inexpressibly vulgar. However, if the British community seemed pleased to have me in their midst, the Greeks were overjoyed, and none more so than the many Theotoky relatives, who welcomed me as if I were a visiting goddess. Within hours of our arrival I had achieved a stature I had enjoyed, so very briefly, in Munich in 1833. This time I fully intended that it should endure for the rest of my life. I had not yet reached an age where one understands that nothing lasts forever.

For the moment, bliss. Even before my arrival Spiro was the island's most famous living son. My beauty, and my wealth transformed us into virtual royalty. We already owned a huge amount of land, and two houses. The town house, while large and interesting enough because of its Venetian design, was for that very reason not the most comfortable, being square and dark and situated in too close proximity to its neighbours. I preferred our country estate, Dukades, where, if the house was smaller, the surroundings were idyllic. I felt I was stepping back in time, for here were the almost feudal conditions that had obtained at Holkham, where all the neighbouring villagers recognized Spiro as their lord and myself as their lady, and where we could do as we liked. All the china and furniture and ornaments I had bought in Paris at last found a home, and I set about creating my own version of Holkham as fast as I could, planting an English garden, establishing a music room for my piano and a library, not only for myself but also to assist Spiro's aspirations, while I also had a workshop set up for him to pursue his bookbinding hobby.

Naturally, I wanted a stable of the best horses I could find, and resumed my cherished morning ride, which I greatly expanded from trotting decorously along crowded bridle paths as in London or Munich to galloping gloriously across open country, leaping hedges and streams as in my girlhood. I was also introduced to a pleasure I had never experienced before – sea-bathing. We had a private beach in a cove on the west coast of the island, called Paleokastritsa. This was a truly beautiful spot, but even its natural attraction could not compare with the delicious freedom of plunging naked into the surf, a pleasure rendered the more exquisite because legend had it that this was the beach where Odysseus, during his lengthy voyage home from Troy, had been washed ashore, rescued the Princess Nausicaa from a sea monster, and enlisted the aid of her father in regaining Ithaca, which was in fact only a few miles away, although it seemed to take him a long time to get there.

When not disporting ourselves, there were the usual ruins to be explored as well as the flower festivals to be enjoyed. These were held in honour of the patron saint of the island, St Spiridion, after whom Spiro was named; and thus we attended them in our carriage, wearing our best, and flying the Theotoky banner.

And we entertained, again on the scale I recalled from Holkham. Our parties soon became famous. Or possibly notorious would be a better description. I know that an Englishman's capacity for consuming vast quantities of port and brandy is well established, but this over-indulgence usually takes place during or after a meal, when the digestion, and the brain, are perhaps better equipped to cope with an influx of alcohol. Our guests in Corfu indulged in a local spirit called raki, which had a strong flavour of aniseed, *before* the meal, with the result that by the time they got to table they were already drunk. On to this dangerous base they proceeded to pour vast quantities of wine, brandy and port, this last being new to them and possibly stronger than they expected, with the result that the evening invariably got out of hand. I am bound to confess that I indulged as much as anyone, even if on occasion I feared for my house and even more for my furnishings and crockery, with good reason. I well remember the night that Spiro hit a priceless antique table so hard that he cracked its marble top. Even more do I recall the evening when our guests decided to indulge in a plate-smashing contest – apparently an old Greek custom – and demolished virtually my entire dinner service. Working on the principal that if you can't beat them the best thing to do is join them, I hurled some plates myself but cleaning up the mess afterwards was, quite literally, a shattering experience. I immediately ordered a new set.

For very nearly two years I was utterly happy on Corfu. Naturally, I wished my family to know of my successful achievement of at least local respectability, and wrote Mama all about it. I would dearly have liked her and Papa to visit and see for themselves how their black sheep had at last found both happiness and social accept- ance, and was the more shocked when Mama replied that she could not come this year, as Grandpa had died. Well, he was ninety years old and had lived a very full life. It was seventeen years since I had seen him, but I could not help feel that an era had ended.

I was depressed for a while after receiving this news, and had hardly recovered when I suffered an even more crushing blow. I received another letter from Mama informing me that Papa had also died. I had not actually known my father as well as I had known my grandfather, and here again we had been estranged for some years, but it is impossible to view the death of a parent without considerable sorrow. At least I could reflect that Mama would be in the safe care of my brothers, and would find considerable solace in her growing number of grandchildren, even if she had not yet, in my opinion, met the best of them all. But this I was determined to put right as soon as it could be managed. Sadly, politics now got in the way of happiness.

Mourning for Grandpa and Papa over, we resumed our blissful existence, but I noticed that during the summer of 1843 Spiro was somewhat preoccupied. I understood that this was to do with developments in Athens, but as I was resolved not to become involved in Greek politics I did not inquire into the cause of his concern. I was therefore the more surprised when on a morning in the autumn, he came into my room where I was dressing for our ride, and announced, 'It has happened! We have regained control of our country.'

This was a profoundly disturbing remark. 'What is it you are saying?'

'There has been a *coup d'état*.' Shades of Paris in 1830! 'This fellow Otto . . . but you know him!'

'I have met the King,' I agreed. 'When he was a boy.'

'You were friendly with his father.'

A masterly understatement. 'Yes, I was friends with Ludwig. But that was after Otto had taken up his duties here in Greece.'

'The man has been a disaster. And that wife of his . . .'

'And you are saying that he has been deposed?'

'No, no. The powers would not allow that. The palace has been surrounded by troops, and he has been given an ultimatum. He must get rid of all these Bavarians who have been running the country for the past ten years, and grant a constitution. What, do you suppose we, who fought so hard to free ourselves from the Turks, will simply submit to being ruled by Bavaria?'

I remembered Ludwig's visit to Greece in 1836, and realized that this crisis must have been simmering for some time. But I still did not see why Spiro should be involved. Nor did I wish him to be. 'My darling Spiro,' I said, 'you are being unnecessarily vehement. *I* do not expect you to accept anything. I am entirely on your side. But will the powers stand for *that*?'

'They appear to have done so. They know we are in the right. And a constitution has been granted, placing Greeks in all positions of authority.'

'Then your friends are to be congratulated. But will you tell me one thing: were you involved in this *coup d'état*?'

'No, no. I was here.'

'But was there any correspondence?'

'Well, I wrote them letters of support. Would you not have had me do that? They are my friends. And they have acted correctly.'

I considered. Otto was Ludwig's son, and, perhaps more important, a Wittelsbach, and while I had to assume that his acceptance of the will of the conspirators had no doubt been on the advice of his father I also knew, from personal experience, that my erstwhile royal lover could bear a grudge, and avenge himself whenever possible. But I could see no point in agitating Spiro all over again by suggesting a future problem which might never arise. 'No doubt they did. Let us hope things will be better from now on. Tell me about the Queen.'

'Her name is Amalia, and she is the daughter of the Grand Duke of Oldenburg.'

'You mean Otto did not marry a Greek princess?' I felt that had to have been a grave mistake.

'There is no such thing as a Greek princess.'

Which explained that: a king had to marry royalty. 'How old is she?'

'Oh, she came straight from school to marry the King, in 1837. That is only six years ago. I doubt she is twenty-one yet.'

Oh, to be twenty-one again: I was now contemplating the dread figure of forty, although with less apprehension than I had thirty. 'Is she handsome?'

'*She* thinks she is.'

'Are there children?'

He shook his head. 'The King contracted malaria soon after coming to Greece, and is never in good health. So his wife has nothing to do but rush about the place – she has enough energy for two – giving orders, commanding things to be built with money the country does not have . . .'

'You are becoming vehement again. Is she likely to come to Corfu?'

'I very much doubt it.'

'Well, then, we shall never have to meet her.'

I was, as always, being over optimistic. The following spring a letter arrived from Athens, commanding Count Spiridion Theotoky to take up residence in the capital and his position as first aide-de-camp to His Majesty.

'Can you not decline?' I asked.

'Decline? One does not decline the King's command. Besides, it is a great honour. To be the King's aide-de-camp . . .'

'Meaning that you will be in constant attendance, and thus in the company of a man, and a woman, you despise.'

'Well . . . it is my duty.'

He was clearly too flattered to regard the appointment dispassionately. 'And I presume I am required to accompany you.'

He frowned. 'Don't you wish to live in Athens? It is our capital city.'

'I am happy here. I am happier here than I have ever been in my life.'

'That is because you have never been to Athens. You will love it there.'

* * *

Despite my protests at leaving my new home for what seemed an indefinite period I was prepared to believe him; to visit Athens had always been my dream. Thus, the disappointment was greater than it should have been. Athens was a dump, saved from being a catastrophe by the presence of the Acropolis dominating the miserable accumulation of decrepit houses at its foot, which contained an equally miserable accumulation of decrepit people and animals. To get there we had to retrace our sea voyage round the Peloponnese, and my heart sank the moment I first looked at Piraeus. The fabled harbour, which had in antiquity housed the Athenian fleet, was a backwater of crumbling docks, rotting fishing vessels, and disintegrating houses.

This first impression was not relieved by the fact that it was raining, and indeed it rained throughout our journey up the historic route to the city, once enclosed by the famous Long Walls, but now as decrepit as everything else in this decrepit country. Looking back, I suppose it was quite fortunate that my first glimpse of Athens should be in the pouring rain, otherwise I might have commanded the carriage to be turned and regained Corfu with all possible haste. The water mist gave the looming Acropolis a grandeur which it certainly possessed, but also shrouded the decrepitude beneath it, and one always had the reassuring certainty that the rain would stop, eventually. What I did not know was that when the rain stopped, for the summer, the flowing water would be replaced by flowing dust, which got everywhere the moment one ventured out of doors, and also covered everything indoors with a dirty film.

The Theotokys not having an Athens town house, indoors for us in the first instance meant the Hotel d'Europe, the only establishment regarded as habitable by visitors. I did not like the look of the place, or its surroundings, for the street outside was penetrated by an open sewer, nor was the hotel itself indicative of any grandeur to match its name, being situated above a bookshop. Our landlord was French, which promised well even if it was disconcerting to be surreptitiously peered at from behind curtains and through half-opened doors, and we were given a very passable meal.

As we had been travelling for several days we were early to bed, Eugenie and Leonidas in the next room – Giorgio slept downstairs – and were quickly asleep, only to be awakened an hour later by a loud noise, bangs and crashes, shouts and screams. Bonzo, sleeping as always beside my bed, began to bark, and Spiro and I both sat up, looking at each other in the gloom. The noise was coming up the stairs, and a moment later there was a banging on our door, accompanied by a woman's cries for help . . . in Italian! Spiro got out of bed and pulled on a dressing gown. I also got out of bed, but it was to locate one of my revolvers. Spiro unlocked the door, and the woman spilled into our midst, wearing a nightgown, her feet bare and her long dark hair flying. 'Help me! Help me!' she cried, still in Italian. 'He will kill me.'

As Spiro did not speak Italian, he was bewildered. I took over, while scooping Bonzo from the floor to tuck him under my arm and prevent him from doing anything rash, such as biting our unwanted visitor. 'Who will kill you?'

At that moment the door was wrenched open again, Spiro having neglected to re-lock it, and our host arrived. 'Where is the bitch?' he demanded. 'I will break every bone in her body.' This seemed to be in line with the woman's own estimation of the situation. However, his immediate intention was arrested by the sight of me. As I sleep naked he did not immediately notice the gun I was carrying, being more interested in everything else that was on view, including the dog in my arms, even in the semi-darkness. I laid down the weapon and placed Bonzo on the bed, in order to put on my dressing gown.

As he was speaking French, Spiro was now able to take part in the conversation, even if he was still trying to cope with our first visitor, who had got behind him and had thrown both arms round his waist while pressing herself against his back. 'Do you know this lady?' he asked, courteously, even if I felt he was stretching the bow a little.

'Lady?' the landlord shouted. 'That is my wife!'

'Good God!' Spiro commented.

I could see that I again needed to take charge of the conversation. 'And do you seriously intend to break every bone in her body?' I inquired.

'He will, he will,' the 'lady' wailed, now using French herself.

'That is no way to treat a wife,' I said severely, drawing on my considerable experience on the subject.

'She is a cheating Maltese bitch!' Which accounted for her use of Italian.

'I must ask you not to use language like that in front of *my* wife,' Spiro requested. 'Otherwise I shall chastise you!'

'I am sorry to have disturbed you, milord. Countess. Give her to me and we will trouble you no more.'

'But her screams will undoubtedly keep us awake for the rest of the night,' I pointed out. 'I must insist that you do not touch her for the duration of our stay in your establishment.'

'No man has the right to come between a man and his wife,' he declared, adding, piously, 'It says so in the Bible.'

'I am sure you are right,' I agreed. 'But the Bible makes no mention of a *woman* interfering, and this I am doing.' I picked up the revolver. 'If we hear one more scream I shall come downstairs and blow your foot off, and then set my dog on you.'

He goggled at the gun, clearly never having seen such a weapon before, and then at me, and then at Bonzo who had resumed a supporting role, uttering some very deep growls. 'The Countess is an excellent shot,' Spiro told him.

The landlord backed towards the door. 'You may go with him,' I told his wife. 'He will not trouble you again.'

'Oh, signora,' she said, releasing Spiro to kiss my hands. 'I owe you my life.'

'Just my sleep,' I assured her again and closed the door behind her.

Spiro and I looked at each other. 'Would you really shoot him?' he asked.

'Yes.' I laid down the revolver, removed Bonzo to the floor, and took off my dressing gown.

Spiro got into bed beside me. 'Have you ever been beaten?'

'No.'

'Not even . . . well . . .'

'By all the men who I have cheated? The answer is still no.'

'Or you would have shot them?' He took me in his arms. 'Remind me never to cheat on *you.*'

We enjoyed a good night's sleep, but, as may be imagined, by the next day the story of our interrupted slumber was all over the city, spread, I have no doubt, by the wife. Equally undoubtedly, it reached the palace; no one could argue that a new force had come to town. We, or at least I, had more important things on my mind. As I had no wish to spend a night longer than necessary in the Hotel d'Europe, however quiet it might have become, we immediately went house-hunting. Athens was divided, almost geometrically, into four quarters, but only one of these, the Neapolis, was regarded as suitable for foreign residents, and was indeed crowded with them. It lay to the right of Hermes Street, the main thoroughfare of the town, which was an extension of the road from Piraeus, and culminated in the royal palace, a rather drab four-square building of yellow plaster, which I later discovered had been laid over walls of the purest marble, mined from the nearby mountain of Pentelicus. I could not imagine what such a connoisseur of architectural beauty as Ludwig must have made of it.

Several of the houses in the Neapolis were available for rent, and although none of them appealed to me, we took one just to get us out of the hotel. But I had no intention of staying in it either. I located the name of Athens' leading architect, and invited him to call. His name was Cleantis, and he was a supercilious fellow, at least when we met. 'You wish me to build you a house, Countess? You have land?'

'I wish you to buy a suitable area for me. It must have a view over the countryside, and easy access to that countryside. Are there such plots available?'

'Oh, there are. But they are very expensive.'

'How expensive? Give me a figure in English pounds.'

'Well, it would of course depend upon the size of the house you wish to build . . .'

'I do not like small houses.'

'Ah. Well, a double plot, for instance, well . . . English pounds . . . we could be talking of at least fifty.'

I kept a straight face. 'I think for the house I have in mind, we will need six plots.'

'*Six!* What, do you mean to build a palace?'

'Yes.' He produced a handkerchief to wipe his brow. 'It must have three floors, twelve bedrooms, four bathrooms, a nursery, a ballroom, a large reception room, a large dining room, a private parlour, a music room, a library, an office, and a workroom for my husband. Oh, and a separate smoking-room. It must be fronted with Corinthian columns – those at the palace were Doric – made from Pentelicon marble and have an entry hall not less than thirty feet by fifteen and a grand staircase. There must also be a stable for my horses and kennels for my dogs. For the house itself you will use marble wherever practical and wood. I wish no plaster. I would like to see your plans one week today. I will make whatever adjustments are necessary then, so that building can commence as soon as possible. I will look at the plots you have selected tomorrow. I will leave it to you to attend to the purchase. Where did you have in mind? It must be a good neighbourhood.'

The handkerchief was hard at work. 'There is land available on Odos Sokratous. But Countess . . . the cost!'

'Give me a figure, again, in English pounds. I merely wish a guide. You can let me have a detailed estimate when you have completed the plans and purchased the land.'

'The cost . . . English pounds . . .' He shook his head. 'What you wish . . .' He pinched his lip. 'I do not think I could do this thing for less than two thousand five hundred.' He looked at me, anxiously.

'That will be satisfactory.'

'You mean . . . I must speak with your husband.'

'What is satisfactory to me will be satisfactory to my husband. As I have said, I will require a detailed analysis of the sum. You may present it with your plans at the end of the week.'

He gulped. 'But, Countess, there is not sufficient time.'

'Make sufficient time, Mr Cleantis. Do you have a bank?'

'Oh, yes, Countess. I have a bank.'

'Very good.' I went to my desk, sat down, and opened my cheque book. 'I will pay you in six tranches, working on three thousand five hundred pounds. Five hundred now.' I wrote the cheque, on my Zurich bank. 'That is to cover the cost of the land. Two hundred and fifty on approval of the plans. Two hundred and fifty when the foundations are laid. One thousand when I regard the work as half completed. Five hundred when I take possession of the house. And the final thousand when I have lived in it for six months and all necessary adjustments have been made. Is that satisfactory?'

'Oh, Countess . . .' He kissed my hand. 'I am forever in your debt.'

'No, no,' I said. 'I am in yours. But only, I hope, for a few months.'

This transaction also reached the palace, I suspect in a matter of minutes.

Spiro had immediately reported to the palace and been informed of his duties, which seemed to be fairly time-consuming. For the moment this did not bother me, as I was occupied with the arrival, from Corfu, of various pieces of furniture, including my piano, my sketching books, and my animals, especially my horses, principally Ghost, my favourite grey, for all of which stables had to be found as there were insufficient at our rented accommodation. There was also the exciting business of superintending the building of our new home, which attracted a great deal of attention, but that was nothing compared with our first Sunday afternoon, when Spiro and I joined the customary promenade on Patissia Road.

Anything less like the Bois de Boulogne or the Munich boulevards could hardly be imagined. If it was not actually raining, the unpaved surface remained muddy and filled with puddles; when we returned home I was forced to consign my gown to the bin. But while I was out . . . the Greeks, like so many other people, had never seen anything like me before, because of my Parisian clothes, my obviously valuable jewellery, and above all, to be quite immodest, my beauty. As on my first appearance at Almack's, as an eighteen-year-old bride, I conquered Athens in an hour. All of this undoubtedly also got back to the palace, where I was naturally required, within a few days of our arrival in Athens, to be presented at court. This was to be a private audience, and to Spiro's surprise, and I think, disappointment, I did not appear as nervous as he felt I should have been. I may say that for all his derogatory remarks in Corfu he had quite fallen for his new and high-profile appointment and was now the most loyal subject of the King. But to me, having been presented at two courts before this one, and both of considerably more importance, the whole affair was a trifle old hat.

This applied only to me. It seemed the whole palace was a-twitter

as I entered, and proceeded, on Spiro's arm, up the grand staircase and into the throne room, where their Majesties awaited me.
When I said this was to be a private presentation, I meant that
I was the only person being presented on this occasion. But the
chamber was filled with people, men in absurd uniforms and
women in outmoded gowns whispering behind their fans. I
ignored them save for a gentle smile as we proceeded up the
centre aisle to stand before the monarchs, where Spiro bowed
and I performed a deep curtsey. I was wearing my latest Paris
creation in pale blue, adorned with diamonds, rubies and pearls,
an ostrich feather in my hat, and I know I was a fairly dazzling
sight. But the sight which most dazzled Otto, as his wife observed,
was my décolletage, which was deep, and if I say so myself,
presented the most beautiful sight in all Greece. This had such
an effect upon the King that he rose from his throne, an unheard
of event in such circumstances, and himself descended from
the dais to take my hand and raise me up. 'Countess Theotoky,'
he said. 'Ianthe! Do you remember me?'

'How could I forget, Your Majesty,' I replied, with supreme
tact.

We gazed at each other. In all honesty, I could not reciprocate
the admiration in his eyes, although I tried. Otto was very obviously Ludwig's son, but he lacked the majesty his father had
always managed to project, this despite the fact that he wore
uniform, a dress Ludwig had seldom adopted. Nor was he actually as handsome as his father, although his looks were not assisted
by the sallow, malarial cheeks, or his tendency to tremble, no
doubt from the same cause. But he had some of his father's charm.
'As I could never forget you, Countess. I would like to present
you to my wife.'

I curtsied again, more briefly. 'Your Majesty.'

I straightened, and engaged in an eye to eye contact. But there
was no friendship here. Amalia was actually much older than Spiro's
estimate, and was in fact twenty-six. She was quite handsome, in
a bold fashion, and had a considerable figure, but it was considerable all over; even when sitting down it could be seen that
she was not very tall; although she had a long body, her legs were
somewhat short. While she could discern, from the situation of
my slim hips, that I had long legs, which gave me a matching

height to her husband's. Equally she could tell at a glance that I was wearing jewellery worth thousands of pounds, whereas hers was certainly not more than a few hundred. 'I am not so privileged as my husband,' she remarked. 'And indeed only heard your name a week ago.' An attempt at a put-down which, as I knew it to be a lie, had no effect on me whatsoever. 'But I look forward to knowing you better.'

'That will be *my* privilege, Your Majesty.'

'I ride most mornings at nine. Will you accompany me tomorrow?'

'I shall be honoured.'

'And you will be able to tell me about this house you are building.'

'She is the best horsewoman in Greece,' Spiro confided when we got home.

'Oh, really?'

'I know your reputation as the best horsewoman in *Europe*, my dearest. But it is not done to outdo a queen.'

He was clearly anxious. I kissed him. 'I shall, as always, be true to my motto.'

He became more anxious yet. He was, in any event, in something of a grouch about the house. Not that he did not like the sound of it; what he disliked was the fact that everyone referred to it as *my* house, which of course it was. He felt it was an insult to his manhood and to his family's reputation that it should be obviously my money – Cleantis, like everyone, had a wagging tongue – which was sustaining our high standard of living, as if it hadn't been my money that had sustained us ever since I had joined him in Paris. I did not take this upsurge of masculine vanity as seriously as perhaps I should, regarding it merely as a passing pique. I had never stinted him a penny that he wished to spend, as we had agreed, but equally as we had agreed, I did not intend to relinquish control over a penny of my income – or my capital.

However, I was aware of the difference between us, just about the first we had ever had, and which I put down entirely to our removal from the paradise that was Corfu to this ghastly place, a move that had been commanded by the King and no doubt his queen. That she should now be attempting to establish me in what she regarded as my proper place, rankled, the more so as I felt entitled to regard her virtually as my step-daughter-in-law. And for three years now I had wallowed in domesticity, without a single challenge to my courage, my personality, my will. Nor could I doubt that I had been challenged. I might have wealth and beauty beyond Amalia's reach, but she would still prove her superiority where it truly mattered. Well, I resolved, that will be over my dead body.

I was up at dawn, arranged Leonidas's day, then dressed in my finest habit with my new silk hat and a blue scarf, mounted Ghost, decorously riding side-saddle, and proceeded to the palace, arriving at five to nine. As I walked Ghost along the street crowds came out to watch me, little boys ran behind me, and I heard one shout, 'The Queen! The Queen!'

'That is not the Queen,' a man corrected him. 'That is the English aristocrat.'

Somehow that sounded far more grand.

The palace yard was littered with horses, grooms, ladies, and gentlemen and officers, quite a few of whom were obviously going to ride with us, but no queen. I reflected that it is a queen's privilege to be late, even as I determined that this queen was resolutely digging her own grave. One of the waiting gentlemen introduced himself to me, and then me to the rest of the would-be riders, who seemed a highly nervous lot, and then Amalia appeared, striding from the palace, twitching the skirt of her habit with her whip, and regarding me with some distaste, although she forced a smile. 'Are you always on time, Countess?'

'I was brought up to believe that it is courteous to be so, Your Majesty.' She glared at me, then mounted, wheeled her horse and rode out of the yard. I followed, and the rest of the party followed me. I had already been for one or two rides in the vicinity of Athens, and had observed that there was very little open country where a horse might really be let loose: all was small fields and orderly rows of olive trees. Amalia threaded her way through these natural obstacles, and I have to say that she handled her mount well, even if I doubted that she would do very well on an English hunting field.

Soon we emerged from the olive groves and discovered ourselves approaching a stream. This was fast-running but by no means wide, certainly not when compared with several of the streams at Holkham. The Queen set her mount at this and sailed across, then drew rein to discover whether I had managed to do the same, only to find me beside her. This brought another glare, which was not alleviated by the applause rising from our companions. We jumped several more streams and then rounded a copse and came in sight of a wall, not particularly high – about six feet – but which blocked the view of what might lie beyond. Amalia set herself at this, but was arrested by a shout from one of the following men. 'No, Your Majesty, no!' he bellowed. 'It is too dangerous!'

The Queen dragged on her reins and brought her mount to a halt. I, at her elbow as I had been throughout our ride, could have done the same, but I did not really regard a six-foot-high wall as dangerous, and so gave Ghost a nudge with my heel. She responded as always and it was only when we were already above the wall that I realized what the man had meant: the ground fell away sharply on the far side. This sort of obstacle is difficult to negotiate when one is side-saddle, but I slapped Ghost with my whip and she came down well, staggered a bit, and then regained her balance as I did mine. Gradually I brought her to a halt, and turned to look back at the wall, lined with faces, both equine and human, the humans cheering and clapping. I inquired after the Queen, and was told that she had gone home.

The Tragedy

'Her Majesty is chagrined,' Spiro told me.

'Because she lacked the courage to jump?'

'Because you knew she would not.'

'You are entirely mistaken, my darling. She knew the ground. I did not. She knew the danger of that wall; the warning shout was clearly pre-arranged. I had no idea what lay before me.'

'You could have broken a bone. You could have been killed.'

'I doubt that either of those possibilities would have bothered her in the least.'

'I cannot believe that. In any event, she was publicly humiliated. We are ruined, socially.'

'What, is His Majesty going to dismiss his aide-de-camp? His Greek aide-de-camp? His *Theotoky* aide-de-camp?'

This was a problem Amalia could not overcome. After the *coup d'état*, which had required the King to be surrounded by Greeks rather than Bavarians, he had chosen, with much publicity, the son and heir of one of the nation's most illustrious warriors. That his choice might have been influenced by his knowledge of the Count's wife was neither here nor there. The choice had been made and was known throughout Greece. For him now to dismiss Spiro would be regarded as backsliding on the agreement made between him and the army, while were it to become known that he had done so at the instigation of his wife would prove to the male-oriented Greek society that he was a weakling. Besides, unlike his wife, he liked me. And more.

Thus, when the invitations went out for the next ball, contrary to Spiro's apprehensions, our names were at the top of the list. Balls at the Greek court were very orderly affairs. All of what might be called the domestic guests were assembled in an antechamber, when, at nine o'clock, we were joined by the King and Queen. We then proceeded, in pairs, down the great hall and into the ballroom, one of the few attractive rooms in this feature-less pile, where the foreign guests were assembled, ambassadors, diplomats and various visitors regarded as worth entertaining. We mingled with these, briefly, until the entry of their Majesties, who followed us. Otto and Amalia moved amongst the guests, greeting the more important ones, then the signal was given, and the ball began with a ceremonial march around the room, the King giving his arm to the most prominent female guest, the Queen to her husband. Needless to say all eyes were on me, as I paraded behind them on the arm of a French school teacher named Edmond About, who later became well known as a satirical writer, and who wrote a great deal about me. But he is one of the very few of his kind I ever liked, because he was honest and told only what he knew, or saw, for himself. Well, most of the time.

The grand march lasted fifteen minutes, then the dancing proper began. I was much in demand, which did not improve the Queen's mood, but the climax came when, just before midnight, the orchestra struck up a polka. My card was entirely full, and I was standing fairly close to the royal couple while I awaited the arrival of my partner, and so could not help overhearing their exchange. 'This is our dance,' Otto said.

'I did not know it was a polka.' Amalia waved her card. 'Why was it not clearly indicated? I hate to polka. It is such a vulgar dance.'

The King looked at her, and then at me, I suspect, in the first instance, merely because I was there. Being me, I spoke without thinking. 'I love to polka, Sire.'

'Well, then . . .'

'But . . .' I fluttered my card, and at that moment my partner hurried up.

'I am sure,' Otto said, 'that Count Mavrocordato would prefer another drink.'

The Count hesitated, glanced at me — I waggled my eyebrows — then bowed. 'Of course, Your Majesty.'

Otto turned out to be a very good dancer, while I excelled myself, earning rounds of applause from the onlookers — everyone else soon stopped dancing to watch my flying skirts and heaving bosom — while Amalia glared at us. 'I must talk with you,' Otto said in a low voice when the music finally stopped. 'There is so much we have to discuss.'

'I am yours to command, Your Majesty,' I said.

I had all but forgotten Madame Normande's prophecy. But could it be possible that this was king number two? I felt quite breathless with anticipation. But this man was Ludwig's son. It would be almost like committing incest. But that was itself a stimulating thought! And if I needed time to consider, it seemed that no one else did. By morning, all Athens was convinced I was the royal mistress. This was the more titillating because so far as anyone knew the King had never before had a mistress, and was supposed to be disinterested in sexual matters. Actually, Otto was as interested in sex as are most men, but the weakness engendered by his malaria left him incapable of evidencing great physical passion. Amalia, who had indeed come straight from a convent to the King's bed, had rapidly formed the impression, from her husband's lacklustre performance, that sexual relations were a time-consuming and embarrassing bore, and as she was not in the least promiscuous, had never sought to have that impression corrected, and so instead turned her undoubted energy to grand architectural or horticultural schemes, regardless of the expense or whose toes she trod on in achieving her aims.

Which is not to suggest that she could not feel jealousy, although in my opinion this was of her position as the King's wife rather than of the man himself. She and I were bound to clash. It was not my fault that the crowds continued to follow me in the streets, cheering and applauding as if I were indeed the Queen herself. Equally, Spiro and I had to have a home. I do not see that I can be blamed for seeking one to match my background and childhood memories. That it cost, in terms of the Greek economy, more than anyone else in the country, including the Queen, could afford, was surely my business. And that when I attended a court function, at which every woman wore her best and her most expensive jewellery, my best should far outshine any other, including the Queen, was again surely not my fault, however tactless it might have appeared to some. It certainly appeared so to Spiro. 'You are determined to ruin me,' he complained. 'And that dance!'

'Would you have me refuse the King?'

'You could have said you did not dance the polka.'

'But I enjoy dancing the polka, and I was about to do so with Count Mavrocordato.'

At that moment neither he nor anyone else knew that I had received a proposition from the King. Nor was I the least sure what I wanted to have happen. I was not really attracted to Otto, physically, while I was very aware that he was eight years my junior. Against these minuses there were two very positive pluses. One was the simple fact that he was the King. The other was the prophecy. Here was number two knocking on my door. I would not have been human did I not consider that if I *did* have an affair with Otto, where might the third king come from?

But more than anything else, he had suddenly emerged as a prod to my always restless spirit. I had supposed, and intended, that it had been laid to rest. But there had never been any hope of that, mainly because Spiro and I had achieved a relationship which was tending towards the humdrum. I enjoyed being his wife as much as I enjoyed being the controlling influence in his life, at least financially, but much as I still found his love-making exquisite, even that was tending towards the predictable. Now, suddenly, I again found myself in the role of the quarry, with that glorious uncertainty as to what would happen to me when I was captured.

I continued my usual life, rode in the morning, accepting the plaudits of the crowd, spent the afternoon amusing Leonidas, in the early evening visited the site of our new home, which was rising rapidly, and in the late evening attended whatever function was available – there was no theatre in Athens. With no other distraction, until, about a fortnight after the famous ball, I was at the site, discussing the decorations with Cleantis, when there was a sudden rustle amongst the workmen, and we both turned to see the King dismounting in the rubbled yard beneath us.

We hurried down to bow and curtsey before the King. 'Cleantis,' Otto said. 'Hard at work, I see. Countess, will you not show me over this fabulous building?'

'It will be my pleasure, Sire. I will see you later, Cleantis.' I did not wish him following us about. 'If you will come this way, Sire. I'm afraid we are still in the very early stages of construction. You will have to use your imagination.'

'I am good at that,' he remarked, somewhat enigmatically.

We threaded our way through various pillars, while I attempted to indicate where each downstairs room – there was no first floor as yet – would begin and end, and the workmen gaped at us and touched their foreheads to their king. 'Is there nowhere we can be alone?' Otto asked, speaking German so that we should not be understood.

'Not here.'

'Then let us go to your rented house.'

'We would not be alone there either, Sire. Is it not possible for me to visit the palace?'

'It would be most awkward if my wife found out.'

'You are the King. And a king . . .'

'Can do as he pleases? That is not a universally accepted point of view. But . . . may I conclude that you would be willing to do as I please, Countess?'

This uncertainty, especially when I had already virtually accepted his invitation, gave me an insight into his personal problems. But, having decided to accept the prophecy in all its ramifications, I said, 'It would be my honour, Your Majesty. I ask only for discretion.'

This was the one thing he could not provide, although he did his best. He procured the use of a house belonging to one of his other aides-de-camp, situated not far from my rented accommodation, to which I could quite comfortably walk. As I was about the best-known woman in Athens, this did not grant me any anonymity on my way to our assignation, and as Otto was also well known, his arrival, on horseback, shortly after mine, tended to confirm what everyone already felt they knew. Nor, I am bound to say, did the event in any way justify the exposure. It was now that I discovered that he was in a severely debilitated physical condition. I presume this was because of his malaria, a disease of which no one knows more than that it drifts on the wind and can strike down prince or peasant indiscriminately. Happily it is unknown in England but I knew it was supposed to have caused the death of Byron, which meant that it did not discriminate against Englishmen abroad. I therefore had more than a passing reflection that I might be endangering myself, although I had never heard it described as contagious.

In the event, I did not contract the disease, but it was an exhausting business trying to cope with the King. I had never shared a bed, at least since my first wedding night, with a man who at the first sight of me naked had not been immediately ready for the fray. That Otto was not was rather off-putting, and I could understand that a virgin bride might find herself wondering what the whole business was about, nor could she have been enlightened by her husband, who did not appear to understand the situation either, and seemed to pin his faith on an unreliable optimism. 'It will happen, Ianthe, dear Ianthe,' he said into my ear. 'All I ask is patience.'

Fortunately, if I had never actually encountered this situation before, I had no doubt that I could correct it, and after some minutes of submitting to his caresses I determined to take matters into my own hands, quite literally. This seemed to alarm him, and then encouraged him into a mood of sublime submission, certainly when I supplemented my fingers with my lips. 'You are unlike any woman I have ever known,' he said.

'I am unlike any woman anyone has ever known,' I told him, no longer having any doubt about that. But then he spoiled the whole thing by wishing to pay me for my services! I declined as politely as I could, while letting him know that I felt deeply insulted. This caused an immediate rift between us, and we did not meet in private again, although he continued to show me every favour when we met in public.

But of course the damage was done, as regards the popular perception of our relationship. I do not know what passed between the King and the Queen, although Otto must have been encouraged by the boost the event gave to his popularity with his people, as the fact that he had at last taken a mistress seemed to rebut the rumours that he was either homosexual or impotent. I had to face Spiro. 'My family is dishonoured,' he complained.

'There is no family in history that has been dishonoured by having one of its members summoned to the bed of a king,' I pointed out.

'That is western morality. In Greece we are more circumspect. I should beat you. I *will* beat you.'

'I really do not recommend it.'

'Or you will shoot me with one of your pearl-handled pistols, eh?'

'Yes, Spiro, I will shoot you with one of my pearl-handled pistols.' We gazed at each other, and he lowered his eyes. 'But I would prefer not to have to do that,' I said. 'You are a much more satisfying lover than the King.'

My intention was to reassure him, but from that moment our marriage was effectively over, even if I did not then wish it to end, for a variety of reasons. I was still very fond of him, and he was still the best lover I had ever known, to that time. And more important than this, I knew he shared my love for Leonidas, and I could not contemplate any action or event that might cause a tug-of-war between us over custody of the boy – while I was aware that as with Didi, my daughter by Felix Schwarzenburg, in such a male-oriented society as that of Greece, a powerful family like the Theotokys would certainly have the law on their side. Thus, I even accepted the information, brought to me by my faithful Eugenie, that my husband was having a series of affairs, something I would never have accepted in other circumstances. But I could no longer respect him as a man, not for anything he did, but for the one thing he had not done. He had not picked up the challenge I had thrown down. Would I have shot him had he taken his belt to me? I simply do not know. I do know that had the situation been reversed, I would have felt obliged to act and the devil take the consequences – the story of my life! What made my husband's conduct the more *un*acceptable was my suspicion that he had submitted to my will, less for fear of a physical confrontation, than a concern that if we really fell out I might cease his allowance.

For nearly two years we settled into a kind of genteel domesticity, much as I had suffered with Edward and then with Karl. And yet at this time I was content. I was regarded as the King's favourite, which I was, as his mistress, which I was not, and more important, as a counterweight to the Queen. All of these, especially the last, made me very popular with the mob. And then the Pelikari came to town.

I encountered them for the first time in the summer of 1844. I should say that summers were very dull in Athens, as they had been in Munich, because those people who could afford it left the city for the country or the islands, a migration caused less by heat than by the concomitant of heat: the open drains and sewers began to stink, the number of flies doubled, and many people became ill.

Despite the discomfort and the supposed risk to our health, and that of Leonidas, Spiro and I spent that summer in the city, mainly because I wished to oversee every detail of the building of my new house. But there was also Athens and the surrounding country to be explored; an unending source of magnificent antiquity. Naturally, I spent a lot of time on the Acropolis, enjoying the view and sketching the ruins. But even more stimulating was my visit to Delphi, which the Ancient Greeks believed was the centre of the world, and which was the home of my favourite god, Apollo. Here too was where the Pythean priestess sat on her tripod and delivered her immortal riddles of prophecy.

I also, as had been my habit in Munich, enjoyed having an afternoon cup of coffee – there was no tea available – in one of the city restaurants, watching the world go by until one afternoon when I found myself surrounded by men, all also drinking coffee, smoking, and all staring at me.

As I had become used to this over the years, I was neither offended nor concerned until one of their number actually sat at my table, without requesting permission.

He was a tall, handsome, but villainous-looking fellow, well built, who sported a great moustache and was, I estimated, old enough to be my father, if only because his hair was quite white. He did not appear to be very clean, and this also applied to his clothes, which might once have been very fine, for he wore the fustanella and matching stockings, both intended to be white, but now a very dingy colour, and the usual red tunic liberally adorned with gold thread, but bearing the evidence of having been *in situ* at his last meal. His red cap, which sported a gold-coloured tassel, was the cleanest thing about him.

I regarded him with extreme disfavour, partly because of his appearance and partly because of his insolence. 'I prefer to be alone,' I told him, coldly.

'But I must speak with you, great lady,' he said. 'I have something most important to say.'

'Then say it,' I suggested.

'I wish to feel your arse. I wish that more than anything else in the world. Will you let me feel your arse? If you will let me, I will put something between the cheeks for you.'

Having never been addressed like that before in my life, I felt quite faint, the more so as he spoke loud enough to be over-heard by his fellows, who applauded, and by everyone else in the restaurant, including the waiters. I immediately realized that were I to behave like a frightened woman I would never be able to set foot in this establishment again. Possibly on this street again, or any street in Athens. I therefore summoned my courage, aware that my cheeks were flaming, as they were wont to do in such circumstances, carefully drained my coffee cup, picked up my reti-cule, opened it, took out one of the revolvers that always lay there, and presented it at his head. And cocked the hammer. He goggled at me, and his companions knocked over their chairs as they started to their feet, while there was a chorus of screams and oohs from the other customers. 'I would like you to leave my table,' I said in a loud, clear voice. 'I would also like you to leave this restaurant, or I shall blow out your brains. I also wish you to understand that if you ever speak to me again, I shall shoot you.'

He pushed back his chair. 'Do you know who I am?'

'I do not care who you are. I have told you what I require you to do. You have ten seconds to obey me, or you are a dead man.'

He gazed at me for several of those seconds, while I tensed my muscles. I was so angry that I believe I would have shot him, but fortunately, just before his time was up, he stood up. 'We shall meet again,' he threatened.

'If we do, it will be your misfortune,' I said. He left, followed by his men.

This event caused a great sensation. As soon as the Pelikari were out of earshot, the proprietor of the restaurant hurried forward. 'Oh, Countess,' he said. 'Are you all right?'

'I would like another cup of coffee.'

He signalled a waiter. 'But . . . do you know who that was?'

'He asked me the same question. No, I do not know who he was. Does it matter?'

'Oh, Countess! That was the bandit king, Cristos Hadji-Petros. He calls himself Hadji because he has made the pilgrimage.'

I found myself becoming interested, both because the word king had a hidden meaning for me, and because of the concept that he was no mere provincial. 'You mean he has been to Mecca? He is a Muslim?'

'No, no, Countess. He is a Christian. Well, in a manner of speaking. His pilgrimage was to Jerusalem.'

'And you say he is a bandit? Then how is he able to walk the streets of Athens, bold as brass?'

'Because he is a great and famous man. He led the resistance to the Turks in the north. They call him the King of the Mountains.'

Once again the use of that evocative word. But at that moment I could not possibly relate such a monster to any view of the future presented by Madame Normande. 'Then the best thing he can do is return to his kingdom,' I suggested.

Otto, when he returned to Athens, was horrified, but less on account of the insult offered to me, in public. 'Would you really have shot him? My dear Ianthe, you could have been murdered by his people.'

'I had six bullets in my revolver, and a second fully loaded weapon in my bag. There were only eight of them, including their leader.'

'And you would have shot them all?'

'I am both fast and accurate.'

He wiped his brow. 'You could have started a revolution.'

'Would you not have quashed it?'

Some more wiping. 'There is no soldier in my army would dare fire on a Pelikari.'

'Then, Your Majesty, I recommend that you set about recruiting some who will.' My opinion of the King, never very high, dipped even lower.

Spiro was no less agitated, and like his king, was at least as concerned about the possible political consequences of my action as about my safety. 'You seem determined to challenge the world.'

'Were that not my intention I would not be lying here now, beside you, as your wife. Is this man really as powerful as everyone seems to think?'

'He is powerful. They call him the King of the Mountains.'

'So I have been told. Which mountains?'

'Those in the north-west. You saw them from Corfu.'

'You mean he is Albanian.'

'No, no. Well, some people call the Pelikari Albanians, but they are actually Greek. There is no proper border up there.'

'But there is a kingdom?'

'Not one recognized internationally. Just a colony of bandits.'

'And this Petros character is allowed to come and go as he pleases. Because everybody is afraid of him.'

'Because everyone respects him. He has been around a long time.'

'I could see that.'

'He was recognized by the Turks. They tried several times to invade the mountains and capture him, but they always failed, at great loss to themselves, so they called him governor and left him alone. Then when the War of Independence began, he declared for Greece, and led his people in the fight. We would not have won without him.'

I was tempted to remind him that they would not have won without the allied naval victory at Navarino in 1827, which had destroyed the blockading Turkish fleet. 'So now he has been given licence to insult defenceless women.'

'It is just their way of speaking. They have no manners. He saw you, he admired your beauty, and, well . . .'

'He wanted to feel my bottom, and said so, in public. You should challenge him to a duel.'

'He admired my wife. That is a compliment to me. As for what he wanted to do to you . . . I have heard that the Pelikari have some very unusual way of making love.'

Now that aroused my interest, but he would not elaborate. However, it seemed that I had made my point. When next I saw Petros, on the street, he gave me a most elaborate bow, while keeping his distance.

And so we come to 1846, the most horrific year of my life. What made it worse was that I myself set up the tragedy that was to engulf me. After spending the summer of 1844 in Athens, and the house being completed, in 1845 we went down to Tinos. This was not the success of my first visit. Rumours of my liaison with the King had reached even the small islands of the Aegean, with the result that Johanne was not as warm as I remembered. So, for 1846, I resolved on a new plan. This was because, at the beginning of the year, my darling Bonzo died. This had not been unexpected, as he was fifteen years old, but it was none the less distressing, and I wished to get right away from Greece for a season.

I therefore contacted an English couple named Stisred, who had a house in a village called Bagni di Lucca in Tuscany. In fact they had two houses; they lived in one and rented the other. I thus secured a summer home. This seemed ideal; Spiro went for the idea, and as we were no longer in the throes of our love affair, and as I had not seen Mama since Papa's death, I invited her to join us. She accepted with alacrity; she was anxious to meet her grandson for the first time. I was delighted at the prospects of a get-together for a whole summer, but was taken aback when she intimated that she would be accompanied by both Margaret and Jane Steele! However, I did not wish to put her off, and reflected that I had always rather liked Jane, my old art teacher, and that there was no necessity for me to put up with any nonsense from Steely.

Spiro, Leonidas, Eugenie, Giorgio and I took the packet from Piraeus and landed in Naples. There was some problem with obtaining transport north – we might have done better to spend another week at sea and gone direct to Genoa – and during our wait Spiro determined that the three of us should have our portraits painted. I cannot for the life of me remember the name of the artist – he certainly never attained any fame – and I do not think he did a very good job on us, while his habit of prattling all the time was irritating. However, I was sitting one morning, inexpressibly bored, when he remarked that the last person he had painted was Prince Felix Schwarzenberg. This coincidence did not immediately interest me, nor could I believe that this fellow knew anything of that now distant affair, but I commented, politely, 'Then you have been to Vienna?'

'Alas, no, Contessa. The Prince is presently residing in Naples. With his family. He is Austrian minister to the Court of the Two Sicilies.' Of which Naples was the capital.

Now I had to make a supreme effort to control my agitation. 'His family? I did not know Prince Schwarzenberg was married.'

This was true, because Felix had not yet met the Princess Windischgratz, at least in an amatory sense. It was also a slip, as hitherto I had indicated that the Schwarzenbergs were only a name to me. However, our artist did not appear to notice. 'The Prince is not married, Contessa. He is occupying a house with his sister, Princess Mathilde, and her ward, Miss Selden.'

The name Felix had selected for our daughter to disguise her true parentage, and under which she had been christened! My heart nearly leapt straight up through my throat, so much so that he peered at me. 'Are you all right, Contessa?'

'I feel a little faint. It must be the heat. We will continue tomorrow.'

He looked somewhat put out, but a moment later I was hurrying down to the Mole, where there was a breeze. I needed this. But I also needed to be alone. Didi – as I had always called her in preference to Mathilde – was in Naples, only a few hundred yards away from where I was standing! What was I going to do? Well, I had to see my daughter, to hold her in my arms, and perhaps . . . But it was something I had to do entirely on my own. Spiro had no idea that Didi existed, but he certainly knew that Felix did, and any suggestion that I might be seeking to renew my acquaintance with him might drive a hammer blow into our increasingly fragile relationship. So then, I thought, if it is going to be done, why not do it now?

It was not difficult to obtain the Schwarzenberg address. I actually had no desire to see Felix again, only my daughter, but I was prepared to do everything necessary to attain that goal. I went up the steps, and rang the bell. The door was opened by a some-what dour-looking flunkey. 'Prince Schwarzenberg is not at home.'

That was a relief. 'I have actually come to see Miss Selden.'

That took him by surprise. 'You know Miss Selden?'

'We have an acquaintance.' An acquaintance!

He held the door wide. 'If you would come in, signora.' Heart pounding, I stepped into a gloomy hallway. 'Please wait here. Take a seat.'

He went off, and I preferred to stand. Inside my gloves, my fingers were clammy. Didi would now be sixteen years old. What would she look like? What would she *be* like? How would she respond to seeing her mother again? Would she remember me?

A door at the end of the hall opened, and I gazed at Princess Mathilde, Felix's sister, as thin and stiff-faced as I remembered. 'Good Lord,' she remarked. 'What are you doing here?'

'I wish to see my daughter.'

'Your daughter!'

'Who you so cruelly kidnapped.'

'And who you have ignored for fourteen years.'

This was not a subject I dared debate. 'I wish to see her. Will you try to prevent me?'

'I have every right to prevent you. You are in my house, where you have no rights at all. I can have you expelled.'

My hand brushed my reticule, in which, as always, there lay my two revolvers. The temptation was enormous to draw them and take what I wanted at gunpoint. But this was not Athens, or even Munich. Here I was neither the Baroness von Venningen nor the Countess Theotoky, merely an itinerant tourist, without friends or powerful protectors, without even a husband on whom I could fully rely for support. So I contented myself by saying, 'Then you would be an unnatural monster.'

She regarded me for several moments, then her face actually softened. 'You must understand, Jane, that Mathilde has been brought up without knowledge of you. She has been told that her parents, great friends of mine, died of typhoid fever in her childhood. She has known nothing else than her life as my adopted daughter. She is happy, and looking forward to a good marriage. Would you now throw her into an emotional turmoil? And she is living with her father, who loves her dearly, even if she regards him an uncle. Can you not see that for you to re-enter her life now would be to ruin it?'

Her appeal touched my heart, perhaps because it was an appeal rather than an attempted snub. Besides, I could not argue with her logic. Whatever crime had established this situation it would equally be a crime to throw my daughter's life into a maelstrom of conflicting emotions, conflicting loyalties. 'May I not at least see her?' I asked.

Mathilde considered. 'If you promise to make no attempt to speak with her or contact her in any way.'

I had no choice. 'I promise.'

'Then come with me.' She led me down the hall into a room which overlooks the inner court. Here there was a garden containing several chairs, and in one of these there sat a girl, reading a book. She wore a broad-brimmed hat which shaded her face, as Mathilde observed. She rang a bell, and the butler appeared. 'Take Sigorina Mathilde a glass of lemonade, Giuliano.' Giuliano bowed and left the room.

'Thank you,' I said.

Mathilde did not reply, but continued to stand beside me at the window. I found that I was holding my breath as we waited. Then Giuliano appeared from beneath us, carrying a tray with a glass. He reached the chair and spoke, and Didi looked up, and smiled. I found tears streaming down my cheeks, as Mathilde saw. 'She is, quite lovely,' she said. 'She is almost as beautiful as her mother.' We looked at each other. 'Believe me,' she said. 'I am so very sorry.' I dried my tears and left. When I got home I hugged Leonidas for a very long time. He was all I had left.

I was glad to leave Naples and travel north, and although my mood remained sombre, perhaps because I could not confide its cause to anyone else, my spirits lifted when we reached our destination. Bagni di Lucca was a delightful spot, quiet and peaceful, and if the house was in a typical Venetian-style, four-square and four-storeyed, it was less gloomy and more airy than most of its type because the central hall had no ceiling, only the roof, rising above all four storeys and containing several glass panels to admit the light. A spiral staircase led from floor to floor, and each floor was fronted by a balustraded gallery. Mama and the Steeles were already there, having travelled overland via Switzerland, and we had a very jolly reunion, even Steely being in the best of humours. They all obviously looked much older than I remembered, Mama's appearance not being enhanced by her black dress – she was still in mourning for Papa. Equally, they were clearly astonished to find that after all my experiences, both emotional and physical, I was virtually unchanged from the girl they recalled, my figure as trimly voluptuous as ever, my hair still a Titian glory, and most of all my complexion unmarked.

Equally, they found Spiro at his most charmingly handsome,

while they quite fell for Leonidas, who impressed them with his looks – he closely resembled me – and his intelligence, as well as his bubbling energy. I look back upon that evening as one of the happiest of my life.

Next morning we all went for a walk, enjoying the village. We called on the Stisreds, but they were not at home, so we left our cards and returned to the house for lunch. Leonidas was clearly tired – we had spent the previous three days travelling – and so we put him to bed in his room on the third floor and then retired ourselves for a siesta, from which we were awakened by the housekeeper, who informed us that Colonel and Mrs Stisred were downstairs, repaying our call. We hastily dressed and went down, followed by Mama and the Steeles. The Stisreds appeared to be a very pleasant couple, and it seemed that we were all speaking at once. The resulting noise apparently awoke Leonidas. I heard him shouting, 'Mama, Mama!' and looked up at the third-floor balcony, to my horror to see him clambering up the balustrade.

'Leonidas!' I shouted. 'Be careful. Get down!' But he kept on climbing. 'Leonidas!' I screamed. All of our heads turned upwards, to watch my son reaching the rim of the balustrade, throw a leg over, hover there for a few terrible moments, and then fall.

The floor of the hall was marble, and he fell head first. This I remember very clearly. But over the following few hours there is a merciful blur. I know that certain things happened. I know that even as I screamed and screamed my brain was refusing to accept the evidence of my eyes. It kept telling me no, no, this cannot be real. I am still in bed, and I am having a nightmare. I know that I scooped the bleeding, mangled body of my son into my arms, and that when Mama and Steely tried to take it from me I struck at them like a wild animal.

I remember being lifted up to my room and put to bed, and I remember a doctor arriving to feed me a sedative. I do not remember the funeral, which in that climate and that time of year had by law to be carried out the next day, but I know I attended. I do not remember what part Spiro played in all this; I did not wish to see him or hear his voice. This was irrational of me, as he could not possibly be blamed for what had happened, but I was not in a rational state of mind. I could only think, all gone, all gone. I had given birth to six children, and they were all gone. It mattered nothing that Heribert might become the next Baron von Venningen, or that Didi might become a princess – due to my wilfulness they were lost to me. After all my maternal mistakes I had determined that Leonidas would be my treasure, the child on whom I would bestow all my love and my care for the rest of my life. And he was dead. I could not doubt that I was being punished by Fate for all the years during which I had rejected convention, laughed at morality, gloried in my indestructible beauty. Perhaps my beauty would remain indestructible, but its joy had turned to ashes.

Looking back, I cannot doubt that for a considerable period I was out of my mind. And yet my brain worked with that cunning and resolve that we are told mad people often possess. I was surrounded by anxious whispers, worried consultations that were hurriedly suspended whenever I entered a room. I became convinced that plans were being laid to confine me in an institution, perhaps even a bedlam. I determined to thwart them. Or more particularly Spiro. Even had my love for him not turned quite cold, I was certain that he was plotting to get his hands on my money. I felt that I could trust no one, not even Mama, save for Eugenie. The French girl had elected to throw in her lot with me and for five years had proved a devoted and utterly faithful companion. 'Will you stay at my side, always?' I asked.

'For as long as you need me, milady.'

'No matter what happens? What I may wish to do?'

'No matter, milady.'

As I was under constant surveillance, certainly whenever I sought to leave the house, I gave Eugenie an order on my Zurich bank. As there was no bank in Bagni di Lucca, she had to find an excuse to go into Reggio, and then we had to wait a fortnight for the money to arrive. I was in a torment of anxiety, as the whispered conferences continued, but I did my best to appear to be recovering from my grief and preparing to resume a normal life, so much so that Spiro even sought my bed. I told him that I could not contemplate sex at that moment, even if my body was crying out for it. And at last Eugenie returned from a visit to the city with her satchel containing enough lira to sustain us for some weeks. The next day she hired two horses, and that night we stole from the house, mounted, and rode out of the village. 'Where are we going, milady?' she asked.

'Away,' I said. I carried nothing save a single satchel, which contained our money, our passports, my two revolvers, and a clipping of Leonidas's hair that I had taken from his dead body, and which is with me still. I was eloping, with my maid.

We went to Rome. I knew that we would be followed, but I by now had considerable experience of running away, and had no intention of being caught. With our head start there would be no possibility of us being overtaken on the road, but as I was not easily overlooked or forgotten once seen, our trail would be simple to follow, especially as I had to present our passports at every border crossing. It took us two days of hard riding to reach a village about ten miles north of the Eternal City. Here we sold our horses – they were not strictly ours but I was in no mood to split hairs – and bought ourselves some new clothes. I use the word new advisedly; they were certainly new to us and by no means as clean as we might have liked. We then walked out of the village, found a lonely copse, and stripped off our habits, donning the Italian peasant costumes, which included voluminous shawls to cover our heads, and most importantly my hair, and walked into the city. As this was not a pastime either of us was accustomed to, over any distance, it took us a whole day, and it was the following dawn before we found ourselves treading the hallowed cobbles. I later learned that Spiro and the men he had summoned to accompany him actually entered the city before us, but he could think of nothing better to do than make a round of the best hotels, where I might have been expected to be found. Instead, Eugenie and I proceeded quietly and unobtrusively, unnoticed in our unlikely garb, and found ourselves rooms in an unfashionable part of the city. 'What now, milady?' Eugenie asked.

'Now? Let us go out, have supper, get drunk, and find ourselves a man. Two men,' I added, as she looked at me questioningly.

Once again I can hear shrieks of angry condemnation echoing on the wind. That a woman in my condition, so recently bereaved, should behave in such a fashion, etc., etc. That is pure humbug.

No doubt, there are women who, finding themselves in my position, would have spent the rest of their lives in mourning, or hurled themselves from a high window. What a waste, not to mention an aggravation of the grief being suffered by one's nearest and dearest. Then there are some who would have entered a convent, which to my mind is comparable with suicide.

I belonged to none of those classes. Throughout my life I had rejected convention, challenged it at every opportunity. On several occasions I had suffered severe rebuffs, which I had considered catastrophic at the time. But I had always picked myself up, turned my back on the past, and strode resolutely forward. Now I had encountered the greatest catastrophe of all, beside which the lesser tragedies seemed meaningless. I had been desolated by the death in infancy of my first two sons, but I had not known either of them well enough to love them as perhaps a mother should. On Leonidas I had lavished everything I possessed, emotionally and physically, and he was gone. I had challenged the gods once too often. But I was not going to lie down and let Fate trample all over me. I knew I still had a great deal to do with my life, perhaps sucked onwards by the still unfulfilled prophecy. But the first step to be taken had to be an utter rejection of the past, a rebirth for the future, and, at least for me, this could only be done in the arms of a man.

I later learned, as my identity soon became known, and indeed we moved to more salubrious surroundings, that I was reputed to have engaged in six marriages during my sojourn in Rome. That this was an absurdity, as even if I could have contemplated marriage to anyone I was still married to Spiro and in Italy divorce is just about impossible, should have been obvious even to the gossip mongers. But I was apparently too good a story to be passed up.

And I cannot deny that I went through several men during my stay in Rome. So did Eugenie. We shared everything, and became far closer to each other than even if we had been sisters. That our behaviour was outrageous I freely admit, but that was my mood of the moment.

Mama, having sorrowfully returned to England, naturally wondered if she had lost a daughter as well as a grandson, but I wrote her as soon as I was settled. I knew it would be useless to attempt to explain my behaviour and could only ask her forgiveness. This she gave readily enough – she did not convey Steely's opinion of the situation – but naturally she begged me to return to Spiro and try to forget the past. This was exactly what I was doing, in my own way, and that way did not include Spiro. Once it was established that I was, after all, in Rome, he naturally turned up, full of reproaches and beseechments. I would not accompany him back to Greece, however. I told him he could divorce me if he wished, but he did not wish, entirely for fear of losing my financial backing, and retired in a very morose frame of mind. While I continued on my merry, or at least, lubricious, way.

I have no doubt that many people, including my family and certainly my husband, concluded that I had finally sunk to the bottom of the barrel, as it were, from which I would never rise, and would eventually succumb to drink and disease. Which but goes to show how little even my nearest and dearest ever knew about my character. I have never enjoyed being drunk, even on those riotous occasions in Corfu, and for all the plentiful and expensive wines with which I plied my guests in my Rome salon I myself seldom had more than a single glass of sherry each evening. Nor have I ever been a gourmet. I enjoy good food, but only in small quantities, and although my table was always laden I preferred to watch my guests enjoying themselves than to over-indulge myself.

As for the guests themselves, I have always – with one grotesque exception – been entirely fastidious in my choice of men. Equally, while I have always enjoyed the act of sex, the more so when the method has been strange to me, I have also always enjoyed witty and intellectual conversation in equal measure. My guests in Rome always included a sprinkling of artists and writers, nearly all of the would-be variety as they had been in Palermo only now I was able to grant them their dearest wish. Yet I was always very mindful of disease. I made it a rule personally to wash the genitals of any would-be bed-mate before allowing him to possess me, a process which delighted them as much as it pleased me. I have no doubt that they were all sadly confused by my refusal to take a penny for my services, but as I was not for sale, any man who attempted to force himself on me, and whom I did not like, was very quickly expelled from my house – my revolvers were never far from my side.

Thus, utter debauchery for two years. Until the morning I awoke with a clear head and a great desire to *do*. I think I may have been restored to normality by the dreadful news coming out of Vienna, and Paris and even Munich, and the utter destruction of poor Ludwig.

I summoned Eugenie, told her to pack our bags, and we set off for Naples to find a ship for Piraeus. It was time to go home.

The Mountain King

My reappearance in Athens in the spring of 1849 caused an even bigger sensation than was usual in my affairs. Over the preceding couple of years my name had seldom been absent from most conversations, the interest in my behaviour being heightened by what Spiro had had to say when he had returned alone, and then by the tales emanating from Rome. No one had ever expected me to dare reappear.

The consternation began almost the moment we stepped ashore in Piraeus. The port captain gaped at me and stammered a greeting, then hurried off to attend to other duties, which consisted principally of sending a messenger galloping up the road to the capital. But as I was, on this occasion, travelling lightly – I had abandoned all my heavy luggage at Bagni di Lucca almost three years before – we were very close behind the galloper.

We went straight to Odos Sokratous. My servants – several of them were strange to me – goggled as I walked into the house, but Giorgio was there. 'Oh, milady . . . Countess . . .' He kissed my hand.

'It is good to see you, old friend,' I said. 'Is the Count home?'

He looked anxious. 'The Count is out at this time.'

I looked past him at the woman standing in the inner archway. 'And who may you be?'

She curtsied. 'I am Madame Zorba, the Count's housekeeper.'

'As of this moment, you are *my* housekeeper, no one else's. You will take your orders either from me or from Mademoiselle Eugenie. I wish to tour the house. After I have had my bath. Have it drawn, please.'

She looked at Giorgio, who gave a surreptitious shrug. Then she went off. I went upstairs into my bedroom. It was perfectly clean and tidy, but the scents were not mine; Eugenie opened the windows wide. We then inspected the wardrobes. Again, the clothes were not mine. I summoned Madame Zorba. 'Have these wardrobes emptied.'

'But milady . . .' she was obviously unsure how to continue.

'You mean you expect the owner to return at some stage? I am sure she will be fully dressed. Have those garments burned.'

She gulped. 'The master . . .'

'I have given you an order, Zorba.' She hurried from the room.

I had a leisurely bath, attended by Eugenie. 'Is it not good to be home?' I asked her.

'Oh, indeed, milady. But . . . is there going to be trouble?'

'No,' I assured her. 'There will be no trouble.' I dressed, and accompanied Madame Zorba and Giorgio on a tour of the house and garden. They were in surprisingly good condition. 'You are to be congratulated. Would you like to continue working here Zorba?'

'Well, milady, the master . . .'

'Pays you very well, I imagine. It happens to be my money. You may retain your position, as long as you remember that.' I was not so pleased with the stables, which had been neglected, and contained only a few scrawny horses. 'Where is my white mare?' I inquired of the only visible groom.

'I do not know, milady. Sold, I think.'

'Find out to whom, and buy her back.'

'But milady, that will cost much money.'

'I will pay him what he paid for it, plus one hundred drachma. If he wishes to haggle, inform him that whoever sold my horse was doing so without my permission, and that therefore he is in possession of stolen goods. Unless these are immediately returned to me, he will be formally charged and sent to prison.' The groom looked at Giorgio and Zorba, received suggestive shrugs, and hurried off.

I had a light meal, then went to the music room, and my piano. Perhaps I had missed this most during my absence. I sat down and played several of my favourite pieces. The piano badly needed tuning, but was actually in better shape than I had expected. I was still playing when I heard movement behind me. 'Ianthe? Can it really be you?'

I turned on my seat. Spiro was as handsome and debonair as

ever, but I could not see his face without also seeing Leonidas.
Besides, I had ample evidence that he had not missed me all that
much. In view of my own conduct I could not blame him for
having sought sex elsewhere, but to have it in my own bed, and
to allow the woman, or women, to use my house as their own,
I found unacceptable. 'Did you expect someone else?'

'If only you had written . . .'

'To enable you to make adequate preparations? Why did you
sell Ghost?'

'Ghost? Oh, the horse . . .'

'My favourite mare.'

'Well . . . I had no idea when you would be coming back. And
she . . . well, she reminded me of you. I will get her back. I
promise.'

'I have already attended to that.'

'Ah! Well, my dearest girl, now that you *are* back . . .' He came
towards me, arms outstretched.

'I do not wish to have sex with you.'

He checked, looking confounded. Then he tried a smile. 'You
are tired, and need a rest . . . I can be patient. Up to a point.'

'I have said, I do not wish to have sex with you.'

'You are my wife.'

'You may divorce me, if you wish. That would probably be
best.'

'Divorce you? I shall not do that. Think of the scandal. Besides,
where would you go? Where would you live?'

'In my house, Spiro. You may examine the title deeds, if you
wish.'

'You think you can throw me out of my own house?'

'I can certainly throw you out of *my* house. However, I do
not wish to embarrass you. The house is big enough for both of
us. If you do not wish to divorce me, you are welcome to continue
living here. But I will regard any attempt to force your attentions on me as rape, and react accordingly.'

'You wish me to stand to one side while you entertain your
lovers.'

'I have no lovers.' At that moment I had no desire ever to have
a lover again. I was exhausted, both emotionally and physically
from the events of the past three years, and wished only to rest.

'However, you are welcome to yours, provided you do not bring
any of them into my house.' He left the room.

The news that I was back, as beautiful and dominant as I had
ever been, had permeated all Athens by that evening. When
next morning, Ghost having been recovered – to my great joy
she was well, and if a trifle gaunt, did not appear to have been
ill-treated – I took my usual ride, the crowds followed me and
cheered me as loudly as ever in the past. I paid a visit to my
local bank and discovered my affairs were in good order, they
having resisted the attempts of Spiro to get his hands on the
regular transfers from Zurich. Then I set about entertaining,
but found my possible circle limited: the palace had declared
me *persona non grata*. I thus sought my company from the ex-
patriot society of the city. Among my regular guests were the
British Minister, Sir Thomas Wyse, the French Minister, Eduoard
Thouvenal, the Austrian Minister, Baron von Prokech-Osten –
all of whom, being their country's representatives, and those
countries being Great Powers without whom Greece could not
exist, were in no danger of being snubbed by the Palace – and
a most handsome young French officer, Baron Roger de la
Tour-du-Pin, whose grandmother, a woman of great beauty
judging by a miniature in his possession, had had a series of
incredible adventures during the original Revolution in France,
time and again avoiding arrest, which would have meant the
guillotine, by the skin of her teeth or the exercise of her wit,
no doubt assisted by her other talents.

   All of these men, and others, were eager to flirt with me,
although I persisted in my self-imposed chastity and allowed none
of them more than an occasional kiss. In this resolve I was assisted,
if that is the right word, by the onset of what is commonly called
the change of life, which left me, for the first time *in* my life
uncertain of my sexual powers. My physician agreed that this
misfortune had overtaken me somewhat early – I was still not
yet forty-three – and hinted that the perhaps oversexed lifestyle
I had practised for so long might have something to do with it,
but then he assured me that it was not such a misfortune after
all, apart from no longer being able to bear children – which to
me *was* a considerable misfortune, at least emotionally – as once

the change was complete I would be able to pursue my pleasures without the fear of pregnancy. I did not altogether believe him, but my salon was soon accepted as the brightest and gayest in Athens, and even my Greek friends began to drift back to my table. Thus, inadvertently, I found myself once more involved in politics.

However, before this happened, I made a new and decidedly unusual friend. I was in the paddock one morning, exercising Ghost, who was now returned to her full health, when Giorgio hurried from the house to inform me that I had a visitor. 'It is the Duchess, milady,' he gasped.

I had heard of the Duchess – she was the only person possessing such a title in the country. Arriving in Greece during my sojourn in Rome, she had attempted, I am sure inadvertently, to steal my thunder. She had built herself a magnificent mansion, even bigger and grander than mine, and as she appeared to have even more money than I, she made quite a splash.

Her title was Duchess of Plaisance, which she had obtained through her marriage to Charles Francois Lebrun, an important political supporter of Bonaparte, who had been ennobled by the great man following the establishment of the Empire in 1804. Sophie was herself an aristocrat by birth, being the daughter of the Marquis de Barbe-Marvois, but she had fitted well into the Imperial Court, and had actually been a lady-in-waiting to Josephine's successor as Empress, Marie-Louise of Austria. However, following the collapse of the Empire, she had abandoned her husband, and her son, who was apparently quite a successful soldier, to undertake a prolonged grand tour of Europe, seeking a prince as husband for her daughter Louise. As she would settle for no lesser rank, this turned out to be a lengthy operation, which was ended with the sudden death of the young woman, still in possession of her maidenhead.

That I had not called on her was not only because I considered her something of a parvenu, certainly in Athens, but because I had been informed that she was quite mad. But she at least promised to be interesting, and as *she* had come to me, I was prepared to receive her. I therefore dismounted and strode into the house, stripping off my gloves as I did so, but still carrying my whip . . . and received a considerable surprise. I knew that she was considerably older than I, but I was unprepared for her size: she had to be about the smallest full-grown woman I had ever seen, not quite five feet tall and as thin as a rake – in fact it was difficult at first glance to be certain there was anyone there at all beneath her large white hat, which she wore with a white linen gown. However disconcerted I might have been, she was clearly delighted. 'My dear Countess,' she said. 'I have so wished to make your acquaintance. You are everything I have been told of you. So tall, so elegant, so beautiful . . . and such a complexion!'

She spoke French, so I replied in kind. 'How nice of you to say such sweet things. I must apologize for my appearance. If you will take a chair I will just go upstairs and change. Giorgio, some wine for the Duchess.'

'No, no,' she said. 'I cannot stay. I but wished to make your acquaintance. But you see, He is waiting for me.'

'Ah,' I said. 'Of course. Although some do say that it is always best to keep a lover waiting, at least for a short while.'

'My dear, I do not have a lover. Heaven forbid! I am speaking of God.'

'Ah!' I said again, seeking some divine inspiration myself.

'He likes me to speak with Him, every morning at noon,' Sophie explained.

'Does He ever reply?'

'Of course He replies. I am His chosen handmaiden on earth.'

'Ah,' I said a third time, completely lost for a reply.

'So I must rush. But we will get together. We must. I feel that we have great things to do together. I will call again, soon.'

'I shall look forward to it,' I lied, fervently hoping that she would soon forget all about me. But in fact events now conspired to keep us apart, at least for a while.

It so happened that the winter of 1849–50 was about the coldest ever recorded in Greece. Snow lay on the Athens' streets for days on end, and everyone was flabbergasted. They were also quite unprepared, and while I merely opted to forego my morning's ride – mainly for fear of Ghost slipping on the icy surfaces – everyone else was decidedly discomfited. No one was more discomfited than the Queen. Lacking the comfort of a husband's passion, and thus the enormous pleasure of holding a babe in her arms, and having built everything she could think of, and been warned that there was no more money for further architectural adventures, she had turned her attention to horticulture, and claimed to possess the best garden in all Greece, filled with exotic plants garnered from all over the Levant and North Africa. Now these were all killed off in a matter of days by the frost.

Being a keen gardener myself, even if I was her bitterest enemy, I could feel sorry for this unhappy event. But suddenly she and her husband were confronted with a far more serious problem: a claim against the Greek government for illegal confiscation of property.

The claimant was named Don Pacifico, who was a Maltese Jew, but nonetheless, a citizen of Great Britain. His importunities against the Greek government had finally aroused the ire of an anti-Semitic mob, who had burned down his house. This had happened just about the time I had returned to Athens, and the event, at the time, had not greatly excited anyone, save for Don Pacifico. He appealed to the British Government. Now, it so happened that at this juncture the Foreign Secretary, on whose desk this petition arrived, was my old friend and occasional dancing partner, Harry Temple, now Lord Palmerston. Always somewhat given to intemperate behaviour, whether in bed or out of it, Harry chose to assume that the Greeks were insulting Great Britain itself, and had immediately got himself into a fine fuss, the upshot being that he dispatched the Mediterranean Squadron of the Royal Navy to Piraeus to enforce the Pacifico claim. The legality of this action, which was only just short of an act of undeclared war, was open to question, and Harry was roundly criticized throughout Europe as well as in Parliament. He defended his action in a truly brilliant speech, in which he used the words *Civis Romanus Sum*, coined in the days of the Caesars, which loosely translated means that any Roman citizen, however humble, is entitled to the full protection of the might of the Roman Empire.

Stirring stuff, if one happened to be under the umbrella. However, Otto, undoubtedly prodded by his wife and encouraged by his intimates, who saw a great opportunity for increasing his popularity with his subjects, determined to resist this intrusion into what was considered a domestic Greek matter. He refused to pay up or even negotiate. Thus far, the business had been fairly low key, conducted at a diplomatic level, and the presence of several British warships anchored off Piraeus merely meant that Athens was flooded with handsome blue-uniformed young officers. Naturally these homed on the most famous house in the city and we had a succession of splendid parties. With one captain, indeed, Robert Drummond, I struck up a great friendship which has persisted to this day, even though he has become Naval Attaché to our gracious Queen, whose favourite person I have never been. I should add here that I was still in the throes of persistent chastity.

However, this state of affairs was too good to last. Harry's bombastic overtures meeting with no response, and realizing that Otto was, in effect, calling his bluff, Palmerston rolled up his sleeves, as it were. Orders arrived for the fleet and were promptly implemented. From being a presence, the Navy suddenly became a power. The entire Greek fleet was placed under arrest, all shipping in Piraeus was impounded and the port placed under an embargo. Suddenly we were indeed confronted with a war!

It never came to this, simply because it could not. There was no way that Greece could oppose the might of Britain, just as, with its always precarious finances, there was equally no way the country could sustain a blockade of any duration. Nor was there any help forthcoming. The crowned heads of Europe, however much they might resent British high-handedness, were still licking their wounds from the events of 1848. The one country which might have interfered, Russia, was following an agenda of its own, which was actually to cause a war in the immediate future – but not over Greece. Thus, after a couple of months Otto's government surrendered and paid up, to the extent of eight thousand pounds, which all but bankrupted it; the Royal Navy returned to Malta, and normal business was resumed.

But, as might be expected, the repercussions were considerable. The Greek people naturally developed a strongly xenophobic attitude which was directed mainly against the British. The situation during the diplomatic stand-off had been very odd. Great Britain and Greece had not been at war, and thus when given shore leave, the officers and men of Her Majesty's Ships, as I have related, had come ashore and explored the antiquities, as well as the tavernas, of Piraeus and Athens, while their officers had gravitated towards the house of the most famous English resident, where they were always sure of a hearty welcome. I did not see that I was doing anyone any harm. These were my countrymen, whose company delighted me: no one could have expected me to turn them away. But my popularity suffered, and after the fleet had departed, I no longer found myself being cheered on the street: I now on occasion found myself being booed. But that was nothing compared with the hostility emanating from the palace. This first manifested itself on the day, not long after the cessation of the blockade, when Spiro marched into my drawing room. 'I have been retired,' he announced. 'I am no longer the King's aide-de-camp.'

'You mean you have been sacked,' I suggested, perhaps unkindly.

'A Theotoky cannot be sacked,' he declared. 'I have been retired. Because I am married to you.'

'That could very well have something to do with it,' I agreed.

'You have ruined me. I knew this would happen, seven years ago. Well, I have come to tell you to pack up. We shall be returning to Corfu.'

I raised my head. 'I have no intention of returning to Corfu.'

'You loved it there.'

'I did, when I lived there with a man I loved, and who I supposed loved me. That man is long gone. I am not sure he ever existed.'

He regarded me with impotent anger. 'I can force you to accompany me.'

'I really do not recommend that you try. Go back to your family, Spiro. Amuse yourself.'

'While you remain here and amuse yourself.'

'I shall try to do so, certainly.'

'I shall never divorce you.' I shrugged, at that moment the matter did not greatly concern me. He went to the door, and paused. 'Will you continue my allowance?'

The nub of the matter. 'Yes, Spiro, I will continue your allowance.'

'You will make it for life.'

'No, I will not do that. It will continue for as long as I see fit.'

Another impotent glare. Then he said, 'Do you know who is to replace me as principal aide-de-camp?'

'It does not interest me.'

'It is that bandit chief, that self-styled King of the Mountains, Petros. Can you believe it?'

'It is a sign of the times,' I suggested, still not very interested.

Summer now being upon us, I decided to go abroad, and wrote Mama asking where we might meet; it was four years since our last tragic time together. She would have preferred England, but I knew I would not be very welcome there, and preferred Switzerland, to which she agreed. So Eugenie and I took to the Alps. Mama was, as usual, accompanied by Steely, but on this occasion it was clearly very necessary – my old governess was now my mother's nursemaid, a task to which she devoted a great deal of tender, loving care, far more than she had ever bestowed on me. But I was, at this late stage, extremely grateful to her. Mama's appearance was a shock. She was, of course, seventy-four years old. But she seemed much older, her hair quite white, walking with a stick, and finding both standing and sitting down a difficult and time-consuming business.

She seemed as glad to see her errant daughter as ever, and had a great deal to tell me about domestic affairs in England, where Edward and Kenelm, and their wives of course, were in the course of producing sixteen grandchildren for her, or nephews and nieces for me. My own tale was a far less happy one, looked at from her point of view, as I had to tell her that Spiro and I had separated, without any hope of a reconciliation. As always, she could not understand how these things happened. But by now she accepted the futility of begging me to seek a return to conjugality. For the rest we had a pleasant time together and I did a great deal of sketching before we parted, promising to keep in close touch in the future. Inevitably, this did not work out.

I returned to Athens in a sombre frame of mind, and to a strangely empty house. My servants were still there, but Giorgio, for whom I had developed quite an affection, had naturally gone with his master, as had Madame Zorba. In addition, most of my friends had moved on, at least partly because of local hostility. I had no

regrets at having burned my boats regarding Spiro, but I had to
consider what I was going to do with my time, with nowhere
to go and no one to entertain. It was now that I received a note
from Sophie, asking, nay begging, me to call. Well, I reflected, it
will at least be a diversion.

I determined to walk, as it was only a short distance, and so
presented myself at the gates of her house. This was, to be honest,
a somewhat vulgar building, in which Grecian columns were
interspersed with odd creations, which gave the impression of
having been added as an afterthought. The gates were unlocked,
which surprised and disturbed me, nor could I see any gardeners
or watchmen within. I pushed the gates open and stepped through,
making a mental note to warn the Duchess to be more careful,
when I was suddenly surrounded by a startling hullabaloo, a
barking and wailing, and a snarling and a gnashing of teeth, and
I saw, advancing rapidly towards me, what could fairly be described
as an army of dogs, of every shape, size and description, but led
by eight white Irish wolfhounds, each of whom was as tall as my
shoulder, and who appeared to be positively slavering in their
anxiety to sink their teeth into my flesh.

I very nearly retreated through the gate, but I had never backed
away from any challenge, and I felt it would be a mistake to start
doing so now. Thus, my hand dropped to my reticule, although
I felt that to shoot one of what I had to presume were Sophie's
pets might get our relationship off to a bad start. I accepted that
this might be necessary, however, and had actually drawn one of
my revolvers when a bell rang very loudly, and to a dog my
assailants halted, the wolfhounds only a few feet away. However,
they remained blocking my path, and I was relieved to see Sophie
emerge from the porch. 'My dear,' she said. 'They didn't frighten
you, I hope.'

Hastily I put away my gun. 'I have a strong heart.'

She had observed my movement, and came up the path towards
me, her faithful guards parting before her. 'You weren't going to
shoot them?'

'Had it been a case of them or me, Duchess, I would have
done so, yes.'

She stood in front of me. 'You are so strong, so bold, so beautiful. How I envy you. You must call me Sophie.'

'And I am Ianthe.'

'Such a beautiful name. Come on, come in.' We threaded our way through the beasts, who I could not help but feel were disappointed in their breakfast, or lack of it, and entered the house, which was another eye-opener, as it strongly resembled the interior of a large church, combined with various aspects of an architect's office, for the various tables were covered in plans and drawings and even models of what looked like mini-Parthenons. 'It is the temple I am to build, you see,' Sophie explained.

'Do you mean a temple, or a church?'

'Oh, a temple. That is His wish.'

'Ah.' I walked around the tables. 'These plans appear to be very thorough. Did He draw them for you?'

'Oh, good heavens, no.' She was clearly amazed at my ignorance. 'He employs men to carry out His works. And women.'

'And when do you commence building?'

'I do not know. He has not told me yet. But come and have a glass of wine, and tell me all about yourself.' We were served by a maid, also dressed, like her mistress – there did not appear to be any men in the house – all in white. But the wine was quite palatable. Sophie asked questions, and I answered them as decorously as I could, having no wish to shock her, which she certainly seemed to be when I had finished. 'Abandoned by three husbands,' she said. 'And you are so beautiful.'

'Well,' I admitted, 'in all honesty, it was I who abandoned them.'

'But you were forced to it. And that dreadful man Schwarzenberg. I met the family, you know, when I served the Empress. Ghastly people. So was the Empress. Imagine, abandoning the Emperor simply because he was forced to abdicate. You know that he is dead?'

'Who?' I had some idea that she was still speaking of Bonaparte, suspecting that a woman like Sophie might very well have considered him to be alive long after the event.

'Your lover. Felix Schwarzenberg.'

'Felix is dead?' I had a profound sense of shock. One is always liable to feel this when hearing of the death of a contemporary, and Felix would only have been just past fifty, an age which was looming on my own horizon, disconcertingly, perhaps, but with no real apprehension of following it with a sudden demise. But

Felix, with whom I had shared so much, and who I had wound up hating so much . . . my thoughts immediately turned to Didi. But she would surely be married and a mother by now, and for me to seek to reappear in her life could only be even more distressing, for both of us, than when I had last seen her.

'Last year,' Sophie said. 'He had married, you know.'

'I had heard.'

'But the rumour is that he had a seizure while dressing to attend an assignation with another man's wife. Men!' she went on. 'I am not surprised that you have given them up.' Actually, after more than two years of chastity I was beginning to feel like some congenial masculine company, even if I had no idea where I was going to find it. She squeezed my hand. 'You will not regret it. I will see to that. I would like you to move in with me.'

This was about the most direct proposition I had ever had, at least to that moment, and it quite took my breath away, if only because I had absolutely no idea what might be involved. But I was desperate for a relationship, having never actually been without one in my life till now, and, besides, it would be an adventure!

In fact, it involved very little of a carnal nature. Sophie had her moods, but then, so did I. What she really wanted was under-standing company, and I was happy to provide this, because I wished some of it in return. Not that I received much. She found more in me to condemn than to support – the story of my life. Thus, she kept trying to make me wear white, as she always did, instead of the colours I so much preferred and was not about to abandon, while she criticized my extravagance, especially my continuing generosity towards Spiro. 'He is a man,' she would say, vehemently. 'It is his business to attend to his own finances.'

I may say that she never made any attempt to use my funds, simply because she was so much more wealthy than I. However, at that time I saw no reason to cast Spiro off entirely. I was still his wife and had no desire to change that situation – at that time I still felt that being a countess had a certain cachet. Looking back, I have no doubt that my brief liaison with Sophie was good for me, if only because it completed my rehabilitation from the death of Leonidas. Had it gone on for any length of time it might have toppled me over into the edge of eccentricity myself, and this very nearly happened, for as she wanted, I moved into her house, much to the concern of Eugenie, who naturally had to accompany me, and who found herself, not for the first time, in an esoteric world which was totally foreign to her essentially earthy nature. And having settled in, I went so far as to put the house on Odos Sokratous on the market, with my usual whole-heartedness, not supposing I would ever wish to live there again.

That Sophie was eccentric, was undeniable. The personal rela-tionship that she claimed with the Deity would alone have made her so. As His handmaiden and high priestess to the exclusion of all other heavenly representatives from pope or patriarch down, she communed with Him every morning, and in everything she did claimed to be carrying out His express will. This was dif-ficult for me, as although I was more often than not required to kneel beside her, Our Lord never deigned to communicate any instructions to me. In view of my irregular religious history I did not blame Him for this, but it did mean that I was required to live my life according to Sophie's interpretation of His will. She waited with increasing anxiety for His choice of site for her proposed temple, which she regarded as her life's work. But her feelings were also tinged with apprehension, for she was convinced that once her duty had been performed she would then die. She carried this apocalyptic view into every aspect of architecture, for while she owned several plots of land, in and around Athens, on each of which she had begun the construction of a building, not one of them was finished, just in case that might be con-sidered a reason for her departure. This apprehension did not in any way deflect her from her assumed duty, and she really intended to get to work on her temple the moment she received the neces-sary instructions. Fortunately, she never did receive the vital message, at least while I was sharing her life.

Differences of character, background, lifestyle, experience and even mental stability apart, we enjoyed each other's company, and we certainly appear to have amused the locals. Edward About, who was still about, if I may be excused the pun – he was to leave Greece the following year – has written that there was no more compelling sight in Athens in 1852 than to see the two foreign aristocrats, the one so tall and beautiful, the other so small and wizened, the one dressed in Paris gowns the other in pristine but very simple white, walking the streets together, invariably accompanied by a pack of ferocious dogs, who certainly protected us from any risk of being waylaid by footpads, but who obeyed every command of their mistress, uttered in the softest of tones. About was a romantic. He has claimed in his writing to have known me quite well – so many people have done that – and I did see him from time to time, but I am afraid that several of the stories he told about me came out of his imagination. There was a tale of an occasion when I was out on my own and was approached by a handsome young man who engaged me in conversation, but he turned out to be a pickpocket who, when he departed, carried my necklace with him. This is true enough, and he was so good at his profession that I was not aware of having been robbed until I reached Sophie's mansion. But I have no recollection of saying, as About claims, when asked how I had permitted such a thing, that when a young man approaches me with admiring glances and conversation, how could I possibly suspect that he was after my *jewels*.

But all things come to an end. Although my house was on the market, a buyer for such an expensive property was hard to find, and it was my custom to return there at least once a week to make sure that my servants were properly looking after the place, keeping it clean and tidy for the delectation of any would-be purchaser, and also to exercise my horses. I was there one afternoon in the autumn of 1852 when my butler informed me that there was a caller. I was upstairs at the time, and hurried on to the gallery to look down at the entry hall, and found myself gazing at Cristoforos Hadji-Petros.

As with other occasions in my life, it is not my intention to offer excuses for what now happened, but I can say that had Cristos watched and waited and planned his appearance it could not have been better timed, certainly from his point of view. I was just becoming bored with Sophie, realizing that I could never share her concept of the relationship between god and human – I inclined to the ancient Greek philosophy, where the gods were awesome and all powerful, to be sure, but at the same time were rollicking creatures who possessed, and indulged, human passions, and could therefore understand such behaviour in mortals, an attitude I do not feel the Christian god has ever adopted. I was also becoming acutely aware that it was a very long time since I had known a man, not since, in fact, I had undergone the change. Obviously this event, with its erroneous suggestion that since one can no longer bear a child one is necessarily no longer a complete woman, can have a profoundly depressing effect on the spirit, and I now also realized that was what had been lying heavily on mine over the past year or so. Now I was recollecting what the doctor had told me, that I would find sex even more satisfying in the knowledge that I could not be impregnated. All I now needed was the man.

Not that, as I looked down on the bandit chieftain, I had the slightest concept that he could fill the bill. His uniform was far cleaner than when last I had beheld him, to be sure, and his hair was somewhat better groomed. But it appeared whiter than I remembered and suggested that he was far too old to perform – I had forgotten Grandpa's remarkable achievements with Anne Keppel. But more than anything else I remembered this lecherous lout was just about the rudest and most vulgar man I had ever met. 'May I ask the reason for your presence, sir?' I kept my voice low. 'It is not welcome here.'

He made an elaborate bow. 'Is not your house for sale?'

I could not believe my ears. 'You wish to buy it?'

'I wish to look at it. Am I not entitled to do that?'

I shrugged. 'You may show the . . . gentleman over the premises, Paul.' And then watched in consternation as Cristos came up the stairs. 'What are you doing?'

'Your man can show me the downstairs later. It is the upstairs interests me.'

I looked at Paul, but he was clearly not about to interfere with anyone possessing Cristos's reputation. And being in my own house, I was not carrying my reticule and therefore my revolvers. On the other hand, they were in my bedroom. 'As you wish, sir,' I said, and as he reached the top of the stairs turned and went straight to my dressing table, where the bag lay, but again to my consternation he reached it at the same time as I, having moved with amazing speed and remarkable softness of foot. Our hands closed on the bag at the same time, and it was removed from my grasp. 'I am not in the mood to be shot today,' he said, his lips against my ear.

I turned, violently, and found myself in his arms; he had dropped the bag on the floor. 'Do you not suppose I can summon assistance?' I asked him, determined to keep calm.

'Not if you value the lives of your servants.' He was moving forward, carrying me with him. His arms were round my waist, and my body was pressed against his, so that I immediately understood that my contempt for his virility was entirely misplaced. My arms were free, and it was a great temptation to scratch his face, but I really had no idea how he might react to that, and I certainly had no desire to have *my* face scratched in return.

I decided to try logic, and reason. 'Do you really suppose you can commit rape and murder, and not be hanged?'

The backs of my knees touched the bed, and I fell across it with him on top of me; I was quite winded. 'I am Cristos Hadji-Petros,' he reminded me. 'Besides, to whom will you appeal? The palace will laugh at you: I am principal aide-de-camp to the King, and the Queen hates you. While the police will turn away from you.'

I realized he was right, and equally that to scream for help would only endanger my people – he would almost certainly have some of *his* people close at hand. Therefore, I was about to be raped, and must put my faith in vengeance, while until that moment came, the best thing to do would be to look on the event as a fresh adventure. I felt, however, that he should know exactly where he stood, or lay – not with any great hope of success as while he had moved off my stomach he was making very free with my breasts, tearing my gown to do so, before sliding his hand down to grasp my crotch very firmly. Thus, I said, in between gasps, 'I intend to kill you.'

'But what a way to die,' he remarked, and rolled me on my face. Even at the age of forty-five my sexual experience had been so conditioned by manners, morals and conventions that I now anticipated nothing more than a beating – another reason for committing murder as soon as possible – nor was my alarm increased when he pulled my skirts to my waist. But then he seized my right leg just above the knee and forced it away from the left, on which he was now lying, up and up until it was virtually touching my breasts. This done, he delivered a couple of hearty slaps to my buttock before sliding his hand between.

My God! I thought, I am about to be sodomized, and gave a convulsive wriggle while attempting to strike behind me. But to no avail, and having satisfied himself that I was ready to receive him – which, to my surprise and, some would say, my everlasting shame, I was – he proceeded to make his entry. But not through the forbidden portal. Instead I found him where all my lovers had gone before, only from a direction I had never previously considered, and with my legs so widely separated, he seemed able to proceed further than any of his predecessors. In addition, although I had not yet had the time to observe his equipment, he certainly seemed larger and longer than any I had known. To cut a long story short – although I would have hated to do that – he transported me in a matter of seconds into a heaven I had never previously experienced. Nor was it a matter of seconds, for he kept on thrusting for what seemed a very long time, although it could only have been a few minutes. By the time he climaxed I had already done so several times, and when he did do so I felt as if my entire body was being flooded with his seed.

We lay still for several moments, while my right leg slowly slipped back into its proper situation, seeking not only a less distended position but also hoping to trap him *in situ*, as it were. However, he had already withdrawn, although he continued to lie against my back for some minutes, panting for breath. Well, so was I. I was also constrained to lie still for I did not know how I could face him, which would necessarily lead to a confession that he had just surpassed every man I had ever known, and that it was a sensation I wished to be repeated, just as soon as possible. Cristos moved first, pushing himself up and then standing. I still would not look at him, as I heard him move about the room. But then he said, 'These are marvellous things. I have never seen guns like them before,' and realized that he had picked up my reticule.

I rolled over and sat up, and saw him examining one of the revolvers with great care. He observed my movement and looked up with a quick smile. 'You said you would kill me. Here.' He reversed the revolver and held it out, butt first. I stared at it in disbelief. 'Do not be afraid,' he said. 'To die, at the hands of such a woman wielding such a weapon, will surely transport me directly to heaven.'

I took the gun, but only to lay it down. 'I think it would be better for you to have dinner with me, and then . . . we could discuss the situation.'

Sophie was alarmed when I did not return that night, and sent one of her women to look for me. As Cristos and I were by then engaged in some very deep conversation indeed, I was unable to receive her, with the result that Sophie herself arrived early the next morning. As Cristos did not take his duties as aide-de-camp sufficiently seriously to abandon the bed of his mistress until absolutely necessary, he was still there, and as Paul did not feel up to refusing the Duchess entry, she discovered us in the most flagrante of delictos, regarded us for a few seconds, then turned and left, pausing downstairs only just long enough to write a note: *I should like an explanation of your disgusting behaviour*, just as if she had been my mother! 'Will she cause trouble?' Cristos asked.

'No,' I said, quite definitely.

'When can I see you again?'

'Tonight. This afternoon. As soon as you are free.'

'You are Aphrodite. You have bewitched me.'

I recalled the name I had been given as a girl. 'I am Aurora, the Light of the Dawn. You have conquered *me*.'

I was astonished, and somewhat regretful, when I thought of all those handsome, dashing men of my youth, and all those beautiful, elegant ladies, not one of whom had ever had the slightest concept of how properly to make love. For Cristos's repeat performances, when he no longer had to fear any opposition on my part, allowed his hands to roam the length and breadth of my body, an intensely stimulating business in itself, quite apart from what was happening between my legs. I had always felt that the act of love as prac-tised in such sterile fashion in the west, was less than perfect, as the missionary position naturally concentrates the entire effort into a very small area, and shuts off nearly all visual contact. Even my sessions with Spiro, which I had then regarded as the ulti-mate, did not allow him to do more than play with my breasts, and that had invariably ceased as we approached a climax. Whereas Cristos's caresses increased in intensity with every thrust, and often continued long after he was spent.

Still, however preoccupied with my latest adventure – as always I was resolved that it would be my last – I did not forget my manners, and after I had bathed and dressed, took myself back to Sophie's. She received me sitting in a vast armchair rather like a queen on a throne. 'Well?' she demanded. 'Have you come to beg forgiveness?'

'Actually, no.'

'What? Do you suppose I can, or will, accept you back after such profligate behaviour? Do you suppose He will ever speak to me again if I were to do so?'

'Probably not,' I agreed.

'So you will get down on your knees and pray for forgiveness, and remain there until I give you permission to rise.'

'I'm afraid I am not going to do that.'

'If you will not, I can have no more use for you.'

'My own sentiments, exactly.'

'What do you mean?'

'That I have come to collect my things, and Eugenie, and return to Odos Sokratous.'

'You . . . you are leaving me?' Her voice trembled.

'My dear Sophie,' I said. 'You have been very kind to me, and I shall always remember you fondly. But we have run our course. You have your temple to build, and I . . . I have my life to live.'

'With that scoundrel? You will be a fallen woman.'

'Happily, I achieved that status twenty-three years ago. But it has been such fun.'

She burst into tears.

I collected Eugenie, to her great relief, and our belongings, and returned home, to throw myself into an orgy of licentiousness which had been so lacking from my life and which I was now prepared to accept was an essential part of my nature. Not that I could have any doubt that Cristos was at least as interested in my wealth as in my body, but then, the same could be said of Spiro. And I did not care, for Cristos could satisfy me in a way no man had ever done before him, nor ever would, or could again, I was certain. As he humoured me so consistently, I was prepared to humour him in return, while never losing sight of my guiding light of not giving up an iota of control over my finances. He continued to be fascinated by my revolvers, and asked me if I would not give him one of them. 'They never leave my side,' I told him.

'But what do you need them for? Who are you going to shoot? If you need protection, my men and I will provide it.'

'I prefer to do things for myself,' I said. 'Well, most things. However, would you like to have a matching pair?'

'You can do this?'

I ordered two Colts from Paris with my next consignment of dresses, together with a large supply of cartridges, as I suspected that he would be doing more shooting than I. He was delighted when they arrived, and immediately retired to the back garden to loose them off several times, and was quite put out when, with a single shot, I shattered the bottle at which he had vainly been aiming. 'Athena!' he said. 'You are a reincarnation of Athena.'

'Once you said I was the reincarnation of Aphrodite,' I reminded him.

'Her too.'

'Well, then, I am unique.' Sometimes I thought I was.

However, as I am not a goddess, I still had to put up with, to paraphrase Shakespeare, the slings and arrows of outrageous humans. Cristos and I in no way publicized our romance. He came to me whenever he was off duty, entering my house as clandestinely as possible, and as I had, to all appearances, gone into perpetual purdah and no longer entertained, I did not see how our relationship would ever leak out. But inevitably it did. Perhaps he boasted of his conquest, perhaps he was seen entering my house by some passer-by, or perhaps Sophie herself spread it about – I would not have put it past her. But it got back to the palace, and the day came when Cristos arrived looking very crestfallen. 'I have been retired,' he said dolefully.

'You? Sacked? I thought you said that could never happen?'

'I have not been sacked.' Clearly this was a word that no Greek was prepared to accept. 'I have been retired from my position as principal aide-de-camp to the King.'

'Oh, Cristos, I am most terribly sorry. But . . .' I squeezed his hands. 'You will be able to spend more time with me.'

'I am to leave Athens.'

'You have been banished? Can they do that?'

'They cannot banish me. But I have been given another appointment. I am to take up my old position as Governor of the
Mountains. There is much trouble up there, and I am to deal
with it.'

'You mean you will again be King of the Mountains,' I cried,
Madame Normande's prophecy flooding back.

He gave a wry smile. 'Perhaps. But it means we will be separated. My headquarters will be Lamia. That is some days away.'

'We shall not be separated. I will come with you.'

'To Lamia? I will have to spend much time in the mountains
beyond.'

'Then I will come with you there, too.'

'I could not permit that. It will be very uncomfortable, rain,
snow – winter will soon be upon us – no roof for our heads . . .'

'But I shall be sleeping in your arms.'

'It will also be very dangerous. If you were to be captured by
those brigands . . .'

I reflected that they could hardly do anything more to me
than he had done, but decided not to say it. 'Who is going to
capture me? Am I not the best shot you have ever seen? Am I
not a reincarnation of Athena and Aphrodite? I sometimes feel I
have a bit of Artemis in me as well: she was a pretty good shot
too.' Although a chaste one.

He shook his head. 'The Queen would never permit it.'

'The Queen will not know of it,' I said. 'You will take up your
post. I will visit Lamia on my own, and we will meet there. All
I ask is that you do not go into the mountains until I join you.'

'I will wait for you.'

'And that you will love me alone, forswearing all other women.'

'This is so important to you?'

'It is all important to me. I will not, I cannot, share my love.'

He took me into his arms. 'Nor should you. You are a goddess.
I swear that I shall love no other woman but you, for the rest of
my life.'

Riding with the Devil

I then had to break the news to Eugenie that we were again going to travel. She looked rather doleful at this. As with my other maids, Lucy and Emma, I had never inquired as to what she did in her spare time, and with whom, but as she was a big, strong, handsome, voluptuous woman, with no inhibitions when it came to sex, I had no doubt that she occupied her time very well. I gained the impression that she had accumulated an almost permanent beau since our return to Athens, and was clearly reluctant to abandon him. 'But think of all those Pelikari,' I told her. 'All dying to get their hands on you.'

'Will they all be like General Petros?' she asked.

'I'm sure of it.' Oddly, this did not seem to reassure her. Being overexcited at the prospect of undertaking the greatest adventure of my life, so far, I did not at the time find anything significant in this. So off we went, only a few days after Cristos, leaving my dogs in the care of my steward, Paul, and taking the road, if an uneven track can be so-called, north of Athens. I personally found the going by no means difficult, for I rode Ghost, although I took along a string of remounts as the poor old girl was getting a little long in the tooth. Eugenie opted for the coach and was terribly jolted.

The countryside was fascinating. For the first couple of days the road followed the coast, and I was able to visit both the famous battlefields of Marathon and Thermopylae. Sadly it took a great deal of imagination and repeated studies of Herodotus, whose *History* accompanied me, to envisage the scene of the immortal battle. This was because the land, over the centuries, had encroached on the sea, and driven it back some distance. The road was reputed to pass over the very ground where Leonidas had fought and died, but while the mountains still rose immediately to the west, the flat, open country to the east would have made it quite impossible for even three hundred Spartans, to have held off the onslaught of ten thousand Persians for more than a few minutes.

Soon after leaving Thermopylae, we turned north-west, leaving the coast behind, and entered ever more rugged and forbidding country, although it remained lush enough, with forests in every direction. We traversed this hill country for two days, finding it empty of life apart from the occasional village or lonely shepherd with his flock and his protective dogs, until on the third morning one of our guides approached me as we breakfasted to inform me that, 'Men coming.'

I was travelling with only Eugenie of my usual entourage, although both the carriage and several mules were laden with my various belongings, which did not, contrary to some rumours, include my grand piano, and had an escort of four guides, who drove the coach and performed all the many and varied menial tasks that go with a camping expedition. Eugenie had been somewhat apprehensive about the wisdom of entrusting our virtues, such as they were, not to mention our lives, to four strange men, but thus far, at least, they had behaved very well, which I put down to the fact that they knew I was going to join the General, as Cristos was universally known, and were not about to risk his wrath. But now they were looking extremely nervous. 'Men?' I inquired. 'You mean the General has sent an escort for us?'

'I do not think these men are from the General, milady.'

'But are we not quite close to Lamia?'

'Another day, perhaps.'

'Then what do you suppose these men wish?'

'I think they have been watching us, milady. They have observed that you have some fine horses. And they have observed . . .' he pulled his nose.

'I see,' I commented. I suppose that if one is going to set out to experience everything life has to offer, one must be prepared to experience rape, but I think it is fair to say that one rape is sufficient for any normal lifetime, however enjoyable it may have been. I therefore opened my reticule, took out my revolvers, and checked that they were both loaded and in their usual perfect working order.

'You cannot fight these men,' protested Boris, the head guide.

'Is there a law against it? You have indicated that they are brigands.'

'They are brigands. But there are a dozen of them.'

'And there are six of us.'

'Well . . .' some more nose pulling.

'Then what do you suggest we do?'

'We could turn back and try to regain that village we passed yesterday.'

'I do not think that would be a good idea. The brigands can undoubtedly ride faster than the coach can travel.'

'We can abandon the coach.'

'And my belongings? And my maid?' I may say that Eugenie was listening to all this, with some concern, although she knew I would never desert her.

'It might slow them up, if they stop to plunder the coach,' Boris suggested.

'And the maid, no doubt. You are a cowardly wretch. As of this moment, you are dismissed my service. Be off with you. All of you.'

They exchanged glances. 'We have not been paid.'

'I hired you to escort me to Lamia. You have not done that. I do not propose to pay you a drachma.' The four men were standing in a semicircle around us. Now they again exchanged glances, and I understood that there would have to be a pre-emptive strike, as it were; should they manage to get hold of either Eugenie or me, we were lost. I therefore presented one of the revolvers. 'Think before you act,' I recommended.

'A woman,' Boris sneered. 'What do women know of guns?' I squeezed the trigger. I could easily have blown his head off, as he was only a few feet away from me, but I had never killed a man in my life – I had never even actually fired at one – and I certainly did not wish to begin in cold blood. So I shot him in the leg. He gave a scream of anguish and collapsed to the ground. His companions now showed a great anxiety to be off, and I had to halt them with another shot. I found myself shaking with released emotion and had a considerable tightness in my chest, but I managed to keep my voice even. 'You must take Boris with you,' I told them. 'Eugenie, give them a bandage from our medicine box, and also some laudanum.'

This she did. They bandaged up their groaning commander, fed him some of the sedative, got him on to the back of a horse, and made off, leaving us two women forlorn. At least, Eugenie considered us forlorn. 'What are we to do, milady?' she asked, looking fearfully at the surrounding hills. 'If there are really a dozen men up there . . . and we have no coachman.'

I secured Ghost to the string of other horses, and secured the entire string to the back of the coach, leaving the line as loose as possible. Then I did the same with the mules. The horses raised no objection; they all knew me and trusted me. The mules were more recalcitrant, and one or two kicked and bucked, but I got them under control, while Eugenie watched. I don't think, after our more than ten years together, that she had any more doubt about my ability to cope than did the horses, but she had never actually seen me in so active a role. 'Now,' I said, panting somewhat and soaked in perspiration, 'I will drive the coach, and you will ride on top.'

'On top?' Her voice was high. 'But milady, I will be exposed.'

'So will I,' I reminded her. 'As for being exposed, I do not believe these men will wish to shoot us. They will be more interested in capturing us. In any event, you can lie on your stomach.'

'Ooh, la, la. Can I not ride inside? Or beside you?'

'No. I need you on top. Do you know how to load these pistols? You have seen me do it often enough.'

'I think so, milady.'

'So, up you get. Here is a box of cartridges. As I pass a gun back to you, you will break it, so, and spill out the empty cartridge cases. Then you will load it again as quickly as possible, and have it ready to give to me when I ask for it. Do you understand?'

'You mean to shoot at these men, milady?'

'If they attempt to block our way, yes.'

'But then they *will* shoot back.'

'At me, not at you.' She did not seem entirely reassured, not having my knowledge of guns – as for instance, I knew that the brigands would have no revolvers, and probably no rifles either, and that my two guns with their rifled barrels would be twice as accurate and have twice the range of any smooth-bore pistol or musket, not to mention about four times the reliability – but climbed on to the coach-top, clutching her box of cartridges as if it were a copy of the Bible, for which I imagine she would gladly have exchanged it.

I reloaded the used pistol, got on to the driving seat, thrust my revolvers into my waistband – they were most uncomfortable – picked up the reins, cracked the whip, and got us moving. And was immediately aware of a problem. Trailing a string of horses and another of mules, and guiding the coach horses and wheels over a rutted track, there was no possibility of riding through any opposition, even had I possessed the strength to control the team at a gallop. But then I reflected, the coach would not be able to outrun a man on a horse anyway; if it came to that, my revolvers would have to do their stuff. I do not remember being afraid. I was supremely confident that I could handle the situation, and while I had a touch of womanly weakness at the thought of poor Boris weltering in his blood, I knew I would act the same in similar circumstances, or in the circumstances I apprehended would soon be upon us. Although I still hoped to get through without bloodshed; if the bandits had ever encountered someone armed with a revolver before, they would surely have the sense not to oppose me. Thus, I guided the team along the track, aware now of the clustering rocks to either side, any one of which might conceal a man armed with a musket, but putting my faith in my assurance to Eugenie, that they would be after our living bodies rather than a pair of carcasses, and in fact I took off my hat and laid it on the seat beside me before pulling out the pins to free my hair and allowing it to float past my shoulders; I wanted them to have no doubt as to the prize that awaited them – if they could take me alive.

We rounded a bend, and saw people in front of us. To my immediate relief I discerned that they were on foot, but then I counted only ten, and realized that the other two would be holding their horses out of the line of any fire. I dragged on the reins and applied the brake, not that, as we had been proceeding at a walk, much pressure was required. Behind me I heard Eugenie muttering prayers in French, but a glance assured me that she had opened the box of cartridges and was prepared to play her part. 'Holloa!' I called. 'Good morning, gentlemen.' One should always be polite. They moved forward. 'Do not approach,' I told them.

'You are the beautiful English lady with the hair of fire,' one of them remarked.

'How sweet of you to say that. But, sir . . .' he was continuing to advance, his fellows behind him. 'I have asked you not to come close.' And I levelled my revolver.

He checked while he studied me, and attempted to discern what support I had, if any; lying flat as she was, Eugenie was all but invisible at a distance. But it was clear that he had not identified the gun as anything more than a pistol. 'You have things that I want, Englishwoman.'

'Tell me what they are.'

'You have money. I will have your money.'

'I am sure we can come to some arrangement,' I agreed, still hopeful of a peaceful outcome.

'You have horses. I wish your horses.'

'My horses are not for sale.'

'But I will take them anyway. And you have a slit. I am sure it is a beautiful slit. I will have that also.'

Well, really, such vulgarity! I all but fainted with embarrassment; certainly I could feel a tremendous heat in my cheeks. But my blush was at least partly caused by anger. 'You, sir, are an ill-mannered lout. I will say nothing more to you. Get off the road, or I shall blow you off it.'

He laughed, and his fellows joined in. 'One woman, with one pistol?' he sneered. I picked up my other weapon with my left hand, although I had never fired with that hand and had no intention of doing so now. 'Two pistols? How many of us can you hit with two pistols?'

It occurred to me that his eyesight could not be of the best, or he would surely by now have discerned that mine were no ordinary pistols. But his ignorance, or short-sightedness, gave me an increased advantage. 'Are you prepared to find out?' I inquired. He gazed at me for several more seconds, but I knew that the die was cast: I had challenged his manhood. I laid down my left-hand pistol. 'Stand by,' I told Eugenie, without turning my head.

The bandit leader shouted something I did not understand and ran at me, followed by his men. I levelled my revolver and brought him down with my first shot, then turned my attention to his friends, cocking, aiming and firing with cool precision. The sounds of the reports echoed into the hills before my hammer clicked on an empty chamber. I passed the now hot weapon back to Eugenie and picked up the second. But the battle was already over. Thanks to my years of practising five of my bullets had struck home, and five men were stretched on the ground. The other five, having never previously encountered such devastating firepower, had taken to their heels. The road was therefore open, but I was now confronted with a problem I had not anticipated: not one of the men I had shot was actually dead, although I could tell at a glance that two of them, including their captain, were very badly hurt. But they were all bleeding copiously, and from the cries and groans were all in considerable pain. I found myself weeping with concern, and when I jumped down my knees gave way and I collapsed to the ground.

'Milady!' Eugenie leaned over the roof, holding my second revolver. 'We must leave this place.'

I regained my feet. 'We cannot abandon these people to bleed to death.'

'They tried to kill us.'

'Actually, we don't know that was their intention. Pass me down the medicine box.' This she did, with obvious misgivings. The bandit leader was only semi-conscious, having been struck in the chest, but one of the others was sitting up, holding his shoulder, which had clearly been broken by a bullet.

'Do not get too close,' Eugenie called.

'I must. Come down. Bring the gun.' She hesitated, then clambered down and joined me, holding the revolver, gingerly, in one hand, and endeavouring to lift her skirts clear of the various pools of blood with the other. 'Present the gun at his head,' I told her.

'Ooh, la la,' she muttered, but obeyed me.

'Now, my good man,' I told the bandit, 'I am going to try to help you. But if you attempt to assault me, my maid will blow your head off. Do you understand me?' He rolled his eyes and looked at Eugenie, who had assumed a suitably severe expression. Maintaining this system, and removing all of the bandits' weapons from easy reach – they consisted mainly of knives and a few antiquated pistols – we did our best for the poor men. But it was obvious that the leader, at least, was not going to live: he was coughing blood as well as bleeding from his wound; my bullet must have penetrated his lung.

Those who could speak begged for water, and we gave them some. 'Now we must leave this place,' Eugenie recommended again.

'We cannot just abandon them to die.'

'What more can we do for them, milady? We cannot take them with us.' I chewed my lip. I knew that they deserved their fate. But my military ardour had entirely dissipated as I had bound up their wounds and listened to their prayers of gratitude; I just could not bring myself to leave them. 'Their friends will not be far,' Eugenie said, understanding the way my thoughts were drifting. 'As soon as we have left, they will come to their comrades' aid.'

I couldn't be sure of that. From the way the survivors had run off I had a notion they might still be running. It was at this juncture that we heard the drumming of hooves. 'Holy Mary, Mother of God,' Eugenie gasped. 'Have mercy on our souls.'

'Back to the coach,' I snapped. 'Quickly.'

We gathered our skirts and ran back to the coach, our only hope of defending ourselves. But we had not got there when at least a score of horsemen appeared behind us. I turned and presented my revolver, and gasped in relief. A moment later I was in Cristos's arms.

Having hugged me and kissed me, Cristos held me at arm's length while he looked around himself. 'What happened?'

'These poor men attempted to rob us.'

'And your people fought them off?'

'No, no. My people ran away.'

'Then who rescued you?'

'No one rescued us. Eugenie and I took care of the business.'

He released me and turned round, counting. 'There were five of them.'

'No, no,' I said. 'There were ten of them. But the other five ran away when I opened fire.'

He turned back again. 'You opened fire? You?'

'I know it was a terrible thing to do. But I didn't see what else I *could* do. I asked them to go away and leave us alone, but they would not. I am very sorry.'

'Sorry?' He gave me another hug. 'You are magnificent! You are Aphrodite! You are Athena! And you are Artemis!'

'And Aurora,' I reminded him.

'One woman!' he shouted, beckoning his followers. 'One woman against ten men, and she slaughtered them.' The Pelikari cheered and all seemed to wish to kiss me.

'Eugenie loaded the guns for me,' I gasped, trying to avert the flood. 'But listen, only one of them is dead, I think. We must get the others to a doctor. They must be seen to. Quickly.'

'They will be seen to, now. You and you, go into those trees and cut some stakes.'

'You are going to make stretchers to carry them?' I asked, somewhat bewildered. 'I would have thought our best course would be to load them into the coach.'

'We are not going to take them with us. We are going to shove sticks up their asses and watch them die.'

'*What* did you say?'

'It is an old custom. We learned it from the Turks.'

'You are speaking of impalement.'

'Yes. That is what we are going to do. You will see. It is great sport.'

'I have never heard of anything so terrible. I will not permit it.'

'You are my woman, and these men tried to lay hands on you. Do you know what they would have done to you if they had captured you? *They* would have impaled *you*, only not on stakes of wood.'

'But they did not lay hands on me. I am sorry, Cristos, but I cannot permit such barbarity.'

'You are my woman . . .'

'And I will remain your woman. But if you murder these men, I am going straight back to Athens.'

He glowered at me for some moments, while his men, and Eugenie, watched us anxiously. Then he grinned. 'All right. If it is so important to you, I will not impale them. I will just cut off their pricks, eh? We shall see how they get along without those.'

'You are speaking of castration?'

'Yes. That is what it is called. That too we learned from the Turks.'

'I will not have these men castrated, Eugenie, help these poor people into the coach.'

Cristos threw up his hands. 'What is the matter with you? These men would have robbed you, raped you, killed you. And you want to look after them?'

'I wish them looked after, yes.'

'And after that?'

'You can lock them up, or make them labour for you, or even set them free. What is their real crime, Cristos? They wanted me for their own. Are you not guilty of the same crime?'

He gazed at me for several seconds, while I held my breath. Then he said, 'You *are* a goddess. Put these men in the coach,' he told his people.

I suspect my arrival in Lamia would in any event have been a triumph, but in the circumstances it was an unforgettable experience. The entire town, and it was quite a sizeable place, surrounded my horse and tried to kiss my feet or even my horse's feet. I was reminded of a painting I had seen of the Queen of Sheba entering Jerusalem. Indeed, I felt like her. I was led to Cristos's house, where I dismounted before a group of women who, in view of our arrangement, I assumed to be servants, and Cristos held my arm to escort me inside. I cannot pretend that the house bore any resemblance to any dwelling I had previously occupied. In its bare earth floors, its damply dripping walls, its entirely open plan, both inside and out, which permitted a variety of animals, fowls, dogs, cats and goats free access, it made the house on Tinos seem like a palace, and might have provided another reason for a hasty return to Athens, but that waiting just inside the doorless doorway there was a small boy.

He had handsome features, but a somewhat thin body, and a not altogether healthy pallor in his cheeks. But he was clearly only a year or so older than Leonidas, when last I had beheld my son. I looked at Cristos, who was beaming with pride. 'This is Eirini. My son.' I turned back to the boy. Somehow it had never crossed my mind that Cristos might have a young son. I could not stop myself from looking to left and right. 'His mother is dead,' Cristos said. 'She was . . .'

I shook my head. 'Do not tell me.' I held out my hands, and

after a quick glance at his father, Eirini came forward and took them. 'I would like to be your mother,' I said. 'If you will permit me. Will you permit me?'

Eirini again looked at his father, and presumably received another nod. 'I would like that very much, great English lady.'

'You must not call me that,' I said. 'You must call me Mama.'

'Yes . . . Mama.' I took him in my arms.

Here was a bliss I had not known for six years. But in fact I count the few months I was enabled to spend in Lamia and the mountains as amongst the happiest of my life. The town itself was on the edge of the rising ground; the mountains were some distance away. But it was the administrative centre of the district, and contained, on a low hill overlooking the houses, an ancient and most decrepit fortress. It was from here that Cristos carried out his duties, but he would not let me live there. He said it was because it was always full of men and he could not guarantee my privacy, but I had no doubt that it was because it was in the fortress that he also administered justice, which was invariably short and sharp and severe, and he did not wish my, in his eyes, soft-centred approach to such matters interfering with his sentences. I accepted this, as while I had felt a sense of personal responsibility for my assailants on the road, I could not possibly undertake such a role for every criminal in the community. I have no idea what eventually happened to the robbers.

That apart, life was glorious. I immediately discerned that my Paris gowns were quite out of the question in my new surroundings, and sent them back to Athens to be stored until my return. I had not been in Lamia more than a couple of weeks when I received a letter from my agent telling me that my house had been sold, and enclosing various documents for me to sign. As I actually made a profit on the transaction, I was suddenly in possession of an enormous amount of ready cash, from which I was able largely to re-equip Cristos's ragtag army with modern weapons, including rifled muskets and revolvers, which made them more than ever certain that I was a goddess come to life.

For clothes, I adopted the very simple costume worn by the Pelikari women, which consisted of a single garment – it could hardly be called a dress much less a gown, but was a sort of enlarged chemise, with a thick black woollen belt, and a scarf-like headdress copiously embroidered . . . and nothing else. I enjoyed this tremendously, as did I enjoy not wearing shoes, or stockings, or any foot covering at all. This meant that one's limbs were constantly covered in mud and dust, but there was no shortage of water for washing. In fact, as we were now into autumn there was a great deal too much water: it rained every day. Eugenie was not happy with these arrangements, but she was a faithful girl and where I led she was always willing to follow, even if as I now wore my hair loose and it was so long, well past my thighs, that I hardly needed to wear clothes at all, she had to spend more than an hour every day brushing it.

Our food was based on lamb, but there were always olives, cheese, yogurt and honey, a most healthy diet. Of course there were no books, and no intellectual conversation of any sort. Once, this would have driven me mad, but that was because, as I now realized, without those aspects of cultured civilization I had been bored stiff. In Lamia there was always too much to be done, principally, in my case, playing with and attempting to educate Eirini – not a difficult task as he was a bright and responsive boy – and when we did decide to call it a day, there was retsina to be drunk – I at last cultivated a taste for it – and cards to be played, a game that could be called a local variety of whist, which consisted mainly of thumping down a superior card with great violence and even greater oaths, always accompanied by a hasty and apologetic glance in my direction.

But Cristos was in Lamia to do a job of work, at least according to his lights. We had only been in residence three weeks when I heard the sounds of a martial gathering, and going outside found some forty men, all armed, gathered outside my house. Cristos had left our bed some time before, and was already in the saddle. 'Is there a crisis?' I asked.

'No, no,' he assured me. 'There is some trouble in the mountains and I must attend to it.'

'Well, wait for one moment and I will be with you.'

'You? We are going to war!'

'That is something I have always wanted to do.'

'Women,' he announced, 'do not go to war.' He might have been addressing the opposition benches in Parliament.

But I had put that sort of hypocrisy behind me. 'I am not women,' I reminded him. 'I am Aphrodite. And Athena. And Artemis. And Aurora.'

'You could get hurt. I absolutely forbid it.'

By now his men were showing signs of amusement at the altercation, while quite a few of the women had gathered to hear what was going on. I had no wish to embarrass Cristos, and so I said, quietly, 'Would you dismount a moment, please, my lord? I wish to speak with you, privately.'

He hesitated, glancing from left to right, then dismounted and stood beside me. 'What do you have to say? I will not be contradicted.'

'I merely wished to ask you a question. This expedition you are about to undertake: will you be firing your guns?'

'Of course.'

'And when you return here, you will have probably used most of your ammunition?'

'That is what ammunition is for. To be used.'

'But it will have to be replaced before you can fight another battle. What are you going to use for money, to buy this fresh ammunition?' He frowned at me. 'I should also point out,' I went on, 'that the ammunition you are about to fire, and the guns with which you intend to fire it, were paid for by my money.'

'And you intend to withdraw your support?'

'By no means. As long as I am permitted to see how my goods are being used.'

'Do you not suppose we can make our own bullets? We have been doing this for years. For centuries.'

'Of course. But can you make *rifled* bullets, to fit your rifled guns, your revolvers?'

'You are a fiend. I should beat you.'

'If you do that, I shall return to Athens. I may even leave Greece. Dearest Cristos, I wish only to ride at your side, be at your side, share your dangers, and triumph at your side.'

He glared at me for some seconds, but I had never been one to lower my eyes. Then he gave one of his enormous grins and embraced me. 'Athena!' he shouted. 'Yes, you will ride at my side, to victory.'

★   ★   ★

We left Eirini behind in the care of the women. I offered Eugenie the choice of remaining as well, but she preferred to accompany me: I think she felt safer in my company, no matter what dangers we were going to face. But there were no dangers, certainly in the beginning, only what some people, I suppose, might regard as hardship. I found it magnificent. We rode across the plain and then walked our horses into the mountains. Most of the time we had to proceed in single file because of the narrowness of the tracks, and often enough we had sheer drops of several hundred feet on one side or the other. It rained incessantly for several days, and then it started to snow, but although the temperature hovered around freezing it never actually plunged much below that, and then only briefly, thus Eugenie's and my bare limbs and toes were not exposed to frostbite.

We bivouacked beneath the stars – or the rain or snow – and I slept in the greatest of comfort in Cristos's arms beneath a shared blanket. What a mockery this life made of the cloistered, convention-ridden existence I had suffered for so long – and which so many of my erstwhile friends and acquaintances were still enduring. Cristos told me that we were seeking some Albanians who had penetrated our mountains, but we did not find them, and after a week our scouts reported that the invaders had retreated across the border. This quite pleased me, as I really had no desire to become involved in any more killing, as was clearly Cristos's intention should he catch up with his quarry. 'Will we now go home?' I asked.

'I think you should do that,' he agreed. 'I will follow shortly.'

'But you are not coming now? Why?'

'You ask too many questions,' he grumbled.

'And I do not get enough answers. Tell me why you are remaining in the mountains.'

'There is work to be done.'

'Then I will stay with you until this work has been accomplished.'

'It is not something for you to see.'

'That is absurd. Tell me.'

His shoulders hunched. 'My scouts report that there is a caravan coming through the mountains. Foreigners.'

'A caravan from where?'

'Who knows? Buda? Vienna?'

'And going where?'

'Athens.'

'And they are coming through the mountains, instead of travelling by ship?' I remembered how Spiro had used sea travel rather than take the risk of encountering the Pelikari on their own ground.

Cristos shrugged. 'Perhaps they do not like the sea. The Adriatic can be very rough.'

'Well, in any case, if they have reached these mountains, they are safe, surely. There is no need for you to protect them.'

'You do not understand. A caravan is full of rich goods. Not to mention rich people.'

The penny dropped. 'You mean to rob them! But they have come to your country as guests.'

'They have not come as *my* guests. I did not invite them.'

I was aghast, and looked around at the waiting men. This time there was no amusement to be seen. I realized that what was involved here was these people's living, regardless of what might have been decreed in Athens. But at least I could perhaps do something to save the unfortunate, and unsuspecting, travellers from the very worst. 'Well, then,' I said. 'Let us go and find these people.'

This was not difficult, our scouts having left two of their number behind to keep an eye on the caravan, and at dusk two days later we found ourselves on a hillside looking down on its campfires. Unlike us, they were travelling slowly and in some style: I counted seven large tents, and there were at least twenty horses, not to mention quite a few mules. As far as could be seen, the entire party was gathered round the main fire, enjoying their supper. 'Do we speak with them?' I asked.

'No, no. We attack them. Now.' He waved his arm, kicked his horse, and charged down the hill. I rode immediately behind him, and Eugenie was immediately behind me. The diners were taken entirely by surprise. They started to their feet, and one or two reached for weapons, but one of these was immediately shot down, and the rest gathered in a group, arms held high. Eugenie and I hurried to the wounded man and did what we could for him – he was not badly hurt – then I joined Cristos, who was surveying his captives. These consisted of the various drivers and muleteers, and four gentlemen, very well dressed in a jaunty fashion, with feathers in their hats and multicoloured waistcoats. They were spluttering at Cristos, but he clearly did not understand them. 'What language is that?' he asked me.

'They are speaking German. And they wish to know the meaning of this outrage.'

'Tell them that they must pay a toll for passing through our mountains.'

I translated, while the men took me in. Then one asked, 'Are you not the Baroness von Venningen?'

'Actually, no,' I said. 'I am the Countess Theotoky. Did you know the Baroness von Venningen?'

'I saw her once. And you are she. I could never forget you. That hair . . .'

'That is very flattering of you. Are you Bavarians?'

'We are from Vienna. But . . .' he looked embarrassed. The Schwarzenbergs had long ago had me banned from entering Austria, with great publicity.

'Water under the bridge,' I assured him.

'But these brigands . . .'

'Yes. I'm afraid you will have to pay the toll.'

'But that is outrageous. We have passports, issued by the Greek minister in Vienna.'

I translated for Cristos, who was showing signs of impatience. 'Tell him that Vienna is a very long way away. I will have their money and their horses.'

'All of them?'

'They may keep four, for themselves. Am I not generous?'

'I do not know if they will think so. However . . .' I explained the situation to my new friend.

'That is outrageous,' he declared again. 'I absolutely refuse.' His companions nodded their agreement.

'They refuse,' I told Cristos.

'How can they refuse? They are in my power. If they refuse, I will burn their balls in that fire. Tell them this.'

'I really think you should do as General Hadji-Petros wishes,' I told the Austrians. 'If you refuse it might get very unpleasant.'

'You will stand by and let this happen?'

'There is nothing I can do to prevent it. However . . . what is the total value of the money and goods you have with you? As well as your horses and belongings. Tell me in English pounds.'

They exchanged glances, and I understood that I was about to be robbed myself. 'Well,' said their spokesman, 'it is not less than three hundred pounds.'

'Very well. Hand over everything they wish to these gentlemen, and I will write you a cheque on my bank in Athens for three hundred and fifty pounds. Will that satisfy you? There is, however, one condition.' They exchanged more glances. 'I wish your words, as gentlemen, that you will carry this matter no further, but will simply cash my cheque, refund and re-equip yourselves, and enjoy your stay in Athens. If you are sensible, you will return by ship. Will you promise this?' They did, and that occasion passed off peacefully; we entertained them to dinner, and I allowed each of them a kiss, which scandalized Cristos but made them very happy, and, I like to think, was the high point of their adventure. I was the only actual loser, and I have no doubt that the travellers dined out on the event for some time.

I was just happy to have avoided any loss of life – I still could not get the memory of the men I had shot out of my mind, even if I knew I would do it again, in similar circumstances. And it was fascinating, when we returned to Lamia, to sit at the general council of the Pelikari, when the booty was evaluated and then solemnly distributed amongst the various members of the community. I was even offered a share myself, but I declined. However, I did not do so well a few weeks later, when the Albanians made the mistake of returning. Naturally Cristos went off in pursuit, and also naturally I went with him. But this time, to my consternation, he did not stop at the border – there was actually no border, just a mutual understanding – but followed the marauders into their own mountains and attacked their village. The Albanians, virtually Pelikari themselves, were not the sort of men to give up without a fight, and it was a bloody encounter. Cristos would not let me accompany the attack, and this time I was happy to obey, as I realized there was nothing I could do to alleviate what was going to happen.

He would also have prevented me from entering the village after his victory, but I insisted, and heartily regretted it. The houses were burning, there were dead bodies scattered everywhere, several of the women had obviously been raped and were in a state of extreme distress, while the most distressing thing of all was the several children who had been orphaned and even seen their parents killed or outraged before their eyes. When I attempted to help some of them, I was reminded that I would do better to attend to our own wounded. 'I would not have had you see this,' Cristos said that night. 'But you are a headstrong woman. So, you must understand that this is the way it has been in these mountains for hundreds of years. When the Turks ruled it was worse. Oh, the crimes that were committed. It was terrible. But it is the way of life.'

'Just tell me that you wish it wasn't so. That if it were possible, you would never seek to take another life.'

'Of course I would like it to be different. When you kill, you must one day expect to be killed. I wish to live forever, loving you.'

Certainly, I realized that Cristos was a scoundrel who in England would probably have been hanged. But Greece, or at least the mountains of southern Macedonia, might have been on a different planet, where the rules and requirements of life were entirely different. I had known what Cristos was like well before I had followed him into the wilds, and in the wilds he had behaved exactly as I had anticipated. If the barbarities he perpetrated, or wished to perpetrate, horrified me, I felt towards them, and him, much as I might have felt towards a lion that had come into my possession. I had no doubt that I could tame him, but I wished to do so without emasculating him. In his wildly romantic lifestyle he was appealing to the primitive in my soul, just as his sexual vigour and his ability to transport me into a sensual heaven whenever we lay naked together carried me to plateau after plateau of ecstasy. I loved him without reservation. Nor was it purely a physical or romantic emotion. I found in him so many qualities I had sought, and never found, in other men. His courage, certainly, his devil-may-care attitude to life, these were characteristics I shared. But more, I felt sure that beneath the bravado and the bluster there lay the heart of a gentleman, at least when it came to me, revealed by the manner in which he always sought to shield me from witnessing the worst excesses of his people, was terrified at the thought that I might be in danger, and understood that he had to deal with me as an equal, which, for a Pelikari, brought up to regard all women as beasts of burden, satisfiers of male lust, and bearers of children and nothing more, was a considerable concession. But more than anything else, he was all mine. I had no doubt that prior to my arrival he had exercised a *droit de seigneur* over all the women in Lamia: that was his nature, and the nature of the society he ruled. But he had never laid a finger on any woman, so far as I could tell, since I had joined him.

And then there was Eirini. I knew that the boy could never replace Leonidas, or even his memory. But as I could never now have another child of my own, I was prepared to make Cristos's son into as adequate a substitute as I could. Even had I not sought such a replacement so desperately, I would still have become attached to him. He was so intelligent, so eager to learn, and so eager to please me, that I sometimes felt he was indeed my own flesh and blood. I believe I would have happily lived in Lamia for the rest of my life, and being me, my thoughts were already turning towards legitimizing my union with Cristos. But it seemed that I was not intended by fate to enjoy any prolonged period of bliss. The new year had just dawned when there came an official letter from Athens.

I have never seen a man so stricken as when Cristos came into our bedchamber carrying the sheet of paper. 'I am retired,' he said.

I sat up. 'From what this time?'

'From here. From my position. From my life.'

'Oh, Cristos.' I held his hand to make him sit beside me, and took the paper from his fingers. It was certainly an official communication, from the Ministry of the Interior, briefly informing General Hadji-Petros that his services were no longer required, and that he was ordered forthwith to lay down his command and retire into private life. 'There is no reason?'

'They do not have to give a reason.'

'Well, then, let us consider what the reason might be.'

'It has to be those Austrian bastards. They have lodged a complaint against me.'

'I do not think so.' As they had been gentlemen I was sure they would have kept their word. Besides, they had lost nothing save a little dignity. 'I think this has come from the King. Or at least the Queen.'

'I have never opposed her.'

'You have, even if you do not realize it. Amalia hates me. I believe she only sent you up here to stop you seeing me. Now she has learned that I am here with you, and this is her revenge.'

He pulled his beard. 'If that is true . . .'

'You must do nothing rash. That would be treason. We must be patient. In the first instance this command must be obeyed. Listen. I will—'

'I will write her.'

'What can you say to her?'

'I will appeal to her magnanimity.'

'You are not going to beg her?!' I was horrified at the idea.

'No, no, I will be very dignified.' I felt it was a mistake, but I let him get on with it. Had I known what he actually wrote I would have been less content. But the immediate result was a complete negative, and he was ordered to be out of Lamia within a week. 'What am I to do?' he wailed. 'Where am I to go?'

'We will go to Athens. If the Queen wants open war, she will have it.'

'Athens? What am I to do in Athens?'

'Why, Cristos, you will be my husband.'

He goggled at me. 'You wish to marry me?'

'Don't you wish to marry me?'

'I wish that more than anything else in the world. But . . . you are the Countess Theotoky.'

'My situation can be rearranged,' I assured him.

And so we returned to Athens, much to Eugenie's relief, at least I supposed so. I took Eirini with me; I was convinced that the life in the mountains was doing his fragile health no good, and besides, I wanted to bring him up as a gentleman. To my astonishment, however, we were also accompanied by a score of Pelikari.

The idea of being ceremonially escorted into the capital certainly appealed to me, but I was a little alarmed when I discovered that they intended to stay. I could have accommodated them all at the house on Odos Sokratous, but that was now sold, so I rented two adjacent houses, placed the brigands in one, and settled Cristos, Eirini, Eugenie and myself in the other.

Our return, in such style, was naturally a sensation, the more so when the Pelikari house became notorious for its late-night drinking sessions, with a great deal of noise, to which more and more of their mountain comrades became attached. It was the Pelikari custom, indeed it was a duty, never to turn anyone away, and soon I had upwards of sixty men and their women enjoying my bed and board – needless to say, I paid for everything. I did not begrudge this, as long as it kept Cristos happy – and kept the Queen's nose out of joint. She responded by a truly underhand action: she published Cristos's letter to her, in which he had declared that far from loving me, he had only accepted my company in Lamia because my wealth had funded his arms and ammunition. I should have been appalled at this disloyalty, and for a little while I was, but Cristos was so apologetic. 'I wished to stay in Lamia, with you,' he said. 'I would have done anything to be able to do that. I had no idea she would ever publish my letter.'

I was prepared to believe him. 'Well, as they say, all is fair in love and war. And it reveals her in a far worse light than it does you.' I was more than ever determined to kick the Queen in the teeth by marrying Cristos in the biggest and most elaborate ceremony ever seen in Athens. But to accomplish this there was a great deal to be done. I made the journey up to Meteora, the wild mountainous area of northern Greece where the geological cataclysms of history had thrown up isolated peaks – the locals call them cones – on the top of several of which are situated monasteries. I was well escorted by a body of Pelikari, and was in no danger until I actually reached my goal, where I discovered that not only were women not welcome in these isolated and all male communities, but that the buildings themselves were inaccessible save by means of a basket hauled up the sheer mountain side by a windlass.

The first problem was quickly overcome when I sent a message up to inform the prior that I had come to discuss a possible endowment for his order – I had already ascertained that these people were as poor as the mice who infested their churches. The second was a business of gritting one's teeth and committing one's soul to the Almighty, or at least to the muscles of the monk winding the capstan. This Eugenie flatly refused to do, and so I went up alone. On more than one occasion in my life I had been in positions of some danger, and there were to be even more dangerous moments in the future, but this was quite the most mind-numbing experience of all, simply because in all the other moments of peril I have endured, my fate has been in my own hands. On this occasion I was entirely dependent upon those muscles, which I had never seen, and which, however formidable, could do nothing about the wind, which although not strong – I gathered that the ascent was impossible in a gale – yet blew the basket, and thus me, to and fro, and on occasion buffeted us against the rock face.

However, I reached the top without mishap, and was assisted over a low wall on to a platform, where I was surrounded by eager, bearded young men, wearing black robes and high black hats, but all very interested in their unique visitor. It was now that I discovered that the muscles on which I had been depending were not in the least extraordinary – and this little fellow would no doubt be responsible for my return journey! I was given a necessary glass of wine, and escorted into the presence of the prior, while having the opportunity to admire the quite exquisite decorations and icons and stained glass windows of the various chapels we passed. The prior was an elderly fellow, who was no less taken by my appearance than his juniors, for I wore for this occasion one of my Paris gowns – not the ideal garment for riding in a basket although I had the idea that it, and my several petticoats, might help to slow my descent if I fell out – and had my hair loose and floating out from beneath my bonnet: he clearly had never seen anything like me before in his life. We had another glass of wine, and then got down to cases. 'Hm,' he said. 'What you wish, Countess, is very difficult. It takes much time.'

'But it can be done?'

'Everything can be done, milady. An appeal to God's good will and guidance, an adequate donation to his charity . . .' he paused.

'How much? In English money, if you will.' I removed my gloves.

'Well, I am sure that for . . .' he paused again to inspect my clothes, my hair, my jewellery and my rings more closely, 'the sum of two hundred pounds it might be possible to ask for heavenly guidance.'

I had taken advice in Athens, and opened my satchel. 'I happen to have that amount with me. In cash.' I placed the two bundles on his desk.

He counted them with a great deal of expertise. 'Blessed be the name of the Lord, and His handmaiden.'

'How long will the decree or nullification take to obtain?'

'Why, I will have it drawn up now.' He rang a bell and gave instructions to the monk who appeared. As this was in legal jargon I had little idea of what he said, but when his aide had hurried off, he beamed at me. 'It will be ready in half an hour.'

'But you said . . .'

'The Lord works in a mysterious way His wonders to perform. When I first heard what you required, I envisaged, as I said, a long and expensive process, but as I counted your money, a divine inspiration came to me. The question is really a simple one. You were granted a nullification of both your previous marriages by a Greek priest in Paris. But he had no right to do this. Such a nullification can only be granted here in Greece. 'So . . .' he put the money safely into a drawer. 'I do not know what is the situation regarding your Bavarian husband, but as far as Greece is concerned, you were not legally married to Count Theotoky.'

'My Bavarian husband divorced me some years ago.'

'Well, then, you are legally free to marry whoever you choose.'

'Just like that?'

'Is that not what you wish, and have come here to obtain? As I have said, the document is being prepared now. You will, of course, no longer be the Countess Theotoky.'

'That is not a problem. Just assure me that this is absolutely legal?'

'There is no one in Greece,' he said severely, 'who would dare challenge a judgement of the Prior of St Stephen.'

'Not even the Queen?'

'Not even the Queen.'

The Promised Land

I had another glass of wine to fortify me, tucked my precious nullification into my reticule, and bade him a fond farewell. As I am bound to confess that my various encounters with religious teachers have left me inclined to scepticism, as regards them if not necessarily their religion, I did have a reflection on my downward journey that having relieved me of two hundred pounds for half an hour's work my recent hosts might be less concerned about my safety than they had been while I was still a prospective customer, as it were. However, I reached the bottom, wind-blown but triumphant.

In this mood I retuned to Athens, where I found everyone in a tizzy, as word of my projected marriage to Cristos had spread. Most people regarded it as mere rumour, as I was still the Countess Theotoky as far as they knew. But when it got abroad that I had obtained a nullification of my marriage, they had to sit up and take notice. Almost everyone was scandalized, the great exception being dear Sophie, who came to see me, expertly avoiding the attentions of various Pelikari, and offered her most sincere congratulations. 'I thought you did not like Cristos?' I had to ask.

'To be frank, my dear, I have never met any man I honestly liked. But if you love him, well . . . and you will be able to get rid of that dreadful Spiro. I never did trust *him*.' She patted Eirini on the head. 'What a dear little boy. I hope his hands are clean.'

She was followed in fairly short order by Spiro himself, all the way from Corfu. 'You cannot do this,' he declared.

'I have done it.'

'You are my wife!'

'It appears that I have never legally been your wife. We have been living in sin. Or at least bigamously.'

'You are saying that our son was a bastard!'

I sighed. 'I am sorry you have brought that up. I have had six children. Only two of them were conceived in wedlock. But I loved them all. I love them still. But I must live my own life.'

Now came the nub. 'And my allowance?'

'I am afraid that ceases as of now. Surely, Spiro, now you are past forty, you can stand on your own feet?'

He glared at me, so angrily I thought he might be going to attack me. But there were several Pelikari within call, and he thought better of it. I thus resolutely looked forward to what I was determined, as usual, would be the last love of my life. Which is not to say that I did not still have some problems with Cristos, and it was now, to my great sadness, that Ghost broke a leg and had to be put down. In fact, all of my horses were growing rather old, and I was informed that the best place to buy a new stable was in Syria: I knew that the Arab strain is the best in the world. I therefore proposed that we should honeymoon in Damascus, and buy horses at the same time. This was, in any event, a part of the world I had long intended to visit. Cristos was not happy about this plan. Syria, Palestine, all of the Middle East, belonged to the Ottoman Empire, and having been so prominent in the fight against that power for Greek independence, he did not think he would be well received. I pooh-poohed this, both on general grounds and because it appeared that there was a looming war between Russia and Turkey, and Great Britain was very much on the side of Turkey. This had less to do with any sympathy for the Ottomans than with the British determination that the Russians should never possess Constantinople, but still, the Porte could not afford to fall out with Britain, as could well happen if they attempted to arrest or manhandle an Englishwoman who happened to be a personal friend, even if, shall we say, a little removed, of the Prime Minister, dear Harry having now achieved the highest office. If he had been prepared to level Athens in defence of an itinerant Jew, it was difficult to envisage what he might do to defend the most famous Englishwoman of her time.

Thus reassured, Cristos began to make preparations for our departure, the day following our wedding. I did the same, and as I was already forming a plan in my mind to explore the Holy Land, and even more, the Heathen Land, which to me was the ancient empire of Palmyra, I sent a fairly large accumulation of trunks down to the ship which would take us to Beirut. The things I could not take, such as my piano, were still in store as they had been since the sale of my house; it was my intention, when we returned, to build myself a new house but I had not yet determined on a location – I was actually leaning towards a return to the mountains, which I reckoned would be one in the eye for Amalia.

However, first things first, and the very first thing was the wedding. I was nearly as excited about this as I had been at my first, perhaps more so. I do like grand occasions, especially when I am to be the centre of attraction. My marriage to Edward had been rather low key. My marriage to Karl, even if it had required two ceremonies, had been for me a somewhat sad affair, as I had known even then that it would never work out. My marriage to Spiro had been positively clandestine, with only Eugenie and Giorgio as witnesses. But this time . . . I was marrying a man I loved more than any of his predecessors, and I was controlling and organizing the event, which I was resolved was going to be the greatest in Athens since the arrival of King Otto, and even greater than that, if possible. Invitations went out to everyone of note in the city, and most of them accepted. I even sent an invitation to the palace, but to this there was no reply.

Thus, the morning before the ceremony I lay late in bed, going over everything in my mind to make sure I had forgotten nothing. I had decided that Cristos should not share my bed for the couple of days before the ceremony as I wished us both to be filled with ardour on the night, but I knew that he had spent last night carousing with his pals, and that today he was leaving the city with his friends to attend a function which would celebrate the end of his bachelorhood – in fact I assumed that he had already left, as I knew he had planned his departure for dawn. I had no doubt that it would be a most drunken affair, and perhaps more than that, but I did not begrudge him this last fling. I was a little concerned that he had taken Eirini, but as he said, the boy had to become a man at some stage, and what better occasion than the wedding of his father?

Having been awake for over an hour with no sign of my morning cup of tea, I rang the bell, and again, but it was still several minutes before Eugenie finally opened my door. I did not wish to reproach her for oversleeping, although I felt that some comment was called for, but before I could speak she ran across the room, dropped to her knees beside my bed, and buried her head in my arm. Only then did I realize that she was weeping, something I could not ever remember her doing before, however considerable some of our past problems. I raised her head, and gazed at an enormous ugly bruise on her cheek, spreading round her eye, which was blacked, to her forehead. 'Eugenie? What has happened?'

'Oh, milady . . .' tears streamed down her cheeks.

I swung my legs out of bed and held her hands. 'Tell me who did this. Your lover? Tell me his name, and I will have him punished most severely.'

'My lover!' She shuddered.

A terrible suspicion crossed my mind. 'You?' I cried. 'You have seduced my husband? You? The woman I have trusted more than any other? I am not surprised he beat you. I will beat you myself.'

'Milady!' she screamed. 'Please. I did not wish it. I have never wished it. From the beginning I did not wish it. I begged him not to. I told him I would tell you, but he said if I did he would cut my throat. Oh, milady.'

I had risen to my feet. Now I sat down again. 'From the beginning? What do you mean, from the beginning?'

'From the day I returned here from the Duchess, milady.'

'I do not believe you.' Empty words. I knew Cristos too well. But I had accepted his word of honour. 'You are a wicked, deceitful woman. You are dismissed from my service.'

'Milady, I beg you, do not send me away. I have devoted my entire life to you. Let me stay. Milady, what was I to do? I knew he would kill me if I refused, or I came to you. But last night, with your wedding so soon, I told him I could not accept him any longer, so he beat me, and then he . . . forced me.'

I knew she was telling the truth. After all his promises! I had to know everything 'You say he came to you after leaving my bed? How could he do that? When he left my bed he was spent. Always.'

'Not for long, milady. He has great powers of recovery. He would say that he came to me because he wanted a real woman after that stuck-up, arrogant bitch. Those were his words, milady. And that is what he said when he took all the other women in Lamia, as well.'

I felt quite faint. All the other women in Lamia! How they must have laughed behind my back! Thus, for all of his endearments, his passion, the only true thing he had ever said was in that letter to Amalia. The only thing he had really wanted from me was the use of my money! I swear that had he walked through the door at that moment I would have shot him dead.

It was Eugenie's turn to ask, anxiously, 'Milady?'

I touched her cheek, and she winced. 'Have something put on this. And then pack our remaining things and have them taken down to Piraeus.'

'But . . . shall I pack your wedding dress?'

'No. We shall leave that behind.'

Part of me wished to remain, and confront Cristos. But I knew that would not do, and not entirely because if he attempted to bluster his way out of his lies and deceptions I knew I *would* shoot him, but equally because I feared that if he threw himself on my mercy and begged my forgiveness, as he had done so often before, I might give in and accept him back. Certainly if he managed to get me into bed.

I knew that I was turning my back on everything I had valued over the past few months. There was Eirini, my plans for a new house, for a new life indeed. At a mundane level there was the time and money I had spent on arranging the wedding. And there would be the cruel laughter of Amalia and her cohorts. But I wanted only to be away, and doing something, anything. I went to my bank, obtained sufficient funds for a journey of some duration and arranged for more to be transferred to the Ottoman Bank in Damascus. I still possessed most of the sale price of the house on Odos Sokratous together with my accumulated funds – to live in Greece, even allowing for my extravagant habits, consumed no more than half my alimony, which continued to arrive every six months, so I had no financial worries. I also gave him power of attorney to find good homes for my animals. Then I went to Piraeus, where Eugenie awaited me on board our ship.

'But we are not to sail until the day after tomorrow,' the captain protested.

'I wish to sail today. Now, in fact.'

'I do not think I can do that, milady. The General—'

'The General is no longer involved. It is I who has chartered this vessel. If you will not put to sea at my request, I wish my money returned, and my luggage put ashore, now. I will find another ship.'

He gulped, but gave the necessary orders; his crew were rounded up and a few hours later the mooring warps were brought in. Eugenie stood at my side as we watched the piers and rooftops of Piraeus falling astern. 'Will he come after us, milady?' she asked.

'I think he will have more sense,' I said.

We smelt Lebanon before we saw it. This was after a journey of three weeks, caused both by contrary winds or lack of winds altogether, as well as the distance, which was over seven hundred miles. But it was an interesting journey, as we threaded our way through the Aegean Islands – there was no glimpse of Tinos – and then round the south-eastern corner of Turkey, actually sighting Herodotus's birthplace of Halicarnassus, which the Turks have renamed Bodrum, with the mountains of Crete looming on our right hand. Then we sailed round the southern side of Cyprus, a much larger island than I had supposed, and found ourselves working slowly to windward, and suddenly enveloped in this delicious scent.

Our ship was not a large one, and the passenger accommodation consisted of a single cabin aft. As Eugenie and I were the only passengers this was not an inconvenience, but the increasing heat was, and we took to sleeping on deck, aft of the helmsman. Thus, we were on deck when we awakened to the sunrise, looked behind us at the dwindling mountains of Cyprus, and took deep breaths. 'The cedars of Lebanon,' the Captain told us. 'It is the sweetest scent in the Mediterranean.'

A few hours later we came in sight of the coast, which was low-lying, although we could make out substantial mountains in the interior, and then of the city of Beirut itself. There was no port and thus we dropped anchor in an open roadstead, and prepared to go ashore.

What was I looking for, after so long and so many miles from Holkham? Well, I can say without qualification that it was not for masculine company. I had spent the voyage brooding on the events of my life, reflecting on my errors, but more on the various members of the male sex who had tormented me for so long. Only one of them had ever dealt honourably with me, Karl, and tragically he had been the only one unable to inspire me with the passion I sought, while even he had attempted to renege on our pre-nuptial agreement. But what, then, lay ahead of me? If I had now learned to despise the sex, men had always provided the driving force for all of my actions; if I had not been running behind one, I had been running away from one – as I was doing now. Without that impulse, what was there? I had no desire to turn into a religious eccentric like Sophie; that was entirely foreign to my nature. Therefore, in the short term, all I could consider was travel, travel, travel and more travel, and thus by constant movement try to control the restless urges of my spirit.

Besides, the desert beckoned. It had been my childhood dream. It was where one of my favourite cousins had perished, albeit some distance away from Beirut. It had also been reawakened in my consciousness by a book I had read a few years before, *Eothen*, by William Kinglake, an evocative account of a journey he had made in Palestine and Syria, and it seemed to me that I could do worse than follow his itinerary, Beirut to Jerusalem and perhaps a look around southern Palestine, then back north to Damascus, from whence I should be able to pick up a caravan for Palmyra. However, there were immediate obstacles. It appeared that there were no relay stations on the route I proposed to take, and therefore I had to hire every animal we required, together with sufficient remounts and replacements. This was a considerable undertaking, because I was accompanied by a great deal of luggage, all of my clothes – these alone occupied five cabin trunks – as well as all the various possessions I had accumulated over the years, largely bric-a-brac but every one of sentimental value, and because the available horses and mules were of very poor quality. It was at this time that I commenced keeping a journal, largely concerned with what I was doing and seeing and where I was going, and how much I was spending – I have always had a taste for detail – but from time to time personal items and thoughts did creep in, and recollections of my past life, although when we left Beirut I had no intention of ever having any deep emotions again. I kept this journal with the idea that it might be of some use either to my family or to those following behind. It bears only a superficial relation to this very personal memoir, which I am compiling for my own satisfaction, enabling me to recall all the many and varied events of my life. I have no intention that *it* should ever be read by anyone else. Heaven forbid!

We left Beirut roughly a fortnight after our arrival, which had been in the middle of April, and proceeded south. The weather was hot, but not as hot, I was informed by the Turkish lieutenant who rode with us, as it would become in a couple of months. In fact, he considered this to be the best time of the year. I should mention that although I was very pleased to have Lieutenant Sigourty's company, he and his men were in no way intended as a bodyguard. The Turkish authorities in Beirut did not consider one necessary, as they claimed that Palestine was a totally peaceful place, and the lieutenant was merely on his way to take up garrison duties in Jerusalem. I should also mention that although the Russian and Turkish governments were still rattling their sabres, the Great Powers were doing their best to dampen things down, and there did not seem to be any immediate prospect of war. The point at issue was officially whether or not the Tsar should be allowed to exercise the right to protect the Christian minorities and pilgrims and their practices inside the Ottoman Empire, specifically Jerusalem with its many holy shrines, a prospect which the Turks vehemently refused to consider. I am bound to say that although there may have been the odd mistreatment of Christian enclaves, it is impossible to imagine the response of a British government to a demand from Turkey that they should send magistrates and even troops to England to protect any Muslim minorities that might be found there.

I am also bound to say that I personally received only the most courteous treatment from the Turks, although this may be because I was far more wealthy in Syria and Palestine than I had even been in Greece, and also because the war did break out before the end of this year of 1853, and as it was known even now that Britain and France would support Turkey, and with force if need be; the citizens of those countries were very popular with the locals.

Unfortunately the Turks, although courteous and even charming to a travelling Englishwoman and her French maid, had limited ideas on how to treat those of their subjects who were not Turks, and even more limited ideas on such things as sanitation and what might be called a healthy ambience. I was mindful of Cristos's claim that he had learned all of his bad habits from the Turks, and in fact we saw sufficient evidence of very harsh punishment meted out to those who broke the law, in which I felt they were a couple of hundred years behind us. However, perhaps sadly, one accepts these things when one can do nothing about them.

But personal hygiene is always with us, and has always been of the utmost importance to me. I quite accepted that when making a long journey over desert it is not possible to have a daily bath, or sometimes even a daily wash, but I did look forward to indulging myself in these necessary pleasures once civilization was regained. This was possible, certainly, but the enjoyment of a wallow was tempered by the fact that the water never seemed quite clean, by the dust and sand that got everywhere and more often than not into places one would have considered quite indecent to explore.

The food was edible, but I will not go further than that. The meat – nearly always lamb or mutton – was stringy, the vegetables poor and invariably overcooked, and wine, this being a Muslim country, unobtainable, while every time one took a glass of water, which it was necessary to do very regularly because of the heat, one felt that one hovered on the brink of dysentery.

Nor did Jerusalem, which we reached after a fortunately short journey, have sufficient of historical interest to offset the drawbacks of the country. Eugenie and I went to all the famous places, where Christ is reputed to have stood, or walked, or preached, or suffered, but to me they lacked the grandeur of the Acropolis or the Greek mountains. Undoubtedly the various shrines had suffered through centuries of Turkish rule, but then so had Greece. Most off-putting was the condition of the streets, littered with manure and dog-dung, and indeed the dogs themselves. Never have I seen such depressing-looking creatures, most of them half-starved with ribs protruding through the skins, barking and snarling over the slightest scrap, while those that had succumbed were left lying in the street to rot. The stench was terrible.

My heart went out to all these desolate creatures, but what could I do? Collect the entire canine population of Jerusalem and carry it off with me? It was a temptation, but as I did not yet know where I was going to find a home I understood that it was not a practical solution. The whole experience was very off-putting. I abandoned any idea of a prolonged visit to southern Palestine, and headed north for Damascus, which I was assured was as beautiful and attractive as Jerusalem was decrepit and disgusting. My experience in the Holy City had quite diminished my ardour for a lengthy stay in this country, but I was determined to make the journey to Palmyra before starting to look for a place to settle. I certainly at that time had no intention of living in any Turkish dominion. I had no idea that I was about to enter the greatest and most satisfying period of my life – after a few hiccoughs, to be sure.

We followed the line of the Jordan River as we went north, principally because this ensured us a constant supply of water, although it did not appear to be of any better quality than in Jerusalem. However, for the very reason that water is an essential of life, we found ourselves in much greater company than earlier. Sometimes we travelled for a day or so with other caravans, at other times we were joined at our night's encampment. It was now that we made our first acquaintance with desert Arabs – the Bedouin. Eugenie was terrified to find our tents surrounded by these dark-visaged desert warriors, or bandits as the Turks referred to them, with their heavily cloaked and veiled women, their flocks of goats, their camels, and above all, their horses. If I had no longer come to Palestine and Syria to buy horses, I could not help but stare in admiration at the quite magnificent beasts which were constantly paraded before our eyes.

I was equally taken with the Arabs themselves, who displayed a general tidiness, cleanliness, and consideration for each other and to strangers wholly foreign to the Turks, and their manners were impeccable. To Eugenie's concern I took to walking from our camp down to the river where the horses were drinking, both to admire them and to converse with their owners. With my gift for languages I had very rapidly picked up sufficient Turkish to carry on a conversation, and even already had a smattering of Arabic. I am sure that my grammar was terrible, and my choice of words not always accurate, but they smiled politely and answered my questions as best they could.

While there could be no doubt that they found me fascinating, there were sufficient non-Muslim women in the country for them not to be distracted by my exposed features, but they were certainly distracted by the features themselves. Equally, did they obviously admire my clothes. But most of all, they were fascinated by my hair. This was not at all new to me, but never had my red-gold tresses been regarded with such awe, and even with some trepidation. I asked a Turkish officer about this, and he told me that to the Arabs, yellow hair is a sign of the evil eye! Well! But I had to assume that my possession of the offensive colour afforded us a considerable measure of protection. No one knew that my trusty revolvers were waiting in my reticule.

We proceeded on our way until we were informed that Damascus was only two days off. When we camped for the evening, as usual I walked down to the water to look at the horses. It was 4 May 1853, a date I shall never forget. For amongst the drinking animals I saw quite the most magnificent stallion I had ever beheld. I knew I had to have him. So I approached the man standing closest, and said. 'That is a splendid animal.'

'It is so, great lady. There is none like him.'

'Is he for sale?'

'How may such an animal be for sale?'

'Everything is for sale,' I told him. 'If the price is right. Name yours.'

'I do not own him.'

'Then who does? Take me to him.'

'I am the owner,' said a deep voice from behind me. 'My name is Saleh.'

I turned, and fell in love.

What can I say? After my betrayal by Cristos, I had resolved never to fall in love again, indeed, never even to get close to another man. But it is impossible to contravene the laws of nature. I had been sexually abstinent before, and for some lengthy periods. This day was only a month, almost exactly, since I had left Piraeus. But the Orient, even the brief glimpse I had so far had of the desert, had had a most powerful effect on my senses, and as I have suggested, I found everything about the Bedouin most attractive. One could almost say that I had fallen in love with an entire people. But I had to be aware that they were of a different race, different religion, different culture . . . and perhaps, most import- antly, that they were generally a small people. But suddenly I was confronted with a paragon. He stood at least six feet, which made him taller than myself, with a matching physique, had the most exquisite features with a carefully trimmed beard and moustache, flashing dark eyes, and sensuous lips. Instinctively I knew he would be the answer to all my dreams. That it was obvious that he was young enough to be my son did not seem the least important. 'Saleh?' I asked.

He gave a brief bow. 'That is my name, great lady.'

For a moment I almost forgot why I was there. Then I regained control of myself. 'I was admiring your horse. He is a magnificent beast.'

Another little bow. 'You are most gracious, great lady. Do you know horses?'

'I know horses. Is he for sale?'

'It is not my intention to sell him. But I might consider it, if the price was right.' While we had been speaking, he had been studying me as closely as I was studying him, and indeed I would say he had already looked me over from a distance before approaching. It was also obvious that he liked what he was looking at.

'Well, then,' I said. 'Name your price.'

'And you will pay it?'

'Yes.'

'Your wealth is unlimited, great lady. I would prefer to discuss our transaction in private.' Inevitably, quite a crowd had gathered.

'Certainly,' I said. 'My tent is just over there.'

'Mine is closer.'

I hesitated but a moment. I had my reticule. 'As you wish.'

Saleh gestured, and I walked in front of him. Not for the first time in my life I had no idea what might be going to happen. I did not even know, in this instance, whether I was again a quarry, or merely a dreamer. He reached past me to raise the flap, and I stepped into a sweet-scented and richly furnished interior. There were two veiled women present, but these he dismissed with a wave of his hand, then he gestured me to one of the cush- ions waiting on the carpeted earth. Getting down to sit virtually on the floor while wearing a riding habit and without revealing one's legs is not the easiest business in the world, but I managed it, sitting to one side, as it were, with both my legs gathered against me.

Saleh sat opposite me, cross-legged, with a great deal less trouble. 'You are like a summer moon, great lady.'

I was suddenly breathless. 'You were to name a price.'

'Which you have agreed to pay.'

A last, momentary, reflection. 'Yes,' I said. 'I will meet your price.'

'I do not seek money,' he warned me.

'Are you then a wealthy man? A sheik?'

'I am not a sheik. But I have been granted good fortune by Allah, blessed be His name.'

'Then tell me what you wish. For the horse.'

'I will show you.'

What followed was perfectly indecent, on several counts. I had met this enchantingly strange man only a few minutes previously, yet I did not demur when he laid his hands on me. Apart from such unforgettable set-tos as my initial intimate encounter with Cristos, the first thing any amorously minded man had done when seeking possession had been to remove all my clothing, the better to appreciate me. Saleh made no effort to do so. And while I had assumed that I had scaled the ultimate heights with Cristos, I now discovered that there was a further achievement yet to be attained, even if I am certain that it has never been sanctioned by the Christian Church, whether Orthodox, Catholic or Protestant.

Moving to sit beside me, Saleh also made no attempt to kiss me. He ran his hands over my hair, then my arms, then my thighs, which I found most stimulating. Then without further ado, he turned me on my side. As I was still waiting to be undressed, this took me by surprise. But then I was further surprised, and frankly, somewhat shocked, when, having grasped my skirts and pushed them up to my waist, he seized my thighs again and raised them from the carpet, at the same time again turning me so that I found myself on my face while still kneeling. Not wishing to bruise my cheeks, I put down my hands and pushed myself up, and found that he had planted my knees on the carpet as well, and was now separating them, as well as my buttocks. I was therefore on all fours, like a dog. And he was between my thighs.

Having been warned that homosexuality was as rife amongst the Arabs and the Turks as it was amongst the English upper classes, I naturally braced myself for the worst, but was instead transported into heaven. I had supposed that no male member could ever explore me more thoroughly than Cristos, but then, Cristos had never approached the ultimate position. Nor had Cristos possessed the longevity, or perhaps the self-control, of Saleh, who I swear remained inside me for ten minutes before allowing himself to climax. By then I had lost count.

'The horse is yours, great lady,' he said, removing himself.

I had collapsed on my face. Now I rolled over, sat up and regained possession of my skirts, and my dignity. But I was already resolved that this could be no chance encounter. 'And what else?' I asked.

He gazed at me for several seconds. 'You wish more?'

'And more.'

'You are a great lady. And I . . .'

'You are a great man, at least in my eyes.'

'You will remain with me?'

'I must go to Damascus. I wish to visit Palmyra. Will you come with me?'

'I cannot venture into that part of the desert. That territory is controlled by the Amazeh. They would kill me.'

This seemed a very odd state of affairs, certainly in view of the open-handed hospitality practised by these people. 'Do they not welcome strangers?'

'Only of their own people. And perhaps, foreigners. Other Bedouin are their hereditary enemies.'

'But do not the Turks rule this land?'

'They claim to do so. But they cannot interfere with our customs. It would be too costly to attempt to change things. And besides, it pleases the Turks to have us continue our age-old feuding. That way, they suppose, we can never unite against them.'

'I see. So each tribe has its own domain, you might say. Which is yours?'

'Here and to the south.'

'You mean Palestine? Bother.' I had no desire to spend any more time in that part of the world. 'Well, if you come with me, I will protect you.'

'I do not believe that can be possible.'

'Trust me. You have said that they do not war upon foreigners. You will be my escort.'

'They would still seek to kill me. And if you attempted to protect me it could cost your own life. I could not risk that. I love you.'

'You say the sweetest things.'

'Besides, I must go into the desert, with my people.'

'When?'

'Within a week.'

'Then I will stay with you for the week.'

Eugenie was scandalized. But I was not to be gainsaid. And so I spent a week in paradise. Which I was determined I would find again. 'Will you return here?' I asked, on our last night together.

'Of course.'

'Then so will I. We will meet here again . . . when?'

'In three months.'

That actually suited me very well, as I was determined to make my pilgrimage, as I considered it, to Palmyra. And now, to have this delightful man to come back to . . . 'Very well. In three months.' I kissed him. 'Then I will stay with you, forever.'

'And I will be yours, forever.'

I kissed him again. 'There is one matter that must be decided. Those women. Are they your wives?'

'I have no wives.'

There was a relief. However . . . 'Do you sleep with them?'

'A man must sleep with a woman.'

'I understand that. But when I come back, they must be gone. I will be your woman. Your only woman.'

He considered this. 'That is not the custom of my people.'

'It is the custom of *my* people – stretching the bow a little, perhaps – and of me in particular.'

Another consideration. Then he shrugged. 'If that is what you wish, great lady.'

'Ianthe.'

'Ianthe. That is a Greek word.' His tone indicated contempt.

'Well, then, you may call me Digby. That is my real name.'

'Digby. You will be my woman, Digby. My only woman.'

'Then will you not give me something to remember you by, until we meet again?'

Was I not outrageous? I was certainly, at that moment, as mad as ever poor Caro Lamb had been. My glimpse of the desert had done that to me, with its evocation of unchanging eternity, of the nearness of the stars on a clear night, and what nights in the desert were not clear? Of a closeness with nature which can never be attained when surrounded by stone walls and civilized manners. I had felt this in the Greek mountains, but it is far more enjoyable to be warm than freezing cold, to be dry than soaking wet. Descartes had once penned the immortal words, I think, therefore I am. My mood was that of, I wish, therefore I have.

Sheer hubris. But what a pleasant feeling. I had just bought the most magnificent horse I had ever seen. But had I not at the same time bought the most magnificent man I had ever seen, who had given me the most magnificent sensations I had ever known? Those three possessions were all I wanted for the rest of my life. I was forty-six years old, and I still believed that life could be that simple to arrange.

Eugenie was sceptical from the start, but she dutifully admired my new Ghost, gave Saleh a penetrating stare, and kept her mouth shut. Then, after a tender farewell, it was on to Damascus! I will freely admit that I was in a state of euphoria, and might, in such a frame of mind, even have found Jerusalem entrancing. But it is not only I who has considered Damascus the most attractive city in the world. Stretching as it does along the River Barada, which bubbles down from the mountains of Lebanon, approaching it from the desert is like entering paradise after a lengthy spell in purgatory. Before the city is even seen, there is the scent, wafted on the breeze like the cedars of Lebanon, but even more sweet-smelling, a compound of perfumes, of countless flower gardens, of the many odours, nearly all pleasant, arising from the many souks which stretched out from the city, every stall laden with irresistible goods. One can buy anything in a Damascus market: a beautiful girl, an exquisite piece of jewellery, a glittering sword, or a splendid horse.

The city's immediately visible beauty, its abundant trees and tumbling streams tends to obscure the even greater beauty that lies behind the various walls, the fabulous palaces and delicious secluded courtyards filled with orange and lemon trees. This was particularly evidenced by the hotel, where we were welcomed by the proprietor, whose name was Dimitri – I assume he was a Turk, perhaps of Russian decent – and shown to very comfortable accommodation, inward turned as in every house but with our veranda overlooking the inevitable delightful courtyard, which in addition to its trees and flowerbeds had a fountain in its centre. I cannot claim that either the food or the wine was outstanding, but at least there *was* wine; Dimitri was happy to dispense with religion, and accept the necessary bribes, to please his foreign guests.

Needless to say, my arrival, long heralded by other desert travellers who had met me on the way and reached the city before me, caused a stir, not least because of the size of my caravan, which, apart from my guides and drivers, consisted of only Eugenie and myself, but which stretched for some distance because of all the luggage I was carrying with me. However, I was used to this and set about my business without delay. In the first instance, after visiting the bank and making sure that my affairs were in order, and also making preparations for the shipping of the rest of my goods from Athens, as soon as I had found a permanent place to live – in which I intended to install Saleh whether he liked it or not – I wished to arrange my visit to Palmyra.

I found the bank manager very dubious about this plan. 'You intend to make this journey by yourself, Madame Digby?'

'My maid will accompany me.'

'But . . . you have no man? No husband?'

'Not at the moment.'

'Then I do not think such an expedition is advisable. It would be better to wait for the formation of a large caravan.'

'And when will that be?'

'Who can tell? It depends on when there are sufficient people wishing to go to Palmyra at the same time.'

'Thank you,' I said, and left. 'How do I go about organizing a caravan to visit Palmyra?' I asked Dimitri; I knew that the men who had accompanied me from Beirut would never venture into that part of the desert.

'You wish to go to Palmyra? That is a very long way. Nine days across the desert.'

'I have been told this. I wish to go to Palmyra, yes.'

'But you have no man.'

I sighed. 'Not even a husband. Why is this so important?'

'Because it is very dangerous. You could be robbed. You could be murdered. You could even be, well . . .'

I refrained from informing him that the last was unlikely to make a vast difference to either my mental or my physical well-being. 'Then how do I get there? People *do* go to Palmyra?'

'In a big caravan, yes.'

'Which may take months to assemble.'

'This is true. But you can stay here until the time. I will make you very comfortable.' He rolled his eyes, having clearly been stimulated by the idea of me being raped by a desert sheik. As I had already enjoyed that experience, even if Saleh was not actually a sheik, I merely smiled at him, and went to see the British Consul, who I was confident would take a more rational view of my situation and requirements.

I was wrong. This gentleman, whose name was Colonel Richard Wood, greeted me courteously enough – he clearly knew a great deal about me – but when I told him what I wished to do he took the same line as everyone else. 'I'm afraid you will have to wait for the formation of a caravan.'

'I wish to form my own caravan.'

'How many of you are there?'

'My maid and I.'

'And?'

'Just my maid and I.'

He regarded me for several moments. Then he said, 'My dear . . .' he hesitated, obviously considering which of my names to use, and then settled for the one on my card, 'Madam Digby, two white women cannot venture into the desert by themselves.'

'Why not?'

'Well . . .' he flushed. 'You would be robbed. You could even be murdered. Why—'

'I might even be raped?' His flush deepened. 'What will be will be. But I do not intend to venture into the desert alone. I will go in a caravan. Surely it is possible to hire a caravan of one's own?'

'That will be very expensive, and will not lessen the danger. To get to Palmyra you must follow the Euphrates River. The desert on this side of the river belongs to the Amazeh tribe.'

'I have been told this. I have also been told that they do not wage war on foreigners. Will they not provide me with protection, for a price?'

'I am sure they will. That does not mean that they will not rob you on the journey. And just across the river are the Gomussa tribes. They are deadly enemies of the Amazeh and often cross over to raid the Amazeh encampments. You could find yourself in the middle of a shooting war.'

'How exciting. Will you put me in touch with these Amazeh people? Are they situated close by?'

'The Mesrab are encamped by the city, at this moment, yes.'

'The Mesrab?'

'They are a tribe of the Amazeh. A small tribe, only about two hundred tents. But they have conducted caravans to Palmyra in the past.'

'They sound the very people I am looking for. Will you arrange for a representative to come to my hotel to discuss terms?'

'No, I will not. I most strongly advise against such a lunatic venture. In fact, I forbid it.'

'What do you imagine gives you that right?'

'As British Consul, I am responsible for the lives of every British subject in Syria.'

'Colonel, it is twenty-four years since any Englishman attempted to protect my life. I have no desire for you or anyone to take up that burden now. Will you secure me an introduction to these Mesrab people, or shall I go elsewhere?'

He glared at me. 'If you choose to disappear into the desert, do not expect me to mount an expedition to rescue you. Nor, I can promise you, will the Turks be the least interested in doing so.'

'I would not dream of expecting it.'

'And I am bound to record that I consider that you are pursuing a course of incredible folly.'

'If you send such a report back to England, sir, you may well be accused of plagiarism.' I rose. 'I shall expect a representative of the Mesrabs to call at my hotel within twenty-four hours. Good day to you, Colonel, and my thanks for your cooperation.'

I left him speechless, but with some confidence that he would carry out my wishes, and indeed I was enjoying my breakfast the next morning, seated on the veranda outside my suite, when I was approached by Dimitri. 'There is someone to see you, Madame.'

'Ah,' I said. 'An Arab gentleman?'

'I believe he is a sheik.'

'Good heavens. I am honoured. Please show him up. Does he have a name?'

'It is Medjuel el Mesrab, Madame. But . . .' he regarded my undressing robe. But it was an all-concealing garment, and I was too excited to wish to delay the meeting by making this Medjuel wait while I changed: he might go away again.

'Show him up,' I repeated.

Very few human beings are prescient, and I certainly am not. Thus it was that this most important moment of my entire life barely scratched the surface of my consciousness. I was aware that I was meeting a very pleasant man, and a surprisingly well educated one, from the manner in which he spoke, as well as from his clothes, which were of the finest quality, from his knee boots of red kid, past his obviously silk striped robe, to his crimson tunic, his burnous, also of silk, around the forehead of which was twisted a strand of camel hair. There was a voluminous sash round his waist, in which were thrust a pair of pistols and a curved Arab sword, called, I knew, a scimitar. His beard and moustache were black and carefully trimmed − I could not at that moment make out his hair. His eyes were also black, his features aquiline and quite handsome. All in all, he made an evocative picture, and I immediately had a desire to sketch him.

But nothing more than that, principally because, I suspect, he was so very small, only a couple of inches more than five feet, with matching hands. For me, a man had to be more than six feet tall and built to match – unless he happened to be a king. And despite the fact that he was armed, neither Medjuel's size nor his demeanour suggested that he would be the least bit dashing – a prime example of how looks can be deceptive.

My inspection of him was therefore far more cursory than my description. He, on the other hand, had clearly never seen anything like me before, as in addition to my undressing gown, which presumably *he* found evocative, my hair was loose and floating down my back – I was not wearing a hat; when I was sitting down in that condition it brushed the floor. Medjuel's countenance was rather dark, otherwise I swear he would have blushed. As it was, he appeared very hesitant and even nervous, as he gave me the Arab greeting of touching his chest, lips and forehead, and then said, in perfect Turkish, 'I beg you to forgive this unseemly intrusion, Madame Digby.'

'It is not at all unseemly, Sheik Medjuel. I was looking forward to meeting you. Do sit down.'

He looked astonished, and glanced at Dimitri, who stood beside him. Dimitri hastily nodded, and Medjuel cautiously sank into a chair opposite me. 'You are very gracious, Madame.'

'Do you really think so? Thank you, Dimitri.' The hotelier looked as if he would have liked to stay, but got the message and left. 'Have you breakfasted?' I asked. 'If not, please help yourself. '

'You wish me to eat with you?'

'If you would care to?'

He regarded me for several moments. Then he said, 'I am not the Sheik. The Sheik is my brother, Mohammed.'

'I look forward to meeting him.'

'But, knowing this, you still wish to share your food with me?'

It was my turn to regard him for some seconds. 'Am I doing something wrong? I have no wish to contravene your customs.'

'Wrong? No. But it is not usual.'

'You mean for a man and a woman to take food together?'

'That, certainly. But for a great lady who is also a Frank, so to honour a humble Bedouin . . .'

'Oh, good lord, Mr Medjuel, I am a guest in your country. It is you who are honouring me by visiting me.' I could see that he was confused, and so asked, 'Do you take tea?' I poured.

Medjuel regarded the cup with some suspicion, then lowered his head to sniff it. 'It does not smell like tea.'

'It is an English brew.'

'It contains alcohol?'

'Good heavens, no.'

He sipped, and resisted the temptation to pull a face. 'It is very nice.'

'I'm glad you like it. You know my business?'

'You wish a caravan to Tadmor.'

'No, no, Palmyra.'

'Tadmor is the Arab name for Palmyra.'

'Oh. Very well. Can you arrange a caravan to Tadmor?'

'You understand that this is a lengthy journey.'

'I was told nine days.'

'And nine back. It is also very dangerous.'

'Please don't start that, Mr Medjuel. Believe me, I have undertaken journeys more dangerous than anything the desert can offer.'

He obviously didn't know how to take that, and did some more considering before resuming. 'For both your safety and your comfort, it will have to be a large caravan. Which means that it will be expensive.'

'I understand. Can you give me a figure?'

He looked at me, and then at the floor, and then at the ceiling. Obviously he was calculating, but I suspected what he was calculating was what my purse would stand. 'It would cost eight thousand francs.'

I did some calculation of my own; eight thousand francs was approximately three hundred pounds, when last I had compared the rates of exchange. 'That will be satisfactory. I will pay you a third now, a third when we reach Palmyra, I beg your pardon, Tadmor, and the final third when we have returned to Damascus.'

He stared at me in consternation. 'You will pay this price?'

'It sounds very fair to me.'

He opened his mouth, and then closed it again. 'When do you wish to leave?'

'As soon as possible.'

'It will take a week to form the caravan.'

'Very good. I will go to my bank this morning and withdraw the necessary money. You may collect the first payment this afternoon. Is that satisfactory?'

He hesitated, as if he would have raised another matter, then changed his mind, considered the tea without drinking it, and stood up. 'You are most gracious, Madame Digby.'

I extended my hand, and after another hesitation he grasped it. He had a firm, dry grip.

The Desert

I got dressed, and went downstairs to locate Dimitri. 'What an odd little man,' I remarked. 'He seemed positively terrified of me.'

'Medjuel el Mesrab is a famed desert warrior, Madame.'

'You could have fooled me.'

'It is possible that he was perturbed by your conduct.'

'My conduct? I am sure I treated him with the utmost courtesy.'

'That is exactly it. Most Franks, and all Turks, treat the Bedouin as an inferior race, quite openly. And to invite him to sit with you, and share your food . . .'

'He didn't actually eat anything.'

'That is because to break bread with a Bedouin, or him with you, means that he must always regard you as a friend, and may never harm you.'

'Then does his refusal to eat with me means that he intends to harm me?'

'It means that he has not yet made up his mind whether or not he wishes to be your friend. And then there is the business of the money.'

'I met his price.'

'Ah, but you see, Madame Digby, you were not supposed to do that. The price he offered was a starting point for bargaining. But you did not bargain. This is incomprehensible to him.' Almost I scratched my head. 'So you see,' Dimitri went on, 'he does not know what to make of you. Would you like me to go behind him and negotiate a lower price?'

'Certainly not. I have agreed a price and I always keep my word.' I left him looking even more confounded than Medjuel.

A week was hardly enough to make all my personal preparations. Medjuel came to see me quite often to keep me up to date on his own preparations, and also to brief me on what

lay ahead. I felt that while he continued to regard me as at the
very least eccentric, he was growing to like me, as I did him.
He told me that I would have to use a camel, as horses could
not last the journey. 'What a shame. And I have recently bought
a new stallion.'

'He will be here when you return. Have you ever ridden a
camel?'

'No.'

'Some people find it very difficult. Especially ladies.'

'You have escorted ladies to Tadmor before?'

'Some years ago my people escorted a great lady. She was a
daughter of the King of England.'

'Hester Stanhope!' I cried.

'That is the name. Do you know this lady?'

Trust Hester to have claimed to be the King's daughter, I
thought, although presumably there was a possibility that her
being the Prime Minister's niece might have been misunderstood
by the Arabs. 'We never met.' I decided against explaining that
she was considerably older than I, as I did not wish the question
of my own age to come up. 'And you say she had difficulty with
the camels?'

'I do not know, I was but a boy then.'

'Well,' I said. 'I shall not.' Nor did I. I gathered my ability to
master these unusual creatures – they were not so very different
to a rather stubborn horse – greatly raised my prestige with the
Mesrab.

Having received his down payment, Medjuel was an enthusiastic
collaborator in my plans. But no one else was, not even Eugenie,
who was of course going to accompany me, and did not find a
camel the least comfortable. Everyone in Damascus followed the
line adopted by Colonel Wood, that I was raving mad. I was even
visited by the governor of the city, General Ahmed, who pointed
out that in view of the political situation, and the necessity of
maintaining the English alliance in the looming war with Russia,
for a high-born English lady to go off and get herself kidnapped
and perhaps murdered by the Arabs could create a difficult situation. 'Have you the authority to forbid me to travel in the desert?'
I asked.

'Well, I suppose I do. But I should not like to have to use it.'

'Then don't. Please let me assure you, General, that there is no one in England who will give a fig whether I live or die.' Except Mama, of course. But I did not see that was any business of his. 'Besides, am I not protected by my hair? I have been told that the Arabs are afraid of yellow hair.' He went away, muttering, and I was ready for the off.

And what an occasion it was. It has been suggested to me since that every departure of a caravan was similarly attended by a comparable ceremony, but I prefer to believe that my departure was a special one, principally because I was in it. We left at four in the afternoon, as by tradition the first day's journey was a short one. I had already tried out my camel, in private, with only Medjuel, two drivers, Eugenie and Dimitri, for witnesses. Now I mounted the animal for the first time in public, my skill and confidence being greeted with loud applause. Eugenie had also practised, but with less success, although she did manage to retain her seat.

Once we were up, the rest of the party mounted, and we were away. I was amazed at our numbers. My actual caravan consisted of twelve dromedaries, ten carrying baggage and food and water. Then there was an escort of twenty men, captained by Medjuel, accompanied by a dozen women, and also riding camels. These I knew about. But with us there seemed to be travelling the entire Mesrab tribe, together with another couple of hundred spectators, screaming little boys, barking dogs, bleating goats . . . 'Am I responsible for feeding all of these people for nine days?' I asked Medjuel.

'No, no. They are not coming the whole way.'

There was a relief. But a large proportion of them came for the whole of the first afternoon, beating drums and blowing trumpets. Not for the first time in my life I felt like the Queen of Sheba, or better yet, a reincarnation of Zenobia, while I conceived that every Arab for a hundred miles, friendly or hostile, would know that I was on my way. However, as Medjuel had promised, the mass went its own way the following day, whether back to Damascus or to their own desert destinations, and we proceeded in our chosen direction. The next four days were sheer heaven. We rose at dawn, generally about four, and after prayers, in which the entire caravan took part, kneeling towards Mecca, and breakfast, proceeded throughout the day, halting for a couple of hours at noon, for midday prayers, a meal, and a brief rest when the sun was at its hottest, before resuming until the early evening. Eugenie and I wore ordinary riding habits and broad-brimmed hats, with veils, but Medjuel thoughtfully supplied us each with a silk burnous, which we could tie over our hats and under our chins, and also allow to flap across our faces and re-inforce the veils in repelling not only the glare but also the drifting sand and the myriad insects that accompanied us.

We stopped for the night, a manoeuvre ordained by Medjuel bringing his camel to a halt and striking the ground with his staff. After evening prayers all was ordered confusion for a few minutes, but in that time our goat hair tents were pitched – by the women, needless to say – and the carpets spread, the cooking fires were lit, and we were drinking tea and eating cold chicken a few minutes later. Being invariably exhausted by our day's labours, and anticipating our early morning start, we were in bed soon after the meal, but Medjuel and I usually found the time for a brief conversation. He still did not eat with Eugenie and I – whether this was because of the differ-ence in our sexes or whether it was because he still had not made up his mind whether he wished to be my friend, I could not tell – but he was certainly interested in my background, such of it as I was prepared to tell him, but of which he clearly could understand very little, while I was fascinated by his know-ledge, not only of Syria and the desert but of the whole Levantine world, as well as his obvious breeding. It turned out that he was married, and had two grown sons – I had no idea of his actual age, although I had no doubt that he was younger than I – and that he anticipated becoming sheik in succession to his brother, who was considerably older, and childless. Perhaps I was a little disappointed in his lack of ambition, his accept-ance that it was the Will of Allah that he should spend his entire life migrating to and fro across this one particular stretch of desert. Apart from the very occasional caravan, the Mesrab spent only a few weeks of the year around Damascus, and the rest with their flocks and guarding their wells. But I understood that it was not an easy thing to change, or even wish to change, a civilization that had obtained for centuries.

For his part, Medjuel was clearly bewildered by the freedom I, a woman who was not yet a widow, enjoyed, but he seemed able to understand something of my restless spirit. 'When you have visited Tadmor, where will you go?' he asked.

'I wish to visit Baghdad. But I intend to make my home in Syria. I am to marry.'

'Ah! To a Frank? Or a Turk?' This last possibility apparently disturbed him.

'A Bedouin.'

Now he was surprised. 'You will do this?'

'Oh, yes. I am in love with him. His name is Saleh. Do you know of him?'

He considered, then shook his head. 'What is his tribe?'

'Do you know, I have no idea. But I believe they are enemies of yours. That is why he is not here now.'

'He would be a trespasser,' Medjuel agreed.

'And for that you would punish him?'

'My people have many mouths to feed, and the desert is not always bountiful. But I will wish you great happiness with your chosen one. He is a man to be envied.'

What a sweet man! I thought.

As on our earlier journey to Jerusalem, hygiene was conspicuous by its absence. There was no privacy, even for the most intimate functions. In this I observed that the Bedouin women, while never allowing anyone, even themselves, a glimpse of any part of their bodies above the waist, were not so fastidious lower down, when it was necessary. Naturally I followed fashion, as did Eugenie, reluctantly. But bathing or changing our clothes was out of the question. This at least saved us a great deal of time in the mornings, as we simply straightened our habits, in which we had slept, ran a brush over our hair, put on our hats and veils, and were ready to mount up. But when, after four days, we came to the oasis of El Quryatein, I felt sure we could do something about ourselves. The oasis was occupied by some rather decrepit-looking Bedouins, who I gathered were subject to the Mesrabs, and there was again no prospect of any privacy, but close by were some

Roman ruins, and when Medjuel told me that it had been a spa in those ancient times, I could not help asking, 'You mean we may have a bath?'

'You wish to bathe?' As usual, he was confounded by my peculiarities.

'When I am not in the desert, I bathe every day.'

He rolled his eyes. 'There is a spring in the bathhouse. But it is very dangerous.'

This dismissively masculine attitude, which I had encountered in so many different forms throughout my life, was not going to deter me, and so Eugenie and I entered the bathhouse, stripped off our clothing, and considered the situation. There was a single small opening in the tiled floor, from which there rose a cloud of hot, damp air, as well as the most appalling stench of sulphur. 'Me first,' I said, and stepped into this cloud. The heat quite took my breath away, and any thoughts of using soap or flannel was out of the question. I stood it for as long as I could, a matter of a few seconds, really, feeling I was being boiled alive, and then stepped away, panting. From Eugenie's squeals she was equally distressed, but we both felt much cleaner, even if it took us some time to get rid of the smell of sulphur.

The following day, as we proceeded on our way, we emerged from a defile into a reasonably open and flat stretch of desert, but were only a few yards clear of the hills through which we had been passing, when we were assailed by a tremendous noise, shrieks and yells, gunfire, and the thudding of hooves, and beheld, coming towards us, perhaps fifty camel riders, clearly bent on mischief.

Our own people uttered shouts to match those of the strangers, but these were of fear, and to a man, and woman, they wheeled their mounts and rode off. Even Medjuel went with them. I was extremely disappointed: my 'escort' seemed concerned only with saving their own skins, with not a thought for our own or for our baggage train. Thus, if I rode behind them I would be abandoning all my goods, not to mention our food and water. This I was not prepared to do. 'Milady!' Eugenie screamed.

'Remember Greece,' I told her, opened my reticule, and took out one of my revolvers. To tell the truth, the approaching

brigands, now only a hundred yards away, were a quite terrifying sight, and I did really suppose that my last moment had
come. But I was determined to go out fighting, and so cocked
and levelled my weapon. I had no wish to kill anyone, as I
remembered the carnage I had created in Greece. Nor did I wish
to hurt a camel; the poor beasts were only doing what was
required by their riders. But I had to do something to halt
the charge, otherwise we were going to be overrun in a matter
of seconds. I therefore fired, levelled, cocked and fired, levelled,
cocked and fired, six times in rapid succession, aiming at the
ground, immediately in front of the approaching host, sending
flurries of sand into the air, while the rapidity of my discharges
no doubt made them feel they were confronted by a body of
trained soldiers. Certainly they came to a halt.

Unfortunately, my own mount was unused to such behaviour
on the part of its rider – I suspect that both Eugenie and I had
been given camels known for their docility. I do not know what
my animal did, but it did it very successfully, and for the first
time in a long time I was unseated. I landed on my feet but with
such a jar that I fell to my knees. I had retained hold of my
weapon, however, as well as my reticule, and as Eugenie hastily
dismounted to join me, I gave her the empty gun, and the box
of cartridges. 'Load that,' I told her, and drew my second revolver.
Then I stood up.

I proposed to address these fellows, and inform them, as I had
done with the Greek bandits, that I would shoot them if they
came any closer, although I was well aware that there is some
difference between ten poorly armed men on foot, and fifty very
well armed men who were mounted, and thus did not hold out
any great hope of success – or survival. As I reached my feet,
however, there was a maniacal series of shouts from behind me,
and Medjuel charged past.

I turned to see what support he had, and discovered that
there was none. But to my horror he continued his attack,
firing his pistols, without hitting anybody, and then drawing
his scimitar. I would have liked to support him myself, but
feared that if I resumed firing I might hit him, when, to my
amazement, the entire enemy force turned tail and fled. After
looking over the recently vacated ground Medjuel turned his

camel and walked it back towards me. 'You fired at them,' he said, his voice incredulous.

'I couldn't think of anything else to do.'

'You, a woman, fired at Bedouin warriors. But you did not hit any of them.' He seemed relieved about this.

'I did not want to hurt them,' I explained. 'But until you arrived, I supposed I would have to. I think you saved my life.'

He dismounted. 'You were not afraid.' It was not a question.

'Well, actually, I was terrified. So was Eugenie. Weren't you, Eugenie?' Eugenie was speechless; she had dropped several bullets on the ground while reloading.

Medjuel picked them up, and then took the revolver from her fingers. 'I did not even know you were armed. And these . . .' he looked from the gun he held to the one in my hand. 'I have heard of these. The Turks use them. They are terrible weapons.'

I took the gun from him. 'I go nowhere without them.'

'You are a woman amongst men,' he declared. I took this as a compliment.

The rest of our caravan soon reassembled − they hadn't gone very far − suitably abashed by their behaviour, and we resumed our journey. If it strikes one that this was a very odd affair, I was later told that it was a subterfuge from start to finish. Apparently the Mesrab had informed some of their compatriots that a wealthy Frankish woman was crossing the desert with only a small escort, and arranged for her − me! − to be robbed. The idea was that if my people ran away until after I had been taken, and came back after the would-be robbers had departed in triumph, they would all, at a later date, share in the spoils. But there were no spoils, because I had spoiled everyone's fun by refusing to lie down with my legs in the air, as it were. Now they were in a state of high anxiety, because if I had inadvertently killed anybody, my escort would have been held responsible and a blood feud would have resulted.

It was even suggested to me, after my return to Damascus, that Medjuel was a party to the plot. This I refused to accept, although I suppose it was likely, but whether he had been or not, his action in returning to aid me when he saw that I was standing my ground was highly honourable, even if, presumably, he knew that none of our would-be attackers was going to harm *him*. In any event, the upshot of the business was entirely in my favour. My fame spread across the desert, and even when, a few years later, I did actually engage in battles with the enemies of the Mesrab, I do not believe anyone ever dared aim a shot at me – certainly I was never hit.

The immediate upshot of the affair was the strangest of all. We continued on our journey, and four days later came to Palmyra. They had been enervating days, as we had travelled very fast, but my exhaustion was completely dissipated when I saw the rose-coloured pillars of the Grand Avenue rising out of the desert, and even more when I beheld the huge archway leading to the Temple of the Sun. I never did accept that it should be called Tadmor. It quite outstripped even the Acropolis. The ruins themselves were magnificent, so redolent of a great and vanished glory, when Palmyra had controlled the trade route from Persia to Egypt. But for me the attraction lay in my imagination. I was treading in the footsteps of Zenobia. I seemed to see her form in every doorway, on every street, and all but filled a new sketchbook with drawings.

My delight at my surroundings was evident, and on our second night in the ruined city – we were due to start our return journey the next day – Medjuel did me the great honour of taking his evening meal with me. 'You are pleased with what you see?' he asked me.

'Oh, it is far more splendid than I ever expected. Do you know, I have dreamed of coming here since I was nine years old.'

'It is always good to be able to make dreams come true. And do you also like the desert?'

'I love the desert.'

'Then . . .' he paused for a moment. 'It would please me very much if you would become my wife.' I was so surprised that for a moment I could not think. This man had never touched more than my hand, much less ever embraced me or kissed me. He watched me for a few seconds. 'I have studied the habits of the Franks, and understand their religion and their prejudices. If you will accept my proposal, I will send my wives away.'

'And your sons?'

'Them too, if you wish it.'

'Oh, Medjuel . . .' I clasped his hand. How to tell this sweet little man that he simply was not my sort, certainly physically. But in any event, it was Saleh I was going to marry. 'You do me great honour. But as I have told you, I am betrothed to another.'

'A man of no importance.'

'A man I love,' I said severely. 'And a man who loves me.'

'I would love you as no other man can. And honour you above all other women. When I become sheik, you would be my sitt.'

'Your *what?*'

'My queen.'

'You mean as sheik you would be a king?' My head was spinning.

'Of the Mesrab, yes. We are only a small tribe, but our territory is large. I would be as much a king as any of the rulers of small city states in Ancient Greece.'

What a prospect! But I had resolved to turn my back on chimeras, or prophecies. I squeezed his fingers. 'Again, I am honoured more than I can say. But the answer must be no. I would like to remain your friend.'

He gazed at me with those deep dark eyes of his, for several moments. Then he freed his hand, stood up, and bowed. 'I am yours to command, Madame Digby.'

I felt close to tears. Equally, I would not have been human had I not reflected that he might seek to take me by force. That night I slept with a revolver beside my head. But I need not have feared. Medjuel was perhaps the most honourable man I ever met, and throughout our return journey was as courteous as ever, more so, in fact, as now he unfailingly ate with me. I felt I *had* made a friend.

The journey back was necessarily anticlimactic. But our entry into Damascus was not. We were greeted outside the city by large numbers of the Mesrab. These were mounted on horses, magnificent beasts, and before I could draw breath Medjuel had leapt from his camel, mounted a horse, and was galloping with the abandon I remembered from my youth at Holkham. Everyone was anxious to greet me, and hear of my adventures: I really felt I had come home. And I was determined to make this my home.

That meant there was a great deal to be done. Saleh, I knew, was still down in Palestine with his people, and would not return for another six weeks at least. That gave me the time to make my arrangements. I took a ship back to Athens.

We travelled as incognito as possible: I had no desire to run into Cristos. I visited my bank, placed my jewellery in safe-keeping, arranged for the sale of various items I no longer needed or wanted, had my remaining good pieces of furniture, including my piano, packed up and made ready for trans-shipment as soon as I had an address, wrote to Zurich for a redirection of my funds . . . and paid one call, to Sophie.

This was a mistake. She seemed pleased enough to see me, and wanted to hear all my adventures, but when I told her I was to marry, firstly an Arab, and a Muslim, and secondly a man only just over half my age, she quite lost her temper, described me as an idiotic adolescent who would undoubtedly come to a bad end, and virtually ordered me out of her house. I was glad to go, if sorry to see the end of a friendship that had been very good for me at the time. But the event made me think. Telling Sophie my plans had been like testing the temperature of the water, as it were. Sophie might have been crazy, but her travels and experiences had made her more broad-minded than most. In view of her reaction, I had to consider the possible attitudes of my mother and my brothers to my marriage to a dark-skinned heathen. I had no doubt that the English, like the Turks, regarded all of our dusky brethren as inferior creatures, principally because they had conquered so many of them with their superior weaponry. This is not a point of view that had ever appealed to me, even before I had met any of these so-called inferior races. My reading as a child and young woman had reminded me time and again of the great empires and profound thinkers and gallant men, and women, who had inhabited Arabia, Egypt, and India while England was still in a totally primitive state. Besides, Zenobia had been an Arab! In her beauty, courage, determination and morality she had far outstripped any English queen, or any Englishwoman, I had ever heard of . . . including myself.

But while I utterly rejected my family's possible prejudices, I had no wish to deepen the rift between them and me, and so I decided not to mention the matter in the letters I wrote home,

but to present them with a fait accompli, which they would have
to accept.

All of this made me more impatient than ever to regain my
beloved. It was necessary in the first instance to return to Damascus,
as I was again travelling with a large collection of trunks and
boxes. I was resolved that Damascus was to be my home for the
rest of my life. But these unloaded in Dimitri's courtyard, I left
Eugenie to start unpacking, mounted Ghost and set off for the
rendezvous, as it was a couple of hours ride from the city. It is
difficult to explain the euphoria which gripped my mind as I
rode beside the river. Partly this was sheer carnal desire. In the
past three months no man save Medjuel had even touched my
hand, except in the most formal of salutes. Now I was stepping
beyond the limits of acceptable behaviour for an English gentle-
woman. Not even Hester Stanhope had actually married an Arab.
But above those reflections was the feeling that I had truly turned
my back on my past and was embarking on the existence for
which I had yearned ever since I could remember. Actually, I
was, but not in any form I had ever anticipated.

When I saw the striped tents of Saleh's people, I nearly shrieked
for joy. I walked Ghost into the midst of the encampment, and
dismounted. Several people recognized me, and greeted me, but
seemed very surprised to see me. I took this to mean that Saleh
had not confided our arrangement to any of his friends and relations, no doubt for fear of their ridicule did I not show up. I had
already identified Saleh's tent, so I led Ghost to it, told him to
wait – I am sure he remembered his surroundings well enough
– lifted the flap, and went in. And gazed, not at Saleh, but at a
young woman, in fact, a girl – she could hardly have been more
than fourteen years old – lounging on the cushions. She had
nothing on, and was really quite exquisite, both in her body, her
long black hair, and her features.

  She sat up in some alarm at my entry, but made no move to
cover herself. 'Who are you?' I inquired.

  'I am Sabla.'

  'I see. And you are Saleh's . . . sister? You really should not lie
about in the nude. It is not seemly.'

'I am not Saleh's sister,' she informed me. 'I am his woman. Like you,' she added, now having identified me, presumably from Saleh's description. 'Why do you not take off your clothes as well?'

I was speechless, and had an urgent desire to strike her. But at that moment the flap behind me opened, and Saleh came in. 'Digby!' he said. 'It is good to see you, after so long.'

I faced him. He was entirely as I remembered him, and revealed not a trace of embarrassment. While I was still not certain whether I was awake or having a nightmare. 'What have you to say to me?' I inquired.

'I have said it.'

'And her?'

'A man must have a woman.'

'I accept that. In my absence. But I am here now. Send her away.'

'I cannot do this. She is my wife.'

'I am to be your wife. But you could not wait.'

'Have I not waited? I am here, as we agreed, at the rendezvous.'

'With another woman. A wife!'

'Why are you so angry? I am allowed four wives. You will take your place beside Sabla.'

'You swore to me that you would love only me!' I knew I was being humiliatingly puerile, but I was very close to despair.

'I spoke in foolish haste,' he explained. 'A man must have as many women as he needs and can afford. Also, a man must not be dictated to by any woman, save his mother. Now put aside this absurdity, take off your clothes, and lie with me. I have waited a long time for this moment.'

My hand brushed my reticule. I had the strongest temptation to shoot him dead. But I did not. I turned and left his tent, mounted Ghost, and rode back to Damascus.

I galloped most of the way, and poor Ghost was exhausted by the time we reached the hotel. Heaven knows, as I have recounted, I have met with some amorous rebuffs in my time, but never had I been at once so hurt and so humiliated. What made it worse was the youth of the girl, and her undoubted beauty. She was young enough to be my granddaughter! For the first time I truly felt my age. Well, that was it, I told myself. I was finished with men, absolutely and forever. I had no desire to return to Europe, certainly after having told Sophie my plans – I could not doubt that they were by now known to everyone in Athens, and that I would be a laughing stock. Besides, even if at that moment I hated all Arabs, I still rated Damascus as my favourite city. I resolved that I would buy a little house with a nice garden, and Eugenie and I would live out our old age in peace and tranquillity.

But my spirit was still seething, and I knew that the next few months were going to be difficult. Thus, when, as I entered the city, I observed what was obviously a caravan about to leave, I wheeled my horse and rode into the midst of the excited people and animals, and dismounted. 'Who commands here?' I inquired.

A somewhat stout fellow, larger in every visible way than the average Bedouin – Saleh excepted – came up to me. 'I am in charge, Madame Digby.'

'How do you know who I am?'

'Everyone knows of the great Madame Digby, so rich and so beautiful.'

The last did something to assuage my shattered spirit. 'And your name?'

'I am El Barrak.'

'Well, El Barrak, where does this caravan go?'

'We are bound for Baghdad, Great Lady.'

'Baghdad?' I cried. 'When do you leave?'

'Within the hour.'

'Wait for one hour more and I will come with you.'

'You wish to go to Baghdad? It is a very long way.'

'Don't tell me. And a very dangerous journey, I suppose.'

El Barrak puffed out his chest. 'There will be no danger while El Barrak commands.'

'That is splendid. Delay your departure for one hour, so that I may change my clothes and fetch my maid.'

'This will cost many francs.'

'I will pay you when you return me here, safe and sound.'

Eugenie, just embarked upon unpacking our belongings, was aghast at being told that we were off on our travels again, but I assured her that this was our last journey before settling permanently.

Dimitri was content to look after our animals and goods and keep our suite; like so many before him, he was beginning to look upon me as a perpetual source of income.

I now undertook a bitter sweet journey. It did not serve its purpose in enabling me to forget Saleh, but it did introduce me to a great many new sights and sounds, and even some new experiences. The journey itself was peaceful and unexciting, as El Barrak had boasted it would be under his aegis. As this was a commercial caravan and not a sightseeing tour, Eugenie and I were the only two Europeans, and were treated with great courtesy by everyone, but especially by the leader. There was no hesitation from El Barrak about making me his friend. He ate with me on our first night out, and every night after that, while taking every opportunity to touch my hands or brush against me. I understood that he could be a looming problem, but then, I have never considered a man's admiration to *be* a problem, and I was badly in need of masculine admiration, if only to restore my self-confidence – I was thinking no further ahead at that moment.

In fact, I spent more of the time in a deep reverie, thinking about Saleh, of course, with a mixture of anger and sadness. I could not imagine myself ever meeting such a man again. Or falling for any man so heavily again. Which I suppose indicates that my resolutions were already weakening. But I also found myself remembering Ludwig, and oddly enough, finding Medjuel intruding on my thoughts. Both, in their widely different ways, had been such perfect gentlemen. Now Ludwig was history. And Medjuel . . . I did not anticipate ever meeting him again, certainly after I had turned down his proposal of marriage.

We gained Baghdad without mishap, after several weeks on the road. There the caravan split up to do its business. 'It will reform in a month's time for the return journey,' El Barrak told me. 'What will you do in that time, Great Lady?'

'Explore Baghdad.'

"But you must have somewhere to stay.'

'Show me to the best hotel.'

'Alas, Great Lady, there is no hotel.'

'Good heavens!'

'But you are welcome to stay at the house of my brother-in-law. That is where I will be staying,' he added, ingenuously.

'I will let you know,' I told him.

'We are not going to stay in an Arab house, milady?' Eugenie asked, anxiously.

'Not if I can help it,' I promised her. 'There is a British Consulate here.'

We found it easily enough, and approached the gate, to be halted by a large Indian sepoy, armed to the teeth. 'Your business?' he asked, brusquely, in French, as he could tell that someone with my hair was neither Arab nor Turkish.

'To see the Consul,' I told him, in English.

He goggled at me, then rang a bell, and various other sepoys appeared, one very resplendent fellow with three stripes on the arm of his red tunic. 'His Excellency is working,' he explained.

'Give him my card.' I handed him the piece of cardboard. 'And kindly admit us. It is very hot.'

We were allowed in to shelter from the sun in a porch. I had no idea who or what I might be about to meet. Thus, I sank into another reverie of times past, from which I was aroused by a shriek from Eugenie. 'Your gun, milady! Your gun!'

I looked up and saw, advancing towards us, a tiger, by no means fully grown, but very nearly so, a splendid if certainly terrifying sight. Eugenie had risen and was standing behind my chair, clearly prepared to perform her usual duty of loading while I fired, and indeed I did open my reticule, but then realized that the beast was followed by an English gentleman.

There could be no doubt about that, whether one considered the somewhat sparse but carefully brushed hair, the little military moustache, the white linen jacket, the carefully creased drill trousers, or the even more carefully polished black shoes. 'Jane Digby?' he inquired. 'Lady Ellenborough? Bless my soul, Lieutenant-Colonel Henry Creswick-Rawlinson, at your service.'

I gave him my hand. 'You are actually speaking of my past, Colonel. Now I am plain Jane Digby.'

'You could never be plain, dear lady. But . . . what brings you to Baghdad?'

'Exploring. What I am actually seeking is a place to stay, for perhaps a month until my caravan begins its return journey to Damascus. I am told there is no hotel in the city.'

'There isn't. But you will stay here, of course.'

'That is very kind of you. But do you not think you should obtain an opinion from you wife, first?'

'I have no wife.'

I considered. But I estimated the colonel to be in every way a gentleman, and as I no longer had any interest in English sexual mores, or, to be frank, in English men, I determined that it would be safe enough. 'Then I shall be pleased to accept your hospitality.'

The month passed very pleasantly. Henry was both erudite and charming. He showed me everything that there was to see in Baghdad, and even took me on a trip down to the delta, a dismal place. He was, in himself, a fascinating character, who had taken it upon himself to display to the Turks and the Arabs the might of the British Empire, and thus lived in unexampled splendour. The Consulate was guarded by a company of sepoys, all apparently selected for their size, who marched behind him every time he left the premises, and when he returned saluted him with a roll of drums. He was accompanied everywhere by his tiger, which certainly encouraged strangers to keep their distance. And he worked in a kiosk set apart from the house, on to the roof of which was constantly poured streams of water to keep the interior cool. I should say that by now the war between Russia and Turkey had broken out, with Britain and France rushing troops and ships to the Black Sea in Turkish support, and there were few people in Baghdad who had any doubts about Britain's greatness, but Henry felt it was no bad thing to keep them in awe.

Sadly, while Baghdad is undoubtedly a fascinating city, I was not in the mood for it. Henry's lifestyle, the amount of silver on his table, the obsequious waiters, the fine wines, combined to remind me of so much of that past on which I had turned my back. This I did not regret, but it had been my intention to recreate much of that past in the house I had dreamed of building in Damascus – to be shared with Saleh. But where was the point in living on a grand scale without a man to share it with? For all Henry's kindness, I was not sorry to leave his house, even if I felt lower than ever as I had no idea to what I was going.

★　★　★

My depression was heightened when, on our return journey, we visited Aleppo, where poor Henry Anson, my cousin, was buried, he having died from an illness contracted in prison following his arrest for attempting to penetrate the mysteries of the ka'aba in Mecca. I knelt beside his grave for some time, the whole of my girlhood seeming to pass before my eyes. My mood was apparent to El Barrak, and it was only a few days later that he visited my tent. Eugenie would have seen him off, but I asked her to leave us, so she went off herself in some disapproval. As always, no excuses, although perhaps I owe some to myself. I was not in love with Barrak. But I needed to be loved, or at least appreciated, to know the comfort of a man and this was accentuated by my present uncertainty. I was coming up to forty-seven years old, and if I still felt seventeen, I had recently had it brutally pointed out to me that, in Arab eyes, I was an old woman. I was even beginning to doubt my own beauty, certainly my own sexuality. Barrak reassured me on every count, and for all his somewhat uncouth exterior, he proved to be a surprisingly gentle and considerate lover. If I knew he could never provide the future, he certainly managed to relieve the present.

Of course, it could not last. Barrak's gentleness towards me did not extend in any other direction. There came the morning I was awakened by a noise outside my tent, and going out, I discovered a stray camel nibbling at my cords. The poor creature was half starved and in a very bad shape. Hastily I secured some milk for it to drink, when I was joined by my lover. 'What are you doing?' he demanded.

'Feeding this unhappy animal.'

'We have sufficient camels.'

'That does not mean we should turn any living creature away to starve.'

'Well, then, we will shoot him. You can show me how well you use your revolvers, eh?'

'Are you a man or a beast?' I demanded in turn. I had always felt put out by the way the Arabs treated these dear creatures, who were so essential to their civilization; this episode seemed to epitomize everything that had been distressing me. 'We will take him with us.'

175

'And I say he will die.'

'If you attempt to harm this animal,' I told him, speaking quietly. 'I will show you how well I use my revolvers. On you.'

By now quite a crowd had gathered, and Barrak was entirely discomfited. But he had heard too much about me to challenge me further. Our romance therefore ended, while, if unable to coerce me, over the next week he used every opportunity to make life difficult, decreeing that we should start our daily ride at four in the morning and continue it until after dark. This was entirely self-defeating, as I had more stamina than most of his people, and they soon began to grumble. He then changed his tactics and attempted to win me back, being as courteous as in the early days of our acquaintance, even halting the march early or beginning it late so that I could explore various Greek or Roman ruins we came across, often accompanying me on these excursions. One of these sites was Baalbek, which I had to admit was perhaps even more splendid than Palmyra; sadly I was still not in the mood to appreciate it. But the final weeks of our journey passed off pleasantly enough, although I was very happy to regain Damascus.

The Barrak episode had made me more determined than ever to settle down, with Eugenie, into a chaste old age. But it so happened that a few days before we regained Damascus, we visited the ancient Hittite city of Hama. This was fascinating in itself, but more importantly it was an Amazeh headquarters, and while we were there, I heard Medjuel's name constantly mentioned, for his brother had died, and he was now the Sheik. I was very happy for him, but no more than that, until, as we reached the environs of Damascus, I saw him approaching us, at the head of several of his people, all mounted, and leading horses. I was delighted to see him, to consider that he had taken the trouble to meet me, and indeed to keep himself so informed of my movements that he knew the exact hour of my arrival, and even more delighted when he presented me with a magnificent mare to celebrate my return. In fact, I was quite overwhelmed, and the more so when Barrak, as we said goodbye, whispered, 'The Sheik means to make you his wife.'

I scarcely slept that night, much to Eugenie's alarm, as she assumed that I must have contracted some kind of desert fever. Well, I suppose I had. The desert had taken over my soul, as had the people who inhabited it, for all their individual faults. I longed to live in it for the rest of my life, providing I could escape to Damascus from time to time. That were I actually to marry a Bedouin would cause the most tremendous scandal, I had had some inkling with Saleh. But my entire life had been surrounded by scandal. I was not going to be put off by that now.

Then what *of* Saleh? I had determined to love him without reservation, providing he would reciprocate, and he had thrown my love back in my face. Would Medjuel be any different? I knew he already had at least two wives. And then there was the very important aspect that I felt for him none of the overwhelming passion I had known with Felix, or Spiro, or even Cristos. Yet he was clearly such a gentle man, as well as being a gentleman!

Unable to make up my mind, I awaited his next visit with some anticipation. But it did not happen the next morning. I remember pacing the verandas and corridors of the hotel in frustrated apprehension. After all, I had only Barrak's suggestion that Medjuel even still had marriage in mind. He did come in the afternoon, and we rode into the desert together, I on my new mare. But we only exchanged pleasantries, and I told him about my visit to Baghdad, without, of course, mentioning my brief fling with Barrak, although I imagine he knew of it. He certainly knew that Saleh was no longer a part of my plans. It was the following afternoon, when we drank tea on the veranda outside my suite, that he suddenly said, 'I have sent my wives back to their people. With their dowries.' Which was the Arab way of divorce.

'Oh,' I said. 'Were they very unhappy?'

'I would say so. But a man has only one life to live.' My own sentiments exactly. 'And when he discovers that Allah has sent him the most sublime gift he could possibly imagine, it would be blasphemy for him to reject it.' I found I was holding my breath. 'I would therefore again like to ask you to be my wife.' He held up his hand as I would have spoken. 'I think it might be wise for you to reflect before answering. There will be many difficulties to be overcome. My people, your people. My religion, your religion. My customs, your customs.'

Total déjà vu. 'There can be no difficulties,' I said, 'which cannot be overcome, if we are both determined to do so.' He kissed me.

The Sadness – and the Glory

As I have indicated, I had had to contend with so many difficulties in attempting to make a success of my previous romantic attachments I did not believe any new obstacles would be insuperable. Well, they were not. But they were far more serious than I had imagined. They began when Medjuel took me to his tribal encampment outside the city to introduce his people to their new sitt. I remembered entering the room full of Venningens when I had accepted Karl's invitation – or had it been Ludwig's command? – to marry him, and been instantly aware of being surrounded by hostility. Now I found myself surrounded by many more people, who appeared to be far more hostile. The women in particular glared at me as if I were an enemy, which was the harder to bear as several of these people had been in the caravan to Palmyra, and by the time we regained Damascus I had counted them my friends. Now I was truly disturbed by my reception, which seemed to be exemplified when I dropped a flower Medjuel had given me, and before I could pick it up, one of the women stepped on it and crushed it into the earth. I retired in tears.

Medjuel was terribly upset. 'They will grow to love you as they grow to know you,' he promised.

'But why do they hate me?' I sobbed. 'They did not hate me before.'

'Before you were a foreigner, offering my people employment. Now you seek to become one of them.'

'*I* seek?'

'It is what I also seek, certainly. And I am the Sheik. So they will accept you. But welcoming you will take them time. It is not so much hate, as mistrust. This is the way of the desert. Since time began strangers have sought to steal our water, our animals or our women.'

'How can I steal your water or your animals? As for your women . . .'

'I know it is absurd. But they do know that you have stolen the heart of their sheik. You must give them time to become used to this.'

I held his hand. 'Tell me what I must do to gain their trust.'

'You must be patient. Although there is . . .' he hesitated.

'Tell me.'

'Your hair . . .'

'It is the evil eye!'

'Another superstition. In time . . .'

'I have no time.' That afternoon I dyed my hair black. As when loosed it now stretched to my ankles, this was a very lengthy operation, but I was pleased with the result. Medjuel was delighted. Eugenie was horrified, but she did as she was required, and dressed it in two plaits. I swear I looked like a young girl again.

The Mesrab themselves were pleased, and I was utterly relieved when El Barrak, of all people, gave a party to celebrate our betrothal, thus announcing *his* approval of the event. This was a great occasion, with sumptuous food, and a mock battle in which two companies of Bedouin charged each other, hurling spears. The objective was to avoid being hit, which was very reasonable, and the men took the opportunity to display their magnificent horsemanship, often riding at full gallop while hanging down beside their mounts. By the end of the evening I was totally reassured.

The difficulties I endured with the Mesrab were nothing compared to the difficulties I encountered with my own people. Obviously marriage to a Bedouin involved legal matters which required sorting out before I actually completed the deed, however much I trusted Medjuel. He showed not the slightest interest in my wealth, although he had to be aware of it. Indeed, when one of his brothers desperately needed money, always scarce amongst the Bedouin, and I discovered that he was having to scrounge every piastre he could from his people to raise the required sum, and told him I would happily give him, or if he insisted, lend him the money, he declined, saying that he could never live off his wife's wealth. But if I became a member of his tribe, and something were to happen to him, I might find myself in a difficult position vis-a-vis his successor, or even more, his sons by his previous wives. There were also matters such as retaining my British nationality, more with regard to avoid placing myself under Turkish than Arab rule, and the retention of my absolute freedom of movement. Thus, I went to see Colonel Wood. I had hoped that after my triumphant return, unharmed, from my expedition to Palmyra, not to mention Baghdad, the colonel would have accepted that not only would I do things my way, but that I would do so successfully. Not a bit of it. In the first instance he stared at my appearance in disbelief. I could not blame him for this. 'What have you done to yourself?' he demanded as he showed me to a chair.

I sat down. 'I have dyed my hair. I am to marry a Bedouin.'

'Are you quite mad?'

'Do you find it necessary to be quite so discourteous?'

He flushed. 'My dear Miss Digby, white women, members of the English aristocracy, do not marry Arabs.'

'I am not marrying any Arab. I am marrying Sheik Medjuel el Mesrab.'

'Do you suppose that makes any difference? I absolutely forbid it.'

'Do *you* suppose that will make any difference?'

He bridled. 'I shall write to your family. To your brother.'

'Neither of my brothers has taken any notice of my existence for some considerable time. They are unlikely to do so now.'

'Edward is still the head of your family . . .'

'He is not the head of *my* family. Now can we get down to business? I came here for your advice on how to proceed in financial matters.'

'The only advice I can give you is not to act in such an insane fashion.'

I rose. 'Then I shall have to go elsewhere.'

'Miss Digby . . . milady . . . please listen to me.'

'That depends on what you have to say.'

'I think that perhaps you do not understand what you are doing. Do you realize that a Bedouin wife has no rights, as to either property or indeed her own person? Your husband has the right to have three other wives, and as many concubines as he can afford.'

'The Sheik has sent away his previous wives. As for my property, I intend to take care of that. Which is why I sought your advice.'

'He will have the right to beat you. And should you, well . . .'

Obviously he had done some investigation of my past. 'Say it, Colonel.'

His cheeks were puce. 'The Bedouin husband has the right to decapitate an unfaithful wife.'

'I will remember that. If you have nothing more to offer me . . .'

He tried one last assault. 'I have to inform you that such a marriage will never be recognized by the Church of England.'

'And I should point out that my first marriage, under the auspices of the Church of England, was not recognized by the Roman Catholic Church in Bavaria, and that my third marriage, in the Greek Orthodox Church, was not recognized by anyone, including the Greek Orthodox Church. But as I always married in good faith, I am sure they were all recognized in Heaven. As will my fourth. Good day to you, Colonel.'

I left him speechless.

But our conversation did give me pause for thought, and discussion. In which I was utterly relieved. 'I do not wish a share in your wealth,' Medjuel repeated. 'What use have I for money. It is only of use in cities, not in the desert.'

'You had use for money a week ago.'

'That was an isolated incident. My brother should not have got himself into debt. And to a Turk!'

'But such a situation may arise again. And you do not spend all of your time in the desert. Let us have a pact, that you will take care of everything in the desert, and I will take care of everything in Damascus.'

He considered. 'You intend to come into the desert with me?'

'Do you not wish me to?'

'It is very dangerous.'

'Do you suppose I am afraid of danger?'

'I know you are not. But this is not a business of defending a caravan. This is a business of defending our wells and our flocks against those who would rob us.'

'I shall ride at your side. If you will stay at my side when we are in the city.' He stroked his beard. 'But when we are in the city,' I went on, 'you will treat me with the respect due to an Englishwoman.' I drew a deep breath. 'In return, I will promise, when we are in the desert, to behave towards you with the subservience of a Bedouin woman, obey all of your laws, follow all of your customs.'

'You are sure you wish to do this? Some of our laws are very severe, our punishments very harsh.'

'I know to what you are referring. I will never betray your bed. This I swear. All I ask in return is that you treat me with respect.'

'Have I ever treated you with disrespect?'

'Never. But you are in love with me. Will you always be?' I could not allow myself to forget that I was older than him.

'I have not loved you yet,' he said quietly.

We quickly put that right. I had actually been postponing the event, principally for fear of being disappointed: I had never actually had sex with a man several inches shorter than myself. But as he practised the Levantine method and approached me from the rear, height did not enter the equation. While he did not lack size in any other direction. As for his fervour . . . I was utterly fulfilled.

So was he. 'I shall love you forever,' he said. I snuggled against him. 'But you understand that I am a man, and a man must have a woman.'

'I am your woman.'

'But there may be times you are not beside me.' I rolled over to face him. 'I therefore require your agreement that as I agree to treat you as an English lady, when you are not here, I may seek another.'

The proposition was not phrased as a request. Nor did it indicate any reciprocity regarding when he might not be at *my* side. In fact, he had just spelled out that any misbehaviour on my part would not be acceptable to him. But I determined that he felt such a stance was a necessary reminder of his ultimate masculine authority. I was in love, and besides, it seemed to me that there was a very simple solution to the question. 'I shall always be at your side,' I told him.

★   ★   ★

But not for the first time in my life I was attempting the impossible. In fact, we were separated almost immediately, and before we were even married: I received a letter from my bank in Athens to inform me that some of the jewellery I had left in safe keeping had been stolen. This did not leave me with a very favourable impression of their safes, and I felt it necessary to return to Greece to sort things out. Medjuel was very upset, but I promised to be back as quickly as possible, and this I did, staying in Athens only long enough to remove all my remaining valuables into my own keeping, and making arrangements to have the rest of my stored furniture shipped to Damascus as soon as possible. I naturally kept a very low profile, as I did not wish to encounter either Sophie, or, Heaven forbid, Cristos, and as far as I know I was back in Beirut before any of my previous acquaintances even knew I had been in their midst. In Beirut I at last found a sympathetic adviser, Mr Heald, the English manager of the Imperial Ottoman Bank, who kept his opinion of my intentions to himself while being as helpful as possible. He introduced me to a Turkish lawyer, who took care of all my problems, drawing up several documents which only required the signatures, in addition to my own, of my future husband and a responsible government official, to afford me lifelong protection. Then it was back to Damascus.

Medjuel and I had a tumultuous reunion. He willingly signed where necessary, and raised no objection when I went to see my old friend General Ahmed, who also signed with pleasure; I suspect he regarded my membership of the Mesrab as a possibly calming influence on these habitually warlike people. A few days later we made the journey to Homs, the Mesrab heartland not far from Damascus, where we were married by a Turkish official. Being a Muslim ceremony, this was the fourth different denominational wedding I had attended as a principal, and I liked it best of all. I was now Sitt el Mesrab.

There was still a good deal of hostility to be overcome, principally from Medjuel's two sons, Schebibb and Japhet, both grown men and naturally resentful of the way their mothers had been ousted, but I was determined to be accepted. I already spoke Arabic passably. Now I entirely adopted Bedouin dress when in their company, wore the voluminous and all-concealing haik, hid my face beneath the yashmak when out of doors, and, far more inconveniently in wet weather, discarded my boots for the high-platform – several inches – wooden clogs, designed to keep one's toes clear of the mud. I even discarded all of my western jewellery, my diamond rings, my ruby bracelets and my pearl necklaces and instead wore simple gold bangles as did my compatriots. My efforts were successful. People warmed to me, even my stepsons, and I found myself being called Mother of Milk, this last being a reference to my complexion, which suggested the local yogurt.

I thus embarked on my fourth marriage with total confidence and contentment, nor were my sentiments misplaced. But there remained a good deal of what might be called adjusting to be done. Religion played a big part in this. It may have been gathered that I had never been a religious person, in the sense that I lived from Sunday to Sunday, believed that the holy day should be the centre of my life, or had ever feared the wrath of God for my misdemeanours, confident that when the time came I could explain them all away. And in fact religion had never impinged on my life, whether in England, in France, in Bavaria, or in Greece. One heard the church bells and more often than not found them an attractive sound. Now I found myself in an intensely religious world, where every day began with the muezzin's call to prayer, and ended likewise, and where such things as fast days, or indeed, fast months, were taken very seriously. This attitude was even held by Medjuel, who every morning, noon and night knelt to face Mecca and perform his homage to Allah as decreed by the Prophet. This left me feeling profoundly isolated, as only Eugenie of my immediate entourage did not take part in the solemn ritual. Of course I could, and I did, kneel in prayer to the Christian version of God, but I had a growing desire for more, for the shared experience of worshipping in a church in the company of others of a similar mind. But I did not know how to accomplish this. I had Wood's word that the wife of a Bedouin sheik would not be welcome in any Anglican church, even supposing there had been such a thing in Damascus. There *were* various Christian gatherings, but none of them could be considered Anglican. This quite distressed me.

There was also the business of Medjuel's nomadic habits, required by both necessity and heredity. As Sheik of the Mesrab he was responsible for the welfare of the entire tribe, for every animal, every well, and indeed every square inch of the territory they claimed as their own. Thus, we had not been married for more than a month before he had to ride off into the desert to see to his people's welfare. Still not knowing me as well as he would later, and fearing to expose me to either danger or hardship, he insisted that I remain behind; he would be back in a couple of months. I was unhappy at his departure, not only because of the separation involved – so much for my determination always to be at his side – but because I knew that if the Mesrab territory had been infiltrated by the men from across the river, he would feel it necessary to mount a reprisal with the consequent risk of battle and death. Medjuel assured me that he would be in absolutely no danger, and on this occasion, being a bride and with our relationship still nebulous, I let him go on his own. I was still settling in as a wife, and I was concerned with domesticity, principally the finding of a home for us, whether it had to be built, which promised to be an almost impossible task, or bought and converted. My thoughts were, as always, ranging towards the ultimate. There was also the arrival of the last of my goods from Athens, which took over almost the whole of Dimitri's hotel. But this was not for sale.

So I spent a desolate two months, wondering every day what Medjuel might be doing, what dangers he might be facing. It did not occur to me to wonder about anything more than that: I was utterly confident of his love. I also had on my mind the problem of informing my family of my latest situation. In fact, I had not yet determined on the best way to do this when I received a letter from my sister-in-law Theresa, telling me that Edward had been very upset to be informed by Colonel Wood that I had so far abandoned decency as to live as man and wife with a Bedouin – the good colonel had apparently not been able to bring himself to recognize the fact that Medjuel and I were married. Theresa begged me to reply and dismiss the rumour as scurrilous gossip. She also informed me that my uncle Lord Digby had finally died, at a very advanced age. Edward had now inherited the title for which he had waited for so long, and was Lord Digby. Unfortunately, while he had at last obtained his title, he could not immediately lay his hands on the capital and income that went with it until all the other bequests had been settled, which required the physical presence of all the beneficiaries. And these included me! The dear old man, of whom I had seen very little since my childhood, had still regarded me as a part of the family. Theresa wrote that even if I did not need any extra capital, Edward would be very pleased if I could see my way to pay a brief visit to England to sign the necessary papers. I got the impression that he was quite desperate, even if I could not help but wonder at his apparent inability to write to me himself. Finally, somewhat pompously, Theresa informed me that in view of Edward's elevation, I was now entitled to call myself the Honourable Jane Digby! She seemed to feel that this would be important to me, as if someone who had been Lady Ellenborough, the Baroness von Venningen, the Countess Theotoky, and was now, most important of all, the Sitt el Mesrab, could possibly have any use for an Honourable before her name. But actually I did find the handle useful, once in my life.

It was very pleasant, after all the disapproval I had endured, to feel that I was still necessary to the well-being of my family, and this being so, I felt that here was a means of achieving a reconciliation. I therefore replied to say that I would come as soon as possible, leaving the question of my current domestic arrangements in abeyance. However, as I could not leave until after Medjuel's return, I took the opportunity to write Mama and inform her that I would be in England before the end of the year, and just to break the ice and test the temperature of the water beneath, that I was married again, to a dear man named Sheik Medjuel el Mesrab.

I awaited a reply with some trepidation, and when it came it was not from Mama, but from Steely! What is more, the envelope was addressed to Countess Theotoky. I felt this was extremely rude. The last thing I wished was to be reminded of that part of my life, and I was furious. Nor were the contents of the letter any improvement. Steely wrote in the coldest terms, not referring to my news at all, and saying that if it was my intention to visit England my mother would be pleased to see me.

I could not believe that Mama had had anything to do with such an attempted put-down, and was in quite a hurry to be off. But it was still necessary to wait for Medjuel's return, and when he did so I was deeply concerned. For there had been a battle with the Gomussa, in which the Mesrab, outnumbered, had only just managed to repel their enemies. Several men had been killed, and many camels driven off. 'I have failed my people,' he said disconsolately.

At that moment I did not know what to say, because now I had to tell him that *I* needed to go away for a few months. He was aghast. 'You are abandoning me.'

'For only a few months,' I protested. 'It is family business. You attend to family business all the time.'

He did not appear reassured. 'Will you ever come back?'

'Of course I will come back. Listen, I will leave everything I possess, save the clothes I need for travel, here in the hotel.'

'Are you not the richest woman in the world? Can you not buy new belongings whenever you choose?'

'Believe me, my dearest, I am not the richest woman in the world. However . . .' I had a stroke of genius. 'Tell me more about this battle. Were you so very outnumbered?'

'They were not so many men. But their guns! They had muskets purchased from the Turks. We had only our jezreels, which are so slow to load and so inaccurate to fire.'

As I had suspected to be the case, but just to be sure . . . 'These muskets the Gomussa used, how were they loaded?'

He frowned at my apparent ignorance. 'The charge and the bullet are inserted into the muzzle, and forced down with a ramrod.'

'Ah! Would you like your people to be armed with modern weapons?'

'The Turks will not sell them to us. Our lands are too close to Damascus.'

'Nor would they be much use to you. Those muskets they sold the Gomussa were out of date, and no longer of any value to them.'

'They were still far superior to our jezreels.'

'Suppose you were to be armed with really modern weapons?' With my interest in guns I kept up to date, through the periodicals I received from England, with all the latest technology. 'The French have just developed a new rifle, called the Chassepot. This is a bolt-action breech-loader, which can fire fifteen shots a minute, and has a range of five hundred yards. At this moment it is the most effective weapon in the world.'

Again he frowned at me, but this time in disbelief. 'To have such guns . . . but how?'

'I will provide them for you. I will buy them and have them shipped as part of my personal luggage.'

'You can do this? You *will* do this?'

'I am the Sitt el Mesrab. Your people are my people.'

Nor did I fail him. But my last visit to England was an occasion I would rather forget. Calamity threatened almost from the moment I sailed from Beirut in a Greek ship of the Papayanni Line, mainly because, on its way to Naples, where I would make my connection for Marseilles, it would naturally stop for a few days in Piraeus, and I still had some unresolved financial matters in Greece. Once the decision to visit England had been taken, I wrote to my bank and various other people to inform them that I would be stopping in Athens for this purpose. Perhaps this was incautious of me. I had forgotten how impossible it is to keep a secret in Greece. Thus, to my distress I discovered Cristos waiting on the dock when I disembarked on 25 November 1856.

I almost turned and went straight back on board – Eugenie indeed was very reluctant to come down the gangplank. But it was too late. He rushed at me, as tall and commanding and handsome as I remembered. 'Ianthe! Can it really be you. But . . . what has happened to your hair?'

I was wearing my pigtails up, beneath a bonnet, but the visible wisps were definitely not Titian. 'I have dyed it.'

He held my arms to kiss me. 'But why?'

'Because I am married, to a Bedouin.'

'I do not believe you. How can you be married to an Arab?'

'I am married, to a Bedouin, because I love him.'

'How can that be? You love me. You have told me this. You are going to marry me. We are betrothed.'

I realized that I had a difficult time ahead. He seemed anxious to carry me straight off to bed. It took me some time to convince him that I *was* a married woman and had no intention of betraying my husband. He pulled out all the stops to have me abandon

Medjuel, tried to convince me that Eugenie had lied about him, and bitterly reproached me for having fled our wedding without giving him an opportunity to defend himself. I have never found it easy to resist an arduous male, and it was a most exhausting week, made worse when he insisted I visited Eirini, who was unwell. In fact, I needed to take but a single look at the boy to know that he was dying. I wept. But I was adamant. I had chosen my course and, I was resolved, my last way of life, and I was not going to abandon it. When I sailed again from Piraeus, I left Cristos standing on the dock, weeping.

Quite apart from this unhappy episode, Greece had ceased to attract me. I no longer had any friends there. Even Sophie had died – I did not discover if this was after, or because, she had finally built her temple – but from my point of view the whole country had changed, for the worse. This was mainly because of the Crimean War. The war itself was now over – I would not like to say who had won – but the Greeks could not forgive the British for fighting on the side of the Turks. Never have I felt so uncomfortable.

That is until I got to England, in December. Eugenie and I landed at Marseilles and crossed France, much to her delight, as she was able to visit her family after so many years. She received a rapturous welcome, as did I, which greatly encouraged me. Then we stopped for a few days in Paris, where I visited my old friend the gunsmith and told him what I wanted. He became very excited. 'The latest in firearms, milady? You mean a Chassepot?'

'Yes. Can you replace them?'

'Oh, indeed. But . . . it is unproven, except in practice. We are trying to sell it to the French Army, but so far without success. You know what these generals are like.'

'I must have it.'

'Of course. Would you like one, or two?'

'One hundred.'

He gaped at me. 'You wish one hundred Chassepot rifles?'

'I will pick them up in three months' time.'

He rolled his eyes.

★   ★   ★

I placed various other orders, including one for a new piano, and then it was on to Boulogne and the Channel packet to Folkestone. I had kept Mama up to date with my arrangements, and I was met on the dock by my old art teacher, Jane Steele. Her greeting was a lot warmer than the weather, which, it being nearly thirty years since I had last experienced an English winter, I found extremely unpleasant. Jane was as charming as I remembered her, all the way to Tunbridge Wells, where Mama was now living with both Jane and Margaret, but while she was careful to ask no questions about my new life, much less my new husband, she was as taken aback as anyone by my new appearance. I was of course wearing European clothes, and, as in Greece, my hair was up beneath my bonnet, but again as in Greece, its new colour was obvious. 'My new people believe that yellow hair is unlucky,' I explained.

She was aghast. 'And you dyed it? Had it turned grey?'

'Of course not.'

'You dyed your hair, your magnificent hair, to please—'

I rested my hand on hers. 'To please my husband and my people. Would you not do as much?' Having never had a husband, it was not a question to which she could reply. But again, I was aware of difficult times ahead.

My first reaction to arriving in Ernstein Villa in Tunbridge Wells was that Steely had feathered her nest very successfully since she had appeared in my life thirty-nine years before, in that she was now in complete control of my mother's household, while living in the greatest comfort herself. But I was as astounded by her appearance as I was distressed by Mama's. Steely had lost weight and was very frail. Mama had put on weight, and was so fat that she moved with difficulty. Even more distressing was the way she, who I remembered always as the calmest of women, had become fretful and querulous. Still, she seemed pleased to see me, after her inevitable initial consternation. 'Jane? Can it really be you? What has happened to your hair?'

'It is all here, Mama. I have dyed it black.'

'But why?'

I gave her the same explanation as I had given Jane, and received approximately the same reaction. Mama seemed unable to comprehend what I was telling her, and Steely looked more like a squeezed-dry lemon with every moment. But I was determined not to lose my temper, and to make a success of the visit, so we spent a couple of reasonably pleasant days together before the storm broke. This was principally the work of Steely, whose character and prejudices had not improved at all with age. I naturally, once our greetings were over and we had passed through a spell of mutual embarrassment, wished to tell Mama all about Medjuel and my life in the desert. But it was impossible ever to be alone with her; Steely was determined on that. And on the subject of my marriage she became quite vituperative, calling Medjuel a 'black' man, as if that was of any more importance than I might have called her a 'white' woman, but far more insultingly, pronouncing that he had to be an ignorant and unpleasant savage. This of a man who had more breeding than she could ever have! I was so angry I nearly left, but did not because I knew this would be the last occasion I would ever be with Mama. But it was not a very happy Christmas, which was equally distressing as I also knew that this would be my last such Christian festival.

Things did not improve with the arrival of Edward and Theresa in January. I had hoped that they, younger than I, would have some understanding that one did not have to be white, Anglo-Saxon and Protestant to be considered an equal, but to my dismay they possessed the same point of view as Steely, and like her would not have Medjuel's name mentioned. Still, Edward gave me a hug and a kiss when we parted after three days.

Edward was replaced by Kenelm, and at last there was a ray of light. I actually anticipated this visit with some apprehension: if Steely and Edward were so prejudiced, what could I hope for from an Anglican minister? But Kenelm was like a breath of fresh air. He actually wanted to know all about Medjuel and my new life, and pored over my sketches of Palmyra and the desert, which Edward and Theresa had refused to look at.

Kenelm's visit was really enjoyable, although sadly he was not accompanied by Caroline or any of his children, and I could not help but wonder if there had been a problem of acceptance there too, but on his departure all was unhappiness again, compounded by news from other quarters. The one quarter from which I wished to hear, Medjuel, keeping me up to date with events in Syria, did not materialize, but, it having been put about that I was 'home', letters poured in from other sources. Karl wrote to inform me that Bertha had had to be confined in an asylum. It may be recalled that as I'd had more than a suspicion that she was actually Ludwig's child I had always had doubts as to her mental stability, but I was appalled that this step had been considered necessary, and was utterly distressed to hear from Bertha herself, begging me to come to her rescue and take her to Syria. This I felt was impossible, as I could not see her fragile health standing up to the life I was proposing to live, but I wrote to Karl and offered to find a home for her in England. He actually agreed to this, and all the arrangements were made, but tragically she sickened and died before she could leave Germany. Hardly less disturbing was a letter from Cristos, informing me that Eirini had also died.

On the credit side of the ledger, I also heard from Heribert, now an officer in the Austrian army, and eager to make at least the epistolary acquaintance of his mother. I replied with enthusiasm, and we have corresponded ever since. But I was very relieved when I finally left Tunbridge Wells to go up to London to sign the necessary papers to complete the disposition of Uncle Edward's estate – from which I emerged considerably more wealthy than before – and, hopefully, find some congenial company. London itself was no improvement on Ernstein Villa. I knew, of course, that Almack's was no more, and that all my old playmates were dead or in their dotage, but I was appalled to observe the way the city itself had changed for the worse. Once it had been gay and chirpy, light and airy. Now it was permanently overlaid by smoke from the chimneys of the factories that were springing up everywhere, while the poverty to be seen on every side was sickening. I kept a very low profile, attended only one public event, a concert by the crazy musician Julien, but there were some compensations. I ran into Bob Drummond, with whom I had become so friendly in Athens, and who had done well, being now the naval aide-de-camp to the Queen. He seemed delighted to see me, and we had a merry reminiscence, while he entirely accepted my marriage. But he did agree that it was unlikely

Victoria would ever consent to receive me, supposing I had any wish to be received.

I also encountered my cousin Fanny Anson, now Fanny Isted, who brought me up to date on Anson affairs, Mama having entirely lost contact with her younger sister, my Aunt Anne Margaret. She told me that her brother George – my first lover – had reached the top of his professional tree, and was now commander-in-chief in India – the Mutiny had not yet started.

I was also gratified to receive a second visit from my brothers, I suspect engineered by Kenelm, determined to effect a reconciliation between Edward and I. He did not actually succeed. Edward tried his best but his innate prejudices could not be overcome. To my joy, however, Kenelm was this time accompanied by Caroline. I discovered that I had been quite wrong in fearing that she had not come to Tunbridge Wells because she had not wished to see me. It had been a domestic matter. Now she was sweetness itself, wanted to know all about my new life, and we formed an attachment which lasted to the end of her life. But I must confess that I was only too happy to get on with the only really enjoyable part of the entire trip, buying what I considered necessary for the happiness of Medjuel and myself.

Then I went back to Tunbridge Wells to say goodbye. This was a sad occasion, because it was also to celebrate my fiftieth birthday. Fifty! When I remembered all the events of the past I was quite overwhelmed. What made it more poignant was that I still felt – and indeed still looked – like that young girl who had eloped with her groom; I certainly still possessed all the energy and determination to enjoy life to the full that she had had. And I was surrounded by utter decrepitude. I knew I would never see Mama again, and this grieved me, but equally I knew that I was no longer her daughter, and had not been for some time. The gulf between us was exemplified when I told her my departure date – the following week – trying for a last time to explain to her the magnificent man, the magnificent country, the magnificent and worthwhile *life* to which I was returning as the Sitt el Mesrab, and she said, 'But Jane, you must stay another week, or you will miss the Henley Regatta!' As if watching some aimless young men paddling up and down a river bore the slightest resemblance, or had the slightest importance, compared to galloping into battle at the head of my people, as I was looking forward to doing. I simply could not think of a reply.

I left England for the last time on 6 April 1857. I had already accumulated a vast amount of luggage – my inheritance from my uncle had made me a wealthy woman even in England – which included a flock of Norfolk turkeys to start a colony of my own, fowl being such an important part of the Bedouin diet. There was also, of course, a stock of books. Then Paris, where the shopping continued. I was annoyed to discover that my new piano was not crated, and indeed would not be ready for some weeks, and would have to follow at a later date, but I bought some more books, including a copy of the new, outrageous novel *Madame Bovary,* by Gustave Flaubert – about a woman who abandoned her husband for love(!), but as it was a moralistic tale, did not find it very amusing – and of course collected the principal object of my journey, a hundred modern rifles, a score of revolvers, and an enormous stock of ammunition. Then it was down to Marseilles a week later to join my ship.

I wrote a last farewell to Mama, regretting that I had not been the daughter she had hoped for, but refusing to regret a moment of my life. I begged her to have no fears for my future, as I had none.

Then I was at sea, and on my way home. I had no doubt of that, either.

Beirut was even more attractive than the first time I had landed here – on my two recent visits I had been in such haste I had hardly noticed anything – and now boasted a new hotel, the Grand Hotel Bassoul, owned, as its name indicates, by a man named Nicholas Bassoul, who had been a dragoman accompanying various tourist parties into the desert. He was delighted to see me, and did his best to make me comfortable, as did Mr Heald, who had masses of new forms and mandates for me to sign, to complete the entire transfer of my finances from both Switzerland and Greece – and now England – to my new and final domicile. But I had thoughts only for Medjuel, and could hardly wait to be on my way. I promised my drivers a bonus if they would travel faster than usual, and my little caravan crossed the mountains at speed, riding day and night, to gain the Blessed City. And my husband.

He had been in the desert, but had been informed of my arrival, and was with me in a few hours. Bliss! But it was short-lived: I had only been back a few weeks when there was a fresh explosion of violence in the desert, and Medjuel had to ride off to war. I was horrified, at least partly because it happened too soon for my arrangements. I had continued my thinking and planning on the homeward voyage, able to concentrate entirely on my future now that I had irrevocably turned my back on my past. My brain was full of ideas, to which Medjuel had seemed receptive, but now he had gone rushing off. What was worse, he again refused to take me with him, as he remained uncertain as to my reception by those of his tribesmen who had not yet met me, or by the reaction of them all at the idea of being accompanied into battle by a woman! I also suspect that for all he knew of me he still doubted my courage and steadfastness when faced with the ultimate test. It was my intention, with the combination of my new guns and my brains, to make the Mesrab, however scant their numbers, into the most formidable force in the desert, but I understood that this could not be accomplished overnight. The rifles, and even more, the revolvers I had brought had not yet been fully unpacked or returned to working order; there had certainly been no opportunity to practise with them, and, in any event, when they were used I wanted to be there. But Medjuel would not wait.

I thus spent a very lonely fortnight, and a very unhappy one too. Because I *had* turned my back irrevocably on my past. And if my new life was to be Damascus and the desert, the centre of it was to be Medjuel. Suppose he were to be killed? The thought haunted me, and I filled my journal with some extravagantly mournful considerations. But on the seventeenth day a messenger arrived to say that the Sheik was alive and well, had gained a victory, and was now on his way home. Another blissful reunion.

Medjuel had also been thinking about my proper place. He had already discerned that it was not in my nature to sit at home and knit as did most women while their husbands rode off to war. He also knew, having seen me in action, that if my courage stood up, I was as good as any man when it came to battle. It was a matter of having my prowess and my unique situation as a woman who was the equivalent of any man in either wealth or ability, accepted by his people. But, like me, he understood that this could not be accomplished overnight. He therefore seized his opportunity, which occurred only a week after his return. He was visited, as I had done, by three Englishmen – their names were Pennant, Raley and Radcliffe – to inquire about a caravan to Palmyra. 'The person you wish to see,' he told them, 'is my wife.'

They were overwhelmed when they discovered who this wife was, while I was equally overwhelmed at being given this important responsibility. I was in any event in a state of euphoria because my piano had finally arrived, and to my delight Medjuel appeared to enjoy hearing me play and sing. Now I threw myself into the business of organizing the caravan, drove a far stiffer bargain than Medjuel had with me – well, they were getting my company as well as their adventure, and the money would, of course, all go to the Mesrab coffers – and set off triumphantly at the head of my party. Medjuel was not to be seen, and my people, no less than my clients, could have no doubt that I was in command. In fact, I knew that he had gone ahead with a strong body to make sure there were no mishaps. What I did not know was that he was arranging a reception for us, and hardly had we come within sight of the Grand Colonnade than we were treated to a typically Bedouin fantasia, with charging horsemen, discharging firearms, blaring bugles, clashing cymbals, and generally deafening noise. My clients were most impressed, and spread the word. Soon more and more people sought our guidance, and to my gratification, all arrangements were left in my hands. This served three purposes. It kept me busy, it increased my popularity with the Mesrab because of the increasing income I brought to the tribe, and, most important of all to me, it increasingly displayed to the warriors that I was capable of leadership, and worthy of being accepted as an equal. As for when the guns were ready and displayed for them, their enthusiasm knew no bounds. Medjuel entirely agreed with me that while the tribesmen should be allowed to practise with their new weapons, and to adopt new tactics, such as, for example, making them understand that a modern rifle, with its great range and accuracy, loses most of its effectiveness when fired from the saddle at a gallop, they should only be allowed to carry the weapons when we were actually at war; they were far too valuable to be discharged at whim as was the Arab custom. Nor were we anxious to let our possession of such an armament become widely known. But for the moment, following the last outbreak of violence, the desert was at peace.

Sadly, not all of our clients, while welcome financially, turned out to be acceptable. I entirely omit from this criticism people like Emily Strangford and her sister; we became good friends and have corresponded regularly since their visit. But Carl Haag was a different matter. I welcomed him with open arms, both because of his reputation as an artist – he was the court painter to Queen Victoria – and because he was by birth a Bavarian, although he had become a naturalized Englishman. I so enjoyed talking with him about the old days in Munich, although he was several years younger than I and had not known me in my heyday. I even persuaded Medjuel to sit for a portrait, despite his religious reservations, and I must admit that it is an excellent likeness. But the lout turned out to be a latter-day Aponyi, and when he returned to England sought additional fame by recounting his meeting with the 'notorious Lady Ellenborough', making me say, and do, things that were quite untrue, and capping it all by claiming that it was he who brought Medjuel and I together! This after we had already been married for four years! Not for the first time I resolved to be more careful about whom I accepted into my home.

But I did, about this time, make the acquaintance of a truly great and lovable man, Emir Abd el-Kader. I had known of him since my first sojourn in Paris in 1830, when I had experienced the revolution, and the city had been excited by the capture of Algiers from what were known as the Barbary Pirates. Naturally, these were not so regarded by their countrymen, who saw them as patriots defending the motherland against the French. I do not wish to become embroiled in points of view, simply to record that the war did not end with the fall of the capital, but continued for another dozen years, the Algerians finding a superb leader in Abd, who emerged victorious, or at least, undefeated, from a score of battles with the would-be conquerors. But at last he had been brought to book and forced to surrender. Sentenced to perpetual exile in the remote island of Reunion in the Indian Ocean, he had recently been released – thanks in part to the intercession of my old friend and near relative by marriage, Bob Stewart, now Marquis of Londonderry (he was the brother of my first husband Edward's first wife) – on condition he did not return to North Africa. Thus, he had opted for Damascus, where he lived in a style almost matching mine, with a fine house and a bodyguard of devoted Algerians. He was also a most educated and cultured man, with a faultless pedigree of nobility, and a delightful companion. I think I can fairly say that he and I were the two most famous people in Damascus.

With the onset of winter, the Mesrab took their camels and headed south as was their custom: neither they nor their animals appreciated cold weather, and frosts were quite common in Damascus. Although I was by now inured to desert hardships, I held to our bargain and remained in the city. To my great joy, Medjuel stayed with me, and we built our house, or rather, created it out of an existing dwelling.

The site was located just outside the city gates, and contained a sprawling, somewhat decrepit building, in typical Turkish style, surrounding a large inner court. I saw its possibilities at first glance, purchased it, and set to work. I divided the house into two parts. The right hand ground floor, looked at from the entrance, was an Arab reception chamber, furnished with soft carpets and luxurious divans, the walls decorated with stands of arms, but no portraits as the Muslim religion forbids the re-production of the human form. Extending from this, at right angles to form one inner wall, was a wing for accommodating visiting tribesmen and their families, which, during the summer, was usually crowded with people and animals, enjoying my hospi-tality. I did not begrudge them this any more than I had begrudged the Pelikari in Athens.

To the left of the entry hall was my domain. Here there was an English drawing room, again carpeted but with upholstered settees and chairs rather than divans, with paintings, mostly my own work to which I constantly added, on the walls, and, of course, my piano. Beyond that was my study-cum-library, where

I spent much of my time. For all the accusations of extravagance hurled at me throughout my life, I kept a very careful set of books, and an accounting of every penny I spent, from clothes through wages to replacements of arms and ammunition, to plants and animals, even down to the sums spent on postage stamps. Above this part of the house was the bedroom in which Medjuel and I sought our mutual heavens.

Needless to say, plants and animals were very important to me. Except for those few happy years in Corfu, I had been apart from them for too long. The inner court was, like the original house, in the Turkish style, with date palms as shade, and a fountain in the centre of the yard. I did not interfere with this essentially attractive scenario, but I appropriated part of it to create an English garden such as I'd had in Corfu – I had agents hunt far and wide for plants. As for animals, I'm afraid I let myself go overboard. I had been bereft for too long. Horses, naturally. Beyond the Arab quarters were the stables, with separate accommodation for camels and horses, and here I built up a considerable string. For domestic pets I naturally turned to cats and dogs, and within a short while had no fewer than seventeen moggies, each with its name printed on its food bowl, while I also had a dozen magnificent dogs who, like Sophie's, responded to my every command. For the garden I could go further afield, and soon had a menagerie of peacocks, gazelles, partridges, turtle-doves, falcons, and, in pride of place, a large pelican. In a fenced area were my chickens and geese, and of course my turkeys; the noise was considerable.

The whole was under the management of Eugenie, who by now spoke Arabic almost as well as I, and who was a stern task mistress as regards discipline. Not that she had an easy task, for the Bedouin women were both independently-minded and not very good at domesticity. I let her get on with doing whatever was necessary to keep them in order, remaining in the background as the ultimate authority, but she sometimes found it all too much, and on one occasion actually threatened to resign and go home. I had to be very patient with her and remind her that this *was* her home, and as she knew that after all of this time she could no more exist without me than I could without her, she soon regained her spirits.

Medjuel regarded all of this with good-humoured if occasion-
ally bewildered patience. I think we were both aware that our
relationship had a fragile side, in which the enormous differences
in our races, our religions, and our innate sympathies might one
day force a considerable rift. But for the moment there was no
crisis, and our mutual love for each other, for the sharing of our
bodies and our passions, kept us in a state of ecstatic happiness.
While our lifestyle, with its sublime mixture of domestic peace
and intermittent action and adventure, the lifestyle I had always
sought and only now found, kept even my restless spirit in check.

While we wallowed in domestic bliss, not everyone else was so
happy. News came in of the Indian Mutiny, which brought both
glory and an untimely end to my old playmate, George Anson.
The army he commanded triumphed in the end, but almost at
the moment of victory he died of cholera; this quite threw me
into a depression for a while. The mutiny ended in 1858, but
then we had problems of our own. The desert had been quiet
for over a year, but now we received news that a brigand named
Holo Pasha was raiding across the river, disrupting the peace of
the Amazeh tribes. This man was apparently known to Medjuel,
who now stroked his beard and said, 'He must be dealt with,
once and for all.'

I had by now gathered that desert warfare, at least amongst
the Bedouin, was largely a matter of galloping about and firing
guns without any real intention of killing anybody. I therefore
found my husband's remark both sinister and exciting. 'What do
you mean?'

'He has murdered some of our people. There can be no holding
back.' His eyes gleamed. 'We will use your guns, for the first time.'

I clapped my hands. 'And I will come with you. For the first
time.'

'I cannot permit that. Suppose you were hit?'

'And I cannot stay here. Suppose *you* were hit? Besides, as you
have just said, they are my guns.'

He considered for several minutes, then nodded. 'You are right.
We shall ride together. And triumph together, or die together.'

Magnificent! Zenobia reincarnated! I have never been so
exhilarated in my life. Not that campaigning with the Mesrab

was an easy matter. In the first place, while our warriors recognized me as their armourer, and also as the Sitt, they could
not stop regarding me as what I was, a woman and the wife of
their sheik. I accepted this, not only because I wanted no discord
but because of my pact with Medjuel: that if he treated me as
a European wife when we were in Damascus, I would be an
Arab wife in the desert. Thus, I happily, over his protests, washed
his feet and attended to his every need – Eugenie had remained
to manage the household.

We moved south in a body four hundred strong, Medjuel and
I riding at the head of our Praetorian Guard of a hundred men
armed with the new rifles, while our picked bodyguard of twenty
were also equipped with revolvers. I had trained and schooled
these men in European tactics; I was now going to find out if
they were capable of such discipline in battle.

We followed the river, never short of information from the
encampments we encountered, but this was always several days
old. It was a fortnight before we came across burned and scattered tents, dead animals, and several dead bodies as well, most
unpleasant in the noonday sun. The survivors of the attack had
been hiding in the rocks and gullies, but when they recognized
us they emerged to give us the harrowing details. Medjuel was
more interested in the whereabouts of Holo Pasha's people. 'They
were here yesterday,' said the refugees' spokesman.

'Did they know of our proximity?'

'They gave no evidence of it, Great Lord. They destroyed us
at their leisure.'

'Can you estimate how many there were?' I asked.

'There were many, Great Lady.'

'More than are with us?'

'At least twice as many, Great Lady.'

I looked at Medjuel, who nodded, and sent out scouts on our
fastest camels

'What is your plan?' I asked.

'To destroy them. I have said this.'

'How will you destroy them, if there are two of them to every
one of us?'

'As soon as we sight them, or their camp, we will charge. With
these rifles they will not stand a chance.'

I suppressed a sigh. After all my training, he could not get the desert tactics out of his system. 'Medjuel, my dearest, if you attack on camels, firing the rifles, you may as well attack with your jezreels. You will throw away your every advantage.'

He frowned. 'But if we do not attack, how do we defeat them?'

'By making them attack us.'

'We cannot force them to do that.'

'I think we can. Will you permit me to advise you?'

He stroked his beard. 'You have fought in a battle before?'

'No.' I could hardly consider my skirmish with Greek bandits a battle. 'But I have read a lot about wars and battles. I know how we can win this one, believe me.'

'By Allah, if you can do this . . .'

'Trust me.'

We proceeded on our way, I at least in a mood of euphoria. Had I not always dreamed of following in Zenobia's footsteps? By evening our scouts came back to us, and said that there was a considerable harka, or body of armed men, only a few miles distant. 'How many?' Medjuel asked.

'Not less than two hundred tents, my lord.'

Which, at say four men to a tent, confirmed the earlier estimate we had been given. Medjuel looked at me. 'We must withdraw and seek support,' Japhet said.

'There are not so many that we cannot defeat them,' I pointed out.

He looked at his father. 'The Sitt is confident of this,' Medjuel said. 'Tell us what we must do.'

'Divide your army.'

'That is madness,' Japhet said. 'We are already outnumbered.'

'Hear me. Send one hundred men out to the west. Tell them they must keep out of sight of the enemy, and not attack until they hear your bugle call. Send another hundred men along the river, but tell them also to keep out of sight until the call.'

Medjuel nodded. 'They will leave at dawn.'

'They must leave now, my lord.'

'It is not possible to fight a battle in the darkness.'

'They are not going to fight tonight. But they must be in position by dawn. At dawn you will send a hundred of your remaining force forward to attack the harka. These men will be armed only with spears and jezreels.'

'You are asking me to send my people to their deaths.'

'They will not be killed. All they must do is ride up to the harka, making as much noise as possible, firing their muskets, and as soon as the enemy are alerted and seek to drive them off, gallop back here as fast as they can. Do you not suppose Holo Pasha will follow, supposing that he has been attacked by only a small force?'

Medjuel nodded. 'He will follow.'

'Then he will rush into the arms of your last hundred men.'

'He will have several times that number.'

'You will have rifles. You will fight dismounted. I will arrange you.'

A last look, then he nodded.

'We will be destroyed,' Japhet muttered.

'You will gain your greatest victory,' I promised him. 'When Holo Pasha charges us, you will blow your bugle, and the two wings will close on his rear. He is the one going to be destroyed.'

Medjuel gave his orders, and his two wings rode off. I knew I was taking a considerable risk here, in trusting them not to attack until the right moment. But I also knew I could win the battle even without them. We advanced as quietly as possible until we heard the sounds of the harka, at perhaps a mile distant. Then we halted. We did not pitch our tents, but bivouacked upon the sand, our weapons at our sides. No fires were lit. I slept soundly, and awoke just before dawn. We said our prayers, ate a hasty meal and I loosed my hair as I had been told the Mesrab women did before a battle, so that it floated in a vast black cloud round my shoulders and down my back. Then I had Medjuel marshal his riflemen – there was no chance of them taking orders directly from me – in a position just behind a low rise, and place them in two lines, the first kneeling, the second standing. Each man had a small bag containing twenty cartridges. I took a rifle myself, and I also had my revolvers, although as usual I kept these concealed. Medjuel had rifle and revolver, and stood beside me, immediately behind the two lines. Then the signal was given, and the decoy attack rode off. 'Are you not afraid?' Medjuel asked.

'I am exhilarated.'

'How long?' Japhet asked.

'Not more than half an hour.'

The decoy had walked their camels to within a hundred yards of the harka before they charged. As instructed they shrieked and yelled, clashed their cymbals and fired their jezreels, setting up a terrible din. The attack having been launched, Medjuel and I went to the top of the rise to watch. Holo Pasha's camp was certainly coming to life, men rushing from their tents, guns being fired. The Mesrab behaved with exemplary discipline; the moment they saw their enemies were astir, they wheeled their mounts and hurried back to where we stood, bringing their camels to a halt beside us, and wheeling as if they intended to charge again.

Now we could hear the shouts of anger and derision rising from the harka, and we saw more and more of the enemy mounting their camels and advancing, shaking their swords and spears and firing their muskets. Medjuel glanced at me. 'Are there enough?' I asked.

'At least five hundred.'

I gazed at the dense mass of camels and men rapidly approaching us. 'Then tell your people to flee again,' I said. 'They need only withdraw out of sight.'

Medjuel gave the order, and his men rode off. The approaching mass shrieked its contempt. 'And us?' he asked.

I nodded. 'They will not stop now. What is the range?'

'Less than a kilometre, and closing.'

'That is ideal. Call up our people.'

He waved the riflemen forward. 'Form your ranks.'

They hurried up the slope to join us. The first fifty obediently dropped to one knee, the second stood behind them. 'Remember,' I said. 'Volley firing.'

'You give the order,' he invited.

The enemy were within three hundred yards, urging their mounts forward and uttering blood-curdling cries. I drew a deep breath. 'First rank, fire!' I shouted.

The fifty rifles exploded as one. The bullets tore into the massed enemy, and at least twenty went down, but the rest hardly checked. 'First rank, reload. Second rank, fire!'

This second deadly hail brought the enemy to a halt. As they were now closer, more men had gone down. But their leaders were calling on them to resume their charge as they could see that both our ranks had discharged their weapons, and by all the rules of the warfare they knew, they calculated it would take us several minutes to reload. They had no idea that for us it was simply a matter of ejecting the spent cartridge and pushing another into the breech. 'Second rank, reload. First rank, fire! My lord, sound the bugle.'

Medjuel gestured at his bugler, who uttered a blast on his trumpet. The enemy were still milling about when the third hail of lead struck them. That was devastating. Their leaders had still assumed that we were firing muskets. To be struck by a fresh volley from apparently empty guns forced them to realize that they were confronted by a force equal to a Turkish regular detachment. They waved their arms to cause a retreat. But before they could be obeyed our two flanking parties charged them, with fiendish shrieks. 'Both ranks fire!' I shouted.

This volley was all but annihilating, and by now a good third of Holo's people were stretched on the sand. Our people reloaded with feverish haste, and looked quite disconcerted when I told them to cease firing. They still did not appreciate the range of the rifles, and that to continue would involve hitting their own comrades, now closing on the rear of the enemy. These broke in every direction, riding for their lives.

Medjuel embraced me. 'You are a woman amongst women!'

'I am a woman amongst men,' I suggested.

The Legend

It was a great victory, but Holo Pasha was not amongst the dead. We pursued and fought quite a campaign, with several more battles. His people knew they could not face our rifles, and were invariably beaten, but he always managed to escape, and eventually returned across the river. Medjuel was quite happy with this outcome. 'He will not trouble us again,' he declared.

Actually, he was right in his judgement, at least in the short term, but now we had to reckon with the repercussions. The story of our triumph spread throughout the land, and of course got to the ears of the Turks, who very rapidly realized that they had a new power in their midst. They did not dare to attempt to disarm the Mesrab: that would have provoked an instant revolt. But they felt that they had to limit Medjuel's activities before they became unstoppable. As he had not broken any laws, either Turkish or of the Koran, they could not arrest him. So with typical cunning, soon after our return to Damascus, where we were greeted as heroes and I was hailed as a goddess, General Ahmed came to call. 'I must congratulate you on your great success,' he said, looking from Medjuel to me.

'The credit belongs to the Sheik,' I told him.

'Of course. And hopefully your victory will bring peace to the desert, at least on this side of the river.' I was immediately suspicious: I knew that it was no part of the Turkish policy to have the desert tribes at peace. 'In fact,' Ahmed went on, 'we would like to offer you the governorship of Hama.'

He paused expectantly, while Medjuel and I looked at each other. I could tell that Medjuel was flattered, but there was nothing I could do save hold my breath.

'Perhaps you would like to consider it,' Ahmed said, and left us to it.

'Governor of Hama,' Medjuel said. 'What an honour.'

'What is so important about being governor of Hama? Do you not already control it?'

'It is an Amazeh stronghold, but it does not belong exclusively to the Mesrab. I am being invited to greatly increase the power and prestige of my people. By the Turks!'

'Does that not concern you?'

'Well . . . they are recognizing my worth. My power.'

'They are seeking to embroil you in intertribal rivalries. Will the people of Hama accept you?'

'If I am appointed by the government . . .'

'Do they love the government? Do they respect the office? Does any Bedouin?' He stroked his beard, and I rested my hand on his. 'I wish only the best for you, my dearest. I wish you to be honoured. I wish your fame to grow. But I also trust the Turks no more than do you. I would only beg you to consider deeply before accepting this post.'

'By Allah!' he said. 'Blessed be His name. You continually astound me with your wisdom. Yes, I will consider long and deeply before accepting. But the first thing I must do is visit Hama, and see conditions there for myself.'

Thus, not for the first time, I was hoist on my own petard. But I could not argue further, nor could I object when he determined that he should go alone; I understood that while I was now accepted by the Mesrab as the most important woman in their history, other tribes did not so see me, as yet, and for him to arrive in Hama with a pale-skinned, blue-eyed infidel in tow, even if my hair was black, would be to invite an immediate hostility. 'I shall only be gone a week,' he promised me. 'A fortnight at the most.'

With that I had to be content, and so busied myself in adding finishing touches to our home. But when a week passed, and then a fortnight, I became agitated. There was absolutely no word from him or anywhere else. I began to envision my husband lying murdered in a ditch. Then I began to envisage him in the arms of another woman, younger and more beautiful than I. I have to confess, as I have illustrated often enough, that I have always been prone to jealousy, and the catastrophe of Saleh still haunted me. Medjuel was considerably older than Saleh had been, but he was still several years younger than I . . . and I was now fifty-two years old. I still felt like a girl, I still in many ways looked like a girl, I still had a girl's energy, still sought sexual satisfaction like a girl, I was still sure that I could make any man happy . . . but the fact was that I was at an age when most Arab wives had long been put aside for a younger bed mate.

It would have been easier had I an intimate to whom I could pour out my heart, and from whom I could receive sympathy. But close as Eugenie and I had become, I could not turn to her, because her experiences, and her observation of mine, had made her profoundly distrustful of all men, and I knew that she would but deepen my depression. I had no friends amongst other foreign women in the city, much as they liked to boast of knowing and visiting me, and were honoured when I visited them, but I had to be aware that they regarded me as a freak, and that they would like nothing better than to be able to whisper that my so ridiculous marriage was breaking down. As for the Bedouin women . . . there was one, named Fatima, the principal wife of another sheik, with whom I was quite friendly, but when I approached her to wonder at Medjuel's long absence without a word, she replied, much as Mama might have done, 'Men are a law unto themselves, Madame Digby. We must wait on their pleasure.'

I found this profoundly disturbing, and became even more agitated. I called on General Ahmed, who was even less helpful. 'I know that the Sheik visited Hama,' he told me. 'But he left there after a week. I do not know where he is now.'

I began riding out into the desert every morning, staring at the horizon in the hopes of seeing him galloping towards me. My heart leapt when on the third day after my meeting with Ahmed, I saw a horseman approaching. As he came closer I saw that it was not Medjuel, but he was coming from the south. I waved him down. 'What news of the Sheik?'

'I have no news, Great Lady. It is said that he is in the desert, with his number two wife.'

I all but fell from my saddle. The entire day seemed to swing about my head. I saw before my eyes all of the men I had trusted so completely, nearly all of whom had betrayed my love. I returned to Damascus in a state of such distress as to terrify those of the Mesrab who were living in my house. After our triumph of the summer, of which they knew the truth, they regarded me not only as the Mother of Milk and their Sitt, but also as their living Nike, or symbol of victory, if only because of the arms I had provided for their warriors to use. Fatima came to see me. 'You do not know what that man told you is true,' she said.

'But you know that my lord has other wives.'

'I know that he *had* other wives, before you,' she said cautiously.

This distressed me even more, as it left open the question of whether he had gone back to one of those earlier women – which had to imply some lack on my part – or whether, as I most feared, he had sought the embrace of some girl young enough to be my granddaughter: I could not get the image of Sabla from my mind. 'I have no more place here,' I declared. 'I will leave.' Without the slightest idea of where I should go.

Fatima was terrified, and I now know that she began laying all manner of elaborate plans to have me stay. She enlisted the help of Sheik Mohammed Dukhi who told me that he knew for a fact that Medjuel was delayed by the illness of a brood mare. This I could accept, with my own love of horses, but only a few days later someone else turned up to say that my husband was looking for stray sheep. I am afraid at this I lost my temper as I realized I was being duped, and ordered Eugenie to start packing. This greatly distressed her, as she had really supposed our travels were over. But now Dukhi persuaded me at least to visit Hama for a festival to celebrate the success of a children's school I had founded. This I could hardly refuse, although I was resolved to leave immediately afterwards. While I was there I was introduced to Sheik Fares ibn Mesiad, who was clearly totally fascinated by me, and began dropping hints that if I was determined to leave Medjuel I would not have to look very far to find a new husband. Fares fared no better than anyone else, as I was totally disinterested in any other man, but he persisted, and was actually telling my fortune, with pebbles – and to his advantage, needless to say – when a horseman arrived . . . with a letter from Medjuel, swearing his undying love, and informing me that he was only a few days away.

All thoughts of leaving vanished, as I rode out into the desert to greet him. Oh, bliss! We delayed our return to Damascus to enjoy a second honeymoon. His late return had been caused, he explained, by the necessity for him to seek out all the various sheiks and consult with them on the wisdom, or not, of accepting the governorship of Hama. To my great relief he had decided against it, but it really meant little to me at that moment. We were together, and I was, and am, the happiest woman in the world.

There remained only one other issue between us, that of religion. This was, I suppose, inevitable. But, in fact, in the very early days of our marriage the question of our opposing faiths did not arise. As I have mentioned, I deeply respected his daily devotions, and was quite envious of them, while he equally respected my prayers. Neither of us made any attempt to proselytize the other, and if there were a considerable number of Christians in Damascus, they were still a small minority of the population, and never impinged on our lives. But then came the great Druze uprising of 1860.

It was a very hot summer and perhaps feelings were in any event running high. But then, no one really knows a great deal about the Druzes, who are a secret society more than a religious sect. They trace their origins back to el-Hakim Bin-Amr, the Sixth Fatimid Caliph, who apparently became disillusioned with the practices of the Sh'ia Muslims, of whom he was one, and instead of attempting to reform them, founded his own, and, as I have indicated, very secret sect. Over several hundred years they had existed in the very heart of the orthodox Muslim world, accepted because they paid their taxes and never sought to cause trouble, while privately practising their beliefs, which, I understand, include some of the tenets of Judaism and Christianity as well as the Koran. Thus, throughout this long period they had been suffered by the various rulers in Damascus: the Muslims have never indulged in the brutal persecution of possible heretical beliefs that has disfigured so much of Christian history. Now they suddenly erupted.

I have mentioned the weather. The previous winter had been the coldest ever recorded in Damascus – shades of Athens in 1850 – with ice and snow everywhere. The result was floods in the spring with the concomitant of ruined crops and drowned animals – and starvation. It was all very sad. Then came the abnormally hot summer, with a great many people woefully out of sorts. The conflagration began in the ancient seaport of Sidon, where three Druze men were found murdered. It was extremely likely that this was the work of common footpads, but somehow the word got around that the deed had been perpetrated by Christians, and the whole Druze sect rose up in anger.

The first I knew of it was when the contagion spread to Damascus a few days later. I was awakened by shots and the clash of steel, by heart-rending screams and shrieks of terror and agony. My first impression was that Damascus had been assaulted by an enemy army, but I could not see how an enemy army could have penetrated into the heart of the Ottoman Empire without us knowing about it. I then recollected tales I had read of the Massacre of St Bartholomew's Day in Paris in 1572. In this I was not so very far wrong. But when I went downstairs it was to find my people going about their tasks without the least concern. It was Eugenie, in a state of considerable agitation, who appraised me of the situation. 'They are murdering all the Christians, milady.'

'Who are? The Turks?'

'The Druzes, milady.'

'But is no one stopping them?'

'I do not think so, milady.'

I hurried off to wake Medjuel, but he was already up. 'We must do something!' I told him.

'There is nothing we can do.'

'People are being murdered out there.'

'It is a fight between two opposing tribes. We cannot interfere.'

In Arab terms he was absolutely right; it was inconceivable that a Bedouin tribe, coming upon two other tribes battling it out in the desert, should attempt to interfere or take sides. 'But these are innocent people,' I protested.

'Are any people truly innocent?'

I stamped my foot. 'Well, I shall do something about it.'

'You are a Christian. If you leave this house you will be killed.'

'We have a hundred warriors living here. They will protect me.'

He shook his head. 'I cannot ask my people to risk their lives in a dispute that does not concern them.'

I was so angry I nearly struck him. 'Then I shall go alone. And be murdered.'

He made no move to stop me.

I dressed, loosed my hair as if I were going into battle, and left the house. Eugenie, in tears, closed the gate behind me; she did not expect ever to see me alive again. As usual, I was not afraid, although I was certainly apprehensive at to what I might find. With good reason. I had barely reached the street when I came across a dying man, his head half severed from his body. At the corner I encountered four thugs crawling over the half-naked body of a woman while she screamed her shame and terror. I drew one of my revolvers and fired a shot over their heads. They leapt to their feet and turned towards me, lips drawn back from their snarling teeth. I realized that I might have to fight for my own protection and levelled my weapon. But then they stopped, and one pointed at me. 'It is the Sitt el Mesrab!'

'The Sitt!' shouted his companions. 'The Sitt!'

'A thousand pardons, Great Lady,' the leader said, and they hurried off.

This behaviour was both gratifying and reassuring. I assisted the stricken woman to her feet, rearranged her clothes, and helped her back to my gate, where Eugenie was anxiously waiting. 'Thank God you have come back, milady.'

'Only for a moment. This woman is in your care until I return.' I took to the streets again, making for the Governor's residence, passing on my way scenes of indescribable horror, often surrounded by ravenous mobs, all of which applauded my presence in their midst.

The sentries allowed me into the palace with obvious misgivings, while General Ahmed regarded me as if I were a ghost. 'Madame Digby? What are you doing here?'

'Visiting you.'

'But . . . you were on the streets? How many men have you?'

'I have no men. '

'You walked those streets, alone? And you are here?'

'I am the Sitt el Mesrab. But as you obviously know what is going on, may I ask why you are not putting a stop to it?'

'How can I interfere?'

'For the sake of Allah, blessed be His name. Are you not the governor of the city, and responsible for the lives of everyone in it? Do you not have a garrison of soldiers waiting for your command?'

'My duty as governor is to maintain Turkish rule. Not become involved in interdenominational strife, or to risk the lives of my soldiers by interfering in matters which do not affect Turkish rule. You are concerning yourself needlessly, Madame Digby. This riot will soon burn itself out.'

'You mean when all the Christians have been slaughtered!'

'I am sure most of them have taken shelter by now. I earnestly recommend that you do the same. You are welcome to remain here until the tumult dies down.'

I left before I lost my temper. In fact, I had already lost my temper, with both Ahmed and Medjuel. I returned to the scenes of carnage, feeling an overwhelming desire to draw my revolvers and shoot every Druze I encountered, while understanding that I could not shoot them all, quite apart from the fact that they continued to cheer me. But I had not gone very far when I heard the sound of rifle shots, and a moment later encountered Abd el-Kader, at the head of a company of his Algerians, escorting several fugitives, and having to fight off the attentions of a mob of Druzes. 'Madame Digby! Jane! What are you doing here?'

'I would like to be doing the same as you, Abd, but I have no support.'

'But you could have been killed!'

'I will provide you with far more protection that your soldiers,' I assured him. And sure enough once I was identified the mob melted away.

'These people are afraid of you?' Abd said, wonderingly.

'No. They worship me. They think I am a goddess.'

We took the fugitives, and several more we found on our way, back to my house. I invited Abd to come in, but he preferred to return to his own palace, hopefully accumulating more refugees on the way. Without me, he did not do so well, and I later learned that he had had to stand a regular siege, which he conducted with his usual military skill. But he gave shelter to some twelve thousand people, which far outnumbered my small contribution.

As Ahmed had prophesied, the riot burned itself out by the

next day, but the death toll was considerable, and those mentally scarred by their experiences even greater. While the exploits of Abd and myself were blazoned across the world's press. This was not to Medjuel's liking. I have never been sure whether his anger was because I had acted without his authority, or because my actions had perhaps thrown his lack of action into a poor light, or whether he felt that the Christians had it coming, present company of course excepted, or if he was simply unhappy at having his house' – *my* house – filled with Christian refugees. He was very stiff, and finally rode off into the desert without me. I rapidly got over my own anger and distress at the massacre, and willingly forgave him out of respect for his religious views. I knew he would come back, as he did when he learned that a new shipment of arms and ammunition, ordered and paid for by me, had arrived. We had one of our tumultuous reconciliations, and he raised no objections when, a couple of years later, my guilt at having for so long rejected or at least ignored the tenets of my background and upbringing, led me to seek the solace of religious company of my own. I had no wish to publicize this, and when I attended a service conducted by a group of missionaries, led by Dr Meschaka, I was heavily veiled and stole into the hall after the service had began to take my place at the very back. But I was noticed, and asked to identify myself. The question was in English, and I replied in the same language without thinking, so that the cat was firmly out of the bag. The missionaries were not going to allow this momentous public evidence of support from the highest quarters to go unpublished. But Medjuel accepted that I wished to follow my own religion as sincerely as he followed his, and soon afterwards I had my own chapel in my house.

I should mention that during Medjuel's absence in the desert, as the reason for his unseasonable departure was well known, I received a visit from one of Sheik Fares' people, bearing a proposal of marriage from his master. I really did not know whether I should be amused, flattered, or insulted. I was amused that he should come snapping at my heels the moment he suspected there might be a rift between Medjuel and myself. I was flattered that at the age of fifty-three I could still command such attention. But I was in the main insulted, not only by the suggestion that I would end my relationship with my husband simply because of a tiff, but by the fact that he had sent a messenger instead of coming himself, and the messenger himself was a most unpleasant fellow, who seemed to think that his master, and therefore himself, was doing me a great favour. I saw him off very rapidly.

Thus, we lived on a level of continuous exhilaration that has been vouchsafed to few people. When necessary we campaigned. Holo Pasha was back, and we had several severe battles. He had now also obtained, from the Turks, modern rifles, and thus we had lost our original superiority, and so were defeated on occasion. But our wits and my military knowledge were greater than his, and we always won the war. There were occasions, in Medjuel's absence, when I led the Mesrab into battle myself, midnight hair streaming behind me, shrieking like any banshee, careless of injury and even death in the excitement of the moment. So my reputation grew, especially as I was never touched by an enemy bullet.

Neither was Medjuel, but that we were not immortal was brought home, at least to me, when he was taken seriously ill with a combination of shivering and a suggestion of paralysis. With my knowledge of western medicine – gained by extensive reading on the subject – I was by now accepted as what might be called the chief medical officer of the tribe, and tended all wounds suffered in battle as well as the various injuries and illnesses endured on our campaigns, thus no one interfered as I consulted my books and my medicine chest, trying both to identify the illness and to discover a cure. I determined that it was typhus, but despite all my efforts he grew worse. 'My father will die,' Japhet said.

'He cannot die,' I protested. 'Medjuel cannot die, before me.'

He pulled his beard. 'But you cannot cure him, Great Mother.'

'I am doing all I can.'

'There are things that even western medicine cannot cure.' I found this very irritating, and was about to send him off when he added, 'But there are desert ways not known to the West.'

I seized his hand. 'You know this sickness?'

'I have seen it before.'

'And you can cure it?'

'I have seen it cured,' he said, carefully. 'Our old men know how it can be done. But . . .' he held up his hand as I would have spoken. 'It may not be to your liking, Great Mother.'

'If you can save your father's life, my husband's life, I will like it.'

'Remember that. And remember too that once the treatment commences, you must not, you cannot, interfere.'

This was a very necessary warning, for what followed was the most harrowing period of my life, to that point. Medjuel's head was shaved, and red-hot irons applied to his skull. I was appalled, and had not Japhet's hand been on my arm I would have been unable to prevent myself from interfering. Yet amazingly, and possibly miraculously, this barbaric treatment worked, and Medjuel recovered his entire health.

We actually had more trouble with the Turks than with either the Gomussa or the desert. Our masters were well aware that I was financing the Mesrab and supplying them with arms, but they dared not touch me for fear of British anger. However, they could touch Medjuel, and they had never forgiven him for declining the governorship of Hama. Thus, there came the day when I was in Damascus and he was in Homs, and a messenger arrived to say that he had been arrested. 'How can that be?' I demanded.

'He has broken the law, Great Lady.'

'Oh, really,' I remarked angrily. The Turkish laws, which often covered the most trivial transgressions, were broken, constantly and every day, by just about every member of the population. No one was ever arrested for doing so. I mounted and rode down to Homs. 'I wish to know the charges against my husband,' I told the commandant. 'And I wish to see him.'

'That is not possible, Madame Digby. No one can be admitted to our cells.'

'Then tell me the charges.'

'The charges will be read out in court.'

'And when will that be?'

'Who can say? Six months, perhaps.'

'Six *months*?'

'The courts are very full at this time.'

I refused either to panic or lose my temper. Instead I used bribery and discovered that the charge had been laid by Sheik Fares, who

since my rejection of his marriage proposal had become our bitterest
enemy, even to the extent of stealing some of our horses. This might
well have led Medjuel into some kind of overreaction. Unlike the
desert, where we were expected and even encouraged to deal with
such matters ourselves, in places like Homs the Turks were very
keen to have everything done by the law, their law, which had much
more to do with who was friends with which Turkish official than
justice, and Medjuel was friends with none of them.

But he was my husband. I remounted my horse, and returned
to Damascus, going straight to Ahmed. 'This is outrageous, and
you know it,' I told him.

'My business is to enforce the law, Madame Digby. Your husband
has broken the law.'

'What law?'

'I am not at liberty to say, until the case comes to court.'

'In six months' time.'

'It may well come to that. But for you, Madame Digby, I will
do my very best to expedite matters.'

'While my husband is beaten and starved in gaol.'

'I give you my word that not a hair of his body will be harmed,
until and unless he is convicted.'

I stood up. 'I do not accept that Medjuel is guilty of any crime
greater than that of defending his own belongings.'

'We shall have to wait and see.'

'I have never been very good at waiting, when the matter is
important,' I told him.

I went to the British Consulate. I knew that my old sparring
partner Wood had been replaced, but I had only met the new
man, Edward Rogers, on one occasion. He now turned out to
be an absolute charmer, as well as a tower of strength, even if he
began somewhat pessimistically. 'If the Sheik really has broken
the law . . .'

'Of course he has not broken any law of the least importance,'
I insisted. 'The Turks just feel that he is growing too powerful.'

'Unfortunately, they are the government.'

'They are not *my* government.'

'Well, of course they are not. You are a British citizen, entitled to all the protection that affords.'

'Civis Romanus Sum.'

'Ah . . . quite. You have not been threatened with arrest, I hope?'

'If I were, you would do something about it, would you not?'

'Of course.'

'So tell me, if my son were to be arrested, would you do something about him?'

'You do not have a son. Here in Syria.'

'Suppose I did?'

'Well, obviously I would take action.'

'Even if, as his father would be a Bedouin, he would not be a British citizen?'

Edward produced a handkerchief to wipe his neck. As with so many men in my life, the combination of my so delicate beauty and my so forceful personality had him out of his depths. 'I would do everything in my power to protect your son, Madame Digby.'

'Then may I ask you another question, Mr Rogers? In most civilized communities, is not a husband regarded as more important than a son?'

'Well . . .' he flushed as he realized where I was going.

'Civus Romanus Sum.'

The next day, as a result of a visit by the British Consul to General Ahmed, Sheik Medjuel el Mesrab, as the husband of the Honourable Jane Digby – the first and last time I found any use for my title – was placed under British protection, and Medjuel came home. The Turks were not very happy about it, and indeed Medjuel was arrested on several more occasions for minor transgressions, but in each case a simple visit to the Consulate procured his release, and we could re-enter our private paradise.

This was the more enjoyable because, while I cannot claim to have achieved respectability in the eyes of English society, they at least could no longer ignore me. My fame grew with every day. And reached its climax when, in the course of a fierce battle in the desert I was unseated and went down in a welter of dust, to be ridden over. I was now approaching sixty, and although with my usual good fortune to which I would add my invariable good health, I received nothing more than bruises, I was incapable of movement for some time, and the battle having moved on, when it finally ended I was discovered to be missing. As a result, the word spread that I was dead.

I was recovered within a few hours, but by then the sensation was already on its way to Damascus, which it reached well before any rebuttal. From Damascus it spread throughout Europe, and by the time we actually returned home there were several newspapers waiting for us, containing my obituary! Reading one's own obituary is supposed to be a rare and uplifting event, and I was certainly prepared to be amused. But I was quite put out when I was referred to as the once notorious Lady Ellenborough, and it was now the spurious story that I had had six husbands in rapid succession while living in Rome in 1846 was first put about, at least in the press.

But however I was still regarded by the public at large, my family were finally prepared to accept me for what I was, and I ceased to be an outcast. Now they became regular correspondents, and even visitors. One of my happiest occasions was when, in 1862, I was visited by my niece, Kenelm's daughter Emily, now Mrs Buxton, in the course of a honeymoon tour of the Holy Land. Entertaining her was such a joy. Equally exciting was to hear from Karl that Heribert was engaged to be married – to Gabrielle Paumgarten, the Erskines' granddaughter, and the daughter of my old friend Gabrielle, whose wedding to the Baron von Paumgarten Karl and I had attended thirty years before. I sent my son a hundred pounds as a wedding present, although the wedding was not to take place for some time. And shortly afterwards I received a visit from the Count and Countess de Boury. The Countess was the daughter of the Countess Lerchfeld, an old friend of mine from my Munich days, and the girl was a friend of Heribert's, and was able to tell me so much about him.

Of course, not all the news was good. One of the most severe penalties of growing old is that so many of the people one has known and loved, or not as the case might be, disappear. I had continued to correspond with Mama, although it was actually with Steely, but there came the day when she wrote to say that Mama had died. It was not unexpected; Mama was eighty-three years old and had been in poor health for a long time. I wept when I read the letter, and said a prayer for her soul, but I was actually more affected by the utterly tragic death of Isabella, George Anson's widow, even if I had never actually met her. This was told me by my sister-in-law Theresa, with whom Isabella had actually been staying. While dressing for dinner, Isabella had picked up what she supposed was a bottle of her tonic and drunk deeply, only to realize that she had in fact imbibed a fatal quantity of laudanum. With admirable courage she had gone down to the drawing room and informed Theresa and Edward what had happened. Edward immediately sent for the doctor, but this took some time, and as the poison began to take effect, Theresa had to walk her friend up and down in the vain hope of fending off the final moment until help could arrive. She was not successful.

I felt this tragedy severely, but there were others much closer to home. Caroline, my so supportive sister-in-law, died about this time. The news was conveyed to me by Kenelm himself, and it was Kenelm, not long after, who wrote to inform me that Steely had also gone. Apparently her end had been quite dreadful, as she had suffered from an illness which caused her unending pain, under the strain of which her mind gave way. This news quite upset me. I forgot our quarrels and her horrid attitude to Medjuel, and remembered only the good times we had shared – there were sufficiently few of these to *be* remembered.

In Damascus, European affairs and crises seemed very remote, but I had to be both alarmed and excited when I heard of the war between Prussia and Austria in 1866, as I knew that old friends, and even relations, could be involved. I was particularly worried about Heribert, but fortunately the war was very brief as the Austrians were resoundingly beaten at Sadowa, and Karl wrote me to say that our son was unharmed.

The very last link with my past seemed to have been severed when I learned that on 28 February 1868 Ludwig had died. I have already recounted the sadness of his fate following his infatuation with Lola Montez, the loss of his throne, the madness of his eldest son. His misery must have been compounded by the expulsion, a few years before, of Otto from the Greek throne. I had actually given an uncharitable smile when I had read the news, unable to resist the reflection that Amalia had finally got her comeuppance, but I could understand how my old lover – who had rescued me from lonely exile – must have felt as his entire dynasty collapsed about him.

*   *   *

By the mid sixties my house had become a shrine for visitors to Damascus. I welcomed them all, and enjoyed the fascination they displayed, not only with me and my house and my pets, and the aura of utter authority in which I moved, but also when, from time to time, I had to leave them to accompany Medjuel into the desert to take part in a campaign.

I especially enjoyed it when my visitors were accompanied by their children. My house was open to all children, and there were always quite a number in residence with their Mesrab mothers and fathers; it was such a joy to have them rushing and screaming about the place, and above all, laughing. I loved them all, and welcomed their adulation. I am afraid I gloried in my fame, even if some called it my notoriety, and even, perhaps, in the way I have outlived all of my critics.

Which is not to say that my generosity, both as regards hospitality and frankness, was not from time to time abused. I am thinking especially of the detestable Burton woman. Richard Burton replaced dear Rogers as British Consul at the end of the decade, and duly came to call. I knew that he had had a somewhat chequered career, which had included some dazzling exploits, such as tracing the course of the Nile, and some distinctly unsavoury ones, including, when stationed in India, spending a great deal of time disguised as a native in the most ghastly Calcutta slums. Some said that he did this to obtain valuable information for the government, others that he sought personal gratification in the most vicious of ways.

I saw no reason to dislike him on those grounds, and indeed I found him entertaining, at once for his knowledge and his wit. He was quite handsome in a dark fashion. Like Edward, my first husband, he suggested hidden secrets. Unlike Edward, he actually did have such secrets, which made him the more attractive. I was particularly interested when he told me that he was working on a translation of the Arabian fable, *The Thousand and One Nights*, which purports to be the tale of the concubine Scheherazade, who, condemned to death by the Caliph Harun-al-Rashid in the Ninth Christian Century, begged for the right to tell her master a story on the night before her execution. This request was granted, and Harun was so fascinated that he postponed the execution for a second night in order to hear another story, and then another

night, and another, until the wily young woman had kept herself
alive for very nearly three years, by which time the Caliph had
fallen in love with her and absolved her of any wrongdoing. This
is a story that has to appeal to any romantic, and the idea of it
being included in English literature delighted me.

But . . . 'You understand, milady,' Richard explained, somewhat
apprehensively, 'that to keep a man like the Caliph, who had every
possible pleasure, or vice, at his fingertips, interested for a thousand
consecutive nights, these stories had to be, well . . .'

'Risqué?' I suggested.

'Extremely so. I'm afraid most people in England would describe
them as obscene.'

I reflected that there were some scholars in England who
regarded even Shakespeare as obscene. Such was the stifling influence of the court of our widowed Queen. 'Can you not tame
them down?'

'Never!' His tone was vehement. 'I do not deal in ex-
purgations.'

'Bravo!' I cried. Whereupon he told me one or two of the
stories himself, and I realized that he knew the risk he was
running. But I was wholly in support, and even supplied him
with some anecdotes of Bedouin methods of love-making, which
he found equally fascinating. But then his wife arrived.

Richard and I were by now firm friends, and Isobel was determined that she also would be my closest European companion.
Although she was twenty years younger than I, there seemed
every reason for us to be close. We had very similar tastes. She
travelled with a collection of animals including a St Bernard pup,
soon had a fine stable, and was quite a witty conversationalist. I
was a bit taken aback when she claimed to be my cousin, but it
appeared that her family, the Arundells, were related to Mama's
first husband, Lord Andover. It is difficult to discern any blood
link there, but I did not object to her assumption of at least
domestic equality. Thus, I lowered my guard with her and discussed
the events of my past freely. Imagine then my disgust when, after
Burton's term of office had expired and they returned to England,
she published a book of memoirs which included a great deal
about me, and even more, like Aponyi of hideous memory, about
what she chose to present as the truth about me, most of which

was utterly spurious gossip. I was so angry that I did something I had never before contemplated in my life: I wrote a letter of refutation to *The Times*, condemning both book and writer for their lies.

The main reason I was so angry about Isobel's falsehoods was that, treating her as a friend and confidante, I had let her into a secret which I had never admitted to anyone else, and would never have admitted to her, had I had the slightest doubt that she would fail to treat it as the confidence I intended. This was the story of the last great crisis of my life, which took place shortly before the Burtons arrived in Damascus.

This near tragedy was entirely my own fault, and had its roots in the many times I had been betrayed by the men I had sought to love. Sadly, as one grows older, past experiences tend to loom larger. I do not think I ever recovered from my treatment by Saleh, and no matter how many evidences of his love shown me by Medjuel, I was still subject to bouts of extreme jealousy, followed by even more extreme depression, whenever we were apart. That this was always dissipated the moment we were in each other's arms did not prevent it from happening at the next separation. Added to this was my tendency to lose my temper when I felt myself to have been betrayed.

It began when Schebibb died. He had always been Medjuel's favourite son, perhaps because he had never been as robust as his brother Japhet. For all that he insisted upon accompanying us on our campaigns, and it was on one of these that he took sick. Medjuel was heartbroken, and I shared much of his grief. Schebibb's wife was not with us, but when we returned to Damascus she was quite overcome. Her name was Ouadjid, and she was an exceptionally beautiful child; I say child because she was not yet twenty years old. With such an age difference between us we had never been very close; I had in fact always felt that, unlike her husband and his brother, who had finally grown to accept me, she had never been able to do so with all her heart. Nevertheless, I mourned for her and with her, and sought only her recovery from her grief while endeavouring to ensure her future. There were no children of the marriage, which was only three years old, and so I suggested to Medjuel that her best chance of restoring her happiness would be for her to marry again. To my surprise, he rejected the idea. 'She is part of my family. Her place is here.'

'Can you really condemn her to live out her life in lonely widowhood?'

'How can she be lonely, living with us?'

'A woman without a man of her own will always be lonely.'

'Ouadjid will not be lonely,' he insisted.

I regretted his attitude, but entirely for the sake of the girl. Then I began to notice that she was indeed not being given the time to be lonely, because Medjuel spent every minute he could spare from his affairs, and from me, in her company. Initially I refused to accept what appeared to be the evidence of my own eyes, but I was surprised and disturbed when we set out on our next campaign, and discovered that Ouadjid was to accompany us. She had never done this before, even when her husband was alive, and I raised the matter with Medjuel. 'We cannot leave her in Damascus all by herself,' he said.

All by herself, in a house constantly filled with people? I found his reply specious, and inevitably my always lurking jealousy began to bubble, and finally surfaced on the day we were riding across the desert, Ouadjid beside me, and she suddenly began to weep. 'Whatever is the matter?' I asked.

'When I ride on the desert, my Mother, I think of Schebibb, and am distressed.'

'Well,' I said. 'I think it is time for you to pull yourself together and start acting like a grown woman instead of a child.'

To my surprise, she reacted angrily. 'What do you know of grief? Have you ever suffered any? With your wealth and your beauty you *buy* happiness, just as you bought the Sheik.'

It so happened that over the past few days I had found myself thinking of Leonidas – the lock of his hair was still in my reticule – and the accusation infuriated me, perhaps because I knew that in many ways it was true. In the event, as on that unforgettable day with Felix in Paris all but forty years before, I reacted violently, swung my riding crop, and caught her across the face, tumbling her from her saddle.

Instantly all was pandemonium. I was surrounded by shouting people – both Schebibb and Ouadjid were great favourites – and the hostility was so evident that I considered my life to be in danger, and I did not even have Eugenie to back me up: she was safely in Damascus. I would have dismounted to assist the girl, being instantly regretful of what I had done, but I felt that if I got to the ground I would at the very least be manhandled. I thus opened my reticule to find my revolvers, even as my heart sickened at the thought that I might have to fire into the midst of these people, who I regarded as my very own.

Fortunately, at that moment Medjuel, who had been riding with our advance guard, returned, having heard the noise. At the sight of him, the tumult somewhat lessened. 'What has happened here?' he demanded.

Japhet answered before I could. He had raised Ouadjid from the ground and was holding her against him. 'The Sitt struck my sister from the saddle, my lord.'

Medjuel looked at me in a mixture of consternation and anger. 'Can this be true? You struck the wife of my son?'

'I acted in haste. I am sorry. She was rude to me, and I overreacted.'

'You struck my son's wife,' he repeated. 'If she was rude to you, you should have told me.'

By now I was growing angry again. 'Would that have accomplished anything?'

'She defies you, my father,' Japhet said. 'She must be punished!'

'Yes,' shouted the people around him. 'She must be punished!'

Medjuel and I stared at each other. I could tell that he was very angry. I now know that it was less at my having struck Ouadjid than at us having our first public difference. 'You must be punished,' he said. 'It is the law.'

For a moment I could not think. I was in a dangerous position, and I could see no immediate solution. I had sworn to be an Arab wife when we were in the desert, and now I had acted as a Frankish wife, and before his people. And I had broken their laws. The temptation was there to draw my revolvers and shoot my way to safety, as I could well have done. But to do that would mean shooting Medjuel first, as he was closest to me. I could not shoot the man I loved. Better to put my faith in the fact that he loved *me*. 'What will happen to me?' I asked.

'You will be flogged,' Japhet said. 'Twenty lashes. It is the law.'

I caught my breath, and looked at Ouadjid; she looked as consternated as myself. She had not expected things to go this far.

'It is the law that she should be flogged,' Medjuel said. 'But it is the prerogative of the Sheik to decide the number of lashes.'

'Then let us bind her and prepare her for punishment.'

'Do not touch her,' Medjuel commanded as they moved towards me. 'I will carry out the punishment. The Sitt will come with me into the desert.'

'There must be witnesses,' Japhet insisted.

'There will be a witness. Ouadjid, you will accompany us.'

The girl hesitated, then slowly remounted.

'This is not the law,' Japhet protested.

'It is my law,' Medjuel told him. 'You . . .' he pointed at one of the waiting women. 'A bag of dates. Haste.'

Food was brought, and a skin of water. 'Now come,' Medjuel said. He wheeled his camel and rode off. Ouadjid and I looked at each other, and then followed. I still could not believe this was happening. But then, I did not know *what* was going to happen.

We rode for some hours, until the camp was completely out of sight, and we were alone in the vast expanse of sand and sun. It was very hot, and I was dripping sweat when at last Medjuel called a halt. 'Dismount,' he commanded, and did so himself. We hobbled our camels, and waited. 'What lies between you?' he asked.

'I was rude to the Sitt,' Ouadjid admitted.

'I struck her in haste and anger,' I repeated.

'This is more than a moment's work,' Medjuel remarked.

Again we looked at each other. Ouadjid had nothing to say. 'It is apparent to me,' I said. 'That you love this child. Perhaps more than me.'

'I love her as the widow of my son. I love you as my wife.'

I looked at Ouadjid.

'My lord has never touched me carnally,' she said. 'This I swear on my dead husband's memory.'

'Then I most humbly apologize.'

'Yet you must be punished,' Medjuel said. 'You struck a member of my house in public.'

'You intend to flog me?'

'It is the law. Unless . . .' he looked at Ouadjid.

'I forgive the Sitt, my mother,' she said.

'Then take her hand, and embrace her.'

This she did, and we sat down and ate and drank, following which Ouadjid went into the desert.

'Would you really have flogged me?' I asked.

'Perhaps. What would you have done if I did?'

'I am sworn to kill any man who ever raises his hand to me,' I told him. 'I would certainly have left your bed.'

'If I had flogged you, my Digby, it would not have been for your crime, but for supposing I could love any woman but you.'

Ouadjid tactfully stayed away another hour.

I was received with acclamation by the Mesrab when we returned for having borne my punishment with fortitude. As Ouadjid was now my closest friend, the truth of it never came out. But the fact of the quarrel between my husband and I did, and my 'punishment' in the desert. Of course people, Isobel to the fore, put the wrong interpretation on the story, and had it that Medjuel had found me in flagrante delicto with another man, and had taken me into the desert and flogged me half to death. As I have said, these stories made me very angry, less because of the implied humiliation I had suffered, than because of the supposition that Medjuel could ever have done such a thing to me – or that I would have permitted it.

But that is several years ago, now. They have been utterly blissful years. Medjuel loves me for what I am, a woman who has a mind of her own and the willpower to match the mind, but who, even when well past seventy, seeks to extract every moment of *life* from every moment of each day – and night. And I have learned that a man does not have to be tall, handsome, and dashing to fulfil my every dream.

I will freely admit there are aspects of my life that I regret and mistakes that for many people would have been catastrophic. I have not been an ideal mother – many would say quite the opposite – but had I not been robbed of Didi and Leonidas when they both were so young I might well have settled into contented domesticity. I have taken part in deeds considered by many to have been unladylike and even unfeminine, but that is because I have never been afraid to make instant decisions and to act upon them. In fact, I can claim that I have never been afraid, save for the occasional fleeting moment.

Above all, I know that I have never been a good Christian, certainly in the eyes of those learned men, clergy and laity, who have spent nigh on two thousand years misinterpreting the words of Jesus Christ to their own satisfaction. But I have never harmed a living creature who did not first attempt to harm me, and I have been as generous as my circumstances would allow to anyone who has sought my aid. When my time comes, I shall face my creator with equanimity . . . and with courage. I regret nothing of my past, save the deaths of four of my children.

And now I will lay down my pen. This is about the hottest summer I can recall, and I do not feel very well today. I shall summon Eugenie, my most faithful friend and companion for more than thirty years, and ask her to sit with me and we shall remember the many adventures we have shared.

Epilogue

The Honourable Jane Digby el Mesrab, Lady Ellenborough, Baroness von Venningen, Countess Theotoky, after a lifetime of almost perfect health, died of dysentery in August 1881, aged seventy-four. She is buried in the Protestant Cemetery in Damascus, where her headstone may still be seen. It is said that her beauty and complexion were as flawless in death as they had always been in life.

Sheik Medjuel el Mesrab went almost mad with grief at her funeral.

There is no trace of Eugenie after her mistress's death.